Daisy's War

Book One of

Robert

Print I
LS Ingram Print 97 046-5
B&N Print 978-0-2286-1047-2
Amazon Print 978-0-2286-1045-8

BWL Publishing Inc.

Books we love to write ...
Authors around the world.

http://bwlpublishing.ca

Dedication

To my friends of the Sheppey History Facebook Group who are the inspiration for this book and were a great help with my research.

Chapter One

Daisy Bishop forced a smile as her sister did a mock curtsy in front of the family, showing off her WAAF's uniform. She wasn't really jealous. After all, as soon as she reached eighteen, she would be joining too.

Sylvia looked beautiful as usual, with her smooth blonde pageboy beneath the cap set at a jaunty angle. The severe uniform jacket did nothing to hide her shapely figure, enhancing it rather. Daisy, trying to smooth her own unruly fair curls, hoped she would look as good when she joined up. She pictured herself coming home and showing herself off to Bob Gardner, the boy next door.

They had known each other all their lives, their friendship deepening into something more serious since she'd left school. Daisy knew that Bob was the only boy for her and she'd been devastated when he announced soon after war was declared that he was joining the army. He' d been gone nearly three months and she had to face the fact that she would not see him for a long time – he might not even get home again before she finally joined up herself.

Her thoughts were interrupted when Sylvia picked up her bag. 'Well, better be off,' she said, kissing her father's cheek and hugging her mother. 'Come and see me off, Daisy?'

They went out by the back gate as usual, taking the short cut through the alley leading to the High Street.

Their progress along the narrow street which was thronged with shoppers this close to Christmas, was hindered by the many friends and neighbours who stopped to wish Sylvia good luck. Everybody knew everyone else in the small dockyard town of Sheerness on the north Kent coast.

When they reached the railway station, the train was just drawing in, hissing steam and belching out clouds of coal scented smoke.

They went on to the platform, the ticket collector waving Daisy on without a platform ticket. Sylvia put her bag down and threw her arms round her sister. 'Look after yourself little sister – and look after Mum and Dad too,' she said. 'I'll write to Jimmy later.' She frowned. 'I wish Mum hadn't insisted on him being evacuated. There haven't been any bombs so far.'

'Don't worry about our Jimmy. He's probably driving them crazy with his antics over there in Wales,' Daisy said. She had to admit she hardly missed her young brother at all. He was always up to mischief, begging Daisy to cover up for him when he got into trouble with their parents. She loved him, but he could be very annoying at times.

Doors slammed and the guard blew his whistle. Sylvia jumped on the train, leaning out of the window to wave.

Daisy stood there for a few minutes after the train rounded the bend and was out of sight. It felt strange to be alone after so many years of sharing a room and being part of a close knit family. She hadn't told anyone about her ambition to follow Sylvia into the WAAFs, knowing her parents would try to dissuade her. She realised it would be hard for Mum and Dad to be alone, but everyone had to do their bit for the war effort. Even Dad, who could no longer work after an accident in the dockyard had left him with a limp and intermittent pain, managed to do odd jobs and when the weather allowed, worked on his allotment, keeping them well supplied with fruit and vegetables and the occasional rabbit.

She walked out of the station and started to make her way home. Instead of going back along the High Street she walked up Beach Street to the seafront. A cold wind blew off the North Sea and she pulled her coat collar up, then thrust her hands into her pockets.

Despite the cold, she enjoyed walking along the prom, looking out at the navy ships that thronged the estuary. She looked across to the hazy outline of Southend, remembering a trip on the Medway Queen, a lovely day out with all the family. Bob was over there at a training camp somewhere in Essex. She shivered. When training finished, he would be sent overseas.

Today the sea was a murky brown as the waves churned up the mud on the sea bottom. In summer it wasn't a lot different, but Daisy and Sylvia and their friends didn't care. They spent most of the summer holidays swimming and lazing on the shingle beach. Would they be swimming here next year?

A shadow fell over her, blocking out the weak winter sun and she glanced up to see an unfamiliar shape suspended in the air. Her heart missed a beat until she realised what it was. She'd heard on the wireless about the barrage balloons which were designed to force enemy planes to fly higher – not that there had been any so far. She gave a little laugh at her momentary fright and walked on. So many changes in such a short time. Everyone said the war would be over by Christmas, just like they'd said about the last one. It didn't look like it though with all the precautions and new rules and regulations, like carrying your gas mask all the time.

She sighed. Tomorrow she would be back at work in the shirt factory, a job she hated. Two years to go before she could apply for the WAAFs and the war might be over by then. In the meantime, she would look around for a more interesting job. She couldn't just leave. Now Dad could no longer work, they were glad of her contribution to the family finances.

Her steps slowed as she reached the path down to the town. She wasn't looking forward to going home and seeing her mother's sadness at saying goodbye to Sylvia. How could she join up too and make her even more miserable?

***

Christmas in the Bishop household was a subdued affair in spite of the sumptuous meal Dora Bishop had prepared. The table was laid with the best china and Daisy had made a holly wreath to surround the tall candle in the middle.

Stan Bishop picked up the carving knife as Dora brought in the roast chicken. A plate of ham followed, together with dishes of vegetables and roast potatoes, all grown on Stan's allotment.

'Looks lovely, my dear,' he said as he began to carve. 'I can't wait to eat it all.'

Dora looked flushed, whether from the compliment or the heat of the kitchen Daisy couldn't tell. Her father wasn't usually one for compliments but perhaps he wanted to cheer her mother up, knowing how she felt with half her family missing from the Christmas table. She had been very quiet this morning and when Daisy went into the kitchen to help she had spotted a tear on her mother's cheek, quickly wiped away.

She had put an arm round Dora's waist and given her an affectionate squeeze. 'We miss Sylvia and Jimmy too,' she said.

Her mother hadn't answered, just kept on chopping cabbage as if she hadn't heard.

Daisy kept quiet after that and set about laying the table.

They finished the first course but none of them had an appetite for Christmas pudding and they went into the front room to listen to the King's Speech on the wireless. His Majesty's sombre words did nothing to lighten the atmosphere although he ended with a message of goodwill to those serving overseas and the hope that they would soon be home with their loved ones.

'That won't be any time soon,' Stan said. 'They've been calling it the phoney war, but my bet is things will start to hot up before too long.'

'Don't say that,' Dora protested. 'I want my Jimmy home and Sylvia.'

'Jimmy's better off where he is,' Stan said. 'I know nothing's happened so far, but you never know. I bet he's having the time of his life on that Welsh farm. He always loved animals.'

Daisy could see that her mother was getting upset at the turn the conversation was taking. 'I saw a barrage balloon on my way home,' she said.

'They're going up all over the place,' her father replied. 'Fat lot of good they are.'

Daisy half agreed with him, but she didn't want to provoke a discussion. Instead, she went up to her room, saying she wanted to write to Bob.

She sat at the little table in the bay window chewing the end of her pencil, wondering what to write. She wanted to berate him for joining the army so quickly. Why hadn't he waited to be called up? They could have had a little more time together. At least Essex wasn't too far away. Perhaps he'd get leave when his training finished.

The thought cheered her a little and she wrote several pages, telling him about Sylvia joining the WAAFs and her ambition to join too when she was old enough. She hoped he'd had a nice Christmas dinner and described their own, saying 'Dad says to make the most of it as rationing will start soon and who knows when we'll get another meal like this.'

She ended by saying she loved and missed him and pleaded with him to write back soon.

When she went downstairs to join her parents, Dad was snoozing in the chair and her mother was knitting. The wireless was on low, playing a piece of music she didn't recognise. She picked up a magazine and curled up on the sofa, trying to lose herself in a romantic story.

***

The shirt factory was still closed the next day and Daisy was bored. Her father had gone to his allotment and she wished she'd volunteered to go with him.

When her mother came downstairs with her hat and coat on Daisy looked surprised. 'Where are you off to? The shops are shut, aren't they?'

'I've joined the WVS, didn't I tell you?' Dora said. 'We're having a first aid meeting. We can't all have a day off. You can come if you like.'

Daisy pulled a face. Not her idea of fun. But what else was there to do? She fetched her coat and followed her mother down the garden path.

To her surprise she enjoyed it. She had thought it would be all old ladies like her mum, but there were a few younger women there. And it turned out to be fun bandaging and putting splints on each other.

Back at the shirt factory the next day, Daisy bent over her sewing machine fighting boredom. There had been a letter from Sylvia that morning enclosing a photo of her with a group of young women. They all looked so glamorous in their smart uniforms and Daisy envied them. Her sister said how much she was enjoying herself in Norfolk and ended by saying she hoped to get leave soon.

The supervisor interrupted her thoughts. 'Daisy Bishop – concentrate. I don't want wavy hems.'

'Sorry,' Daisy muttered. Oh heck, told off again. She should be doing something useful like her mum. She would have to find another job – and soon, before she died of boredom.

Chapter Two

'Have I got to wear this horrible thing?' Daisy dangled the shapeless off-white cap between finger and thumb as if it was a dangerous snake. It looked like the turban her mum wore when doing the housework. She shook her curly locks which it had taken ages to tame that morning. 'It'll squash me hair.'

She had given notice at the factory and joined the NAAFI which was situated just inside the garrison behind the guard room. If she was too young to join the WAAFs, at least she'd be doing her bit for the war effort.

She had hoped for a dainty little frilled cap like those girls in Lyons Corner House wore, with a white frilly apron to match, but the beige overall and shapeless cap were a disappointment.

'You're not here to look glamorous, my girl,' the supervisor said. 'Your job is to wash up, peel carrots and chop cabbage.'

Daisy scowled and pulled on the hideous overall, jamming the cap on her head. Was this why she'd left the shirt factory?

'Tuck your hair in, cover it right up,' the supervisor instructed. 'The customers don't want hair in their dinner.'

What have I let myself in for, Daisy asked herself. She would've looked more glamorous if she'd joined the Land Army. Well, she had no choice now. Besides, she'd only signed on as a NAAFI assistant for the duration of the war or at least until she was old enough to join the WAAFs like her sister. Better get on with it then.

'I'm Muriel Green but you call me Mrs,' the supervisor said hurrying her through to the kitchen. At the far end, a row of ovens and hobs was presided over by a man in Army uniform covered with a chef's apron and hat. A young man, also in uniform, looked up from rolling pastry and winked. Daisy looked away quickly and followed Mrs Green to the line of deep metal sinks under the window. Piles of dirty crockery adorned the draining boards either side of each sink. 'Make a start on that lot,' she said, smirking.

'Doesn't anyone else work here then?' Daisy risked a cheeky grin.

Mrs Green smiled and took pity on her. 'Don't worry, Lily will be here soon. She'll show you the ropes.' A burst of laughter came from the canteen and Daisy glanced through the hatch hoping for a glimpse of Bob. She could hardly believe it when he'd finished his training a few days ago and turned up on her doorstep, telling her he'd been posted to Sheerness Garrison here just up the road. What were the chances? That was her main reason for joining the NAAFI . She might even see Bob when she was at work, she thought hopefully.

Her mum had been furious when she'd given in her notice at the factory. 'Why give up a well-paid job to be a glorified waitress?' she'd asked.

'I'll be doing my bit for the war,' she'd said, and Mum had seemed to accept that. If only she knew, Daisy thought, as she filled the sink with hot water and poured in a good measure of Teepol. This new stuff made washing up much easier. 'Thank goodness I don't have to use washing soda like Mum,' she murmured.

Still, she hadn't bargained on spending all her time washing dishes. Not only did it seem she was what her dad would call a skivvy, the lowest of the low, but even if Bob came into the canteen, her chances of seeing him had sunk to zero. She couldn't even hope for a glimpse of him through the window. Her view was of a brick wall and, if she craned her neck, a glimpse of sky.

As she scrubbed at the greasy plates with their dried-on residue of egg yolk and bean juice she let her mind wander to her last meeting with Bob. She was still cross that he hadn't waited for the call-up, but she couldn't help feeling proud when he'd come home on leave in his smart new uniform. They'd walked along the seafront hand in hand gazing out at the Royal Navy ships in the estuary.

And now, here he was, stationed in Sheerness garrison just up the road from her home. Her heart gave a little skip at the thought that she was bound to see him soon. But then she sighed. It wouldn't be for long. The regiment would soon be embarking for France and who knew what would happen?

She added more hot water and plunged another pile of plates into the sink. One thing about this sort of job, she thought, it left her mind free to daydream. She started to hum *'I've got my Love to Keep me Warm'*, lost in thoughts of her last date with Bob. She imagined herself in his arms as they waltzed round the Wheatsheaf Hall, he in his smart uniform, she in her best blue dress. And tonight, they were going out again.

She started to sing, holding the dish mop up to her face as if it were a microphone, then did a few dance steps. As she whirled round, she spotted the assistant chef grinning and came to a stop, her face reddening.

'Need a partner?' he asked with a cheeky grin. 'I'm Harold. I'm no Fred Astaire but I'm partial to a dance.'

'No thanks. I've already got a partner,' she said.

'Suit yourself.'

'Tompkins, get on with your work, you lazy so-and-so,' Sergeant Shiner shouted across the room.

Harold jumped to attention and went back to stirring the big vat of soup.

Hiding a smile, Daisy turned back to her pile of dishes just as the door opened and a girl came in pushing a trolley loaded with more dirty crockery.

'Hello, I'm Lily,' she said. 'I'm supposed to show you the ropes.' She nodded towards the stack of newly washed crockery. 'Looks like you didn't need to be told.'

'Mrs Green told me to get on with it.'

Lily picked up a tea cloth and began drying the plates, stacking them neatly on a shelf. As they worked, she spoke quietly, 'That's Cook Sergeant Shiner over there, but you call him Chef when he's in here. Outside it's Sergeant. He's got big ideas, thinks he's working in some posh hotel up in London. And Harold, Private Tompkins, the other one, you want to watch him. Fancies himself, he does.'

'I noticed - we've already met,' Daisy said.

Lily went on to explain what the work entailed and who she'd be working with. 'Mrs Green's all right. Strict, but if you get on with your work...' She paused. 'What made you join the NAAFI?' she asked.

Daisy didn't feel she could confide the real reason. 'Got fed up with the shirt factory,' she said. 'What about you?'

'I was stuck home looking after the little ones. My mum was ill after the last baby but she's OK now. So I grabbed the chance of a proper job, told them everyone has to do their bit.'

'That's what I told my dad,' Daisy said. 'I didn't think I'd be stuck in the kitchen though. I hate washing up.'

'Peeling spuds is worse,' Lily said.

'I thought I'd be serving, dishing up the meals and that.'

Lily smiled. 'I know – you wanted to be out there eyeing up the soldiers and sailors.'

Daisy tossed her head. 'Certainly not,' she retorted.

'I'll believe you, thousands wouldn't.' Lily laughed. 'Anyway, what's wrong with that? You've got to have a bit of fun in life.'

'Don't you have a boyfriend already then?'

'Chance'd be a fine thing. If I was allowed out to the pictures or anywhere, I had to take my little brother and sisters, give Mum a bit of a rest. Who'd want to go out with me with them hanging on?' Lily shrugged. 'What about you?'

Daisy felt herself blushing. Her relationship with Bob was too new to talk about. She'd known him since they were children and they'd always been friends. But things had changed when he joined the Army. He'd become more serious, more grown-up, she supposed. When he'd gone off to Aldershot for his training, he had begged her to write to him. 'I want you to be my girl,' he'd said, 'to be here when I get home waiting for me. You will, won't you?' He'd kissed her then, her first real kiss and it had stirred up all sorts of feelings she had only previously imagined.

Lily gave her a little push. 'Go on then, who is he?'

'No one special.' Daisy tried to sound nonchalant. It would have been true a few months ago. Bob lived in the same street and they'd played out with all the other kids after school. He was just one of the gang. But then, she had to admit, he had always been a bit different to the other lads, protecting her from bullying, sharing his sweets with her and helping her with her school work.

Lily shrugged and picked up another plate. 'Better get on or we'll have Mrs G on our backs.'

***

Daisy's hands were red, and her fingers wrinkled from the hot water but despite the discomfort she found she was enjoying the work. Lily was a cheerful companion and kept her entertained with gossip about the other NAAFI girls, as well as the Catering Corps personnel. She was going to like working here, she thought.

As they worked, Lily told her that she'd lived in the town all her life. 'In Hope Street, with mum and dad and two sisters plus a baby brother,' she said.

'I live up the other end of town. My sister's in the WAAFs and my little brother's evacuated to Wales so there's just me now.'

'Wish my lot had been evacuated,' Lily said with a little laugh. 'It gets a bit crowded in our house.'

'Why weren't they?'

'Mum didn't want them to go. And she was right – there's been no bombs.'

'I don't think Mum wanted Jimmy to go, but Dad insisted,' Daisy said.

The morning passed quickly as they were so busy and there was no time for more chat. As fast as one lot of crockery was dried and put away, the kitchen doors would swing open and another trolley full would arrive pushed by a girl in a white overall. She only stopped long enough to introduce herself.

'I'm June. See you at dinner time.' Then she was gone.

Daisy gazed longingly at the swing doors wishing she could go and help clear the tables. If Bob wasn't on duty, he was sure to come in even if only for a packet of cigarettes. She turned to Lily. 'Will we always be working out here?'

'The new ones have to do a stint in the kitchen. Mrs G likes to see how hard we work, how we shape up. If you're lucky she'll take a shine to you and let you serve.'

'What about you? You've been here longer and you're still a kitchen skivvy.'

Lily twisted her hands in her overall. 'She won't let me near the customers. I'm too clumsy. I spilt gravy on a sergeant and he bawled me out something awful.'

'It wasn't your fault. Anyway, you're not clumsy. You've been doing OK as far as I can see.'

'I know, but when I get out there with all the noise and chatter, I get nervous and keep dropping things. Besides, I prefer it in the kitchen. I know what I have to do and I just get on with it.'

Daisy glanced towards the end of the room. The other workers ignored her and she was a little disappointed that they had not bothered to introduce themselves. She had hoped they would be friendly and she would enjoy the same camaraderie that she had with her co-workers at the shirt factory. Perhaps she shouldn't have left there after all. But then she thought of Bob and how near he was. The barracks was just a few yards down the road beyond the parade ground. She could hear the shouts of the sergeant major as he drilled the men and could picture Bob out there, smart in his uniform, arms swinging, chest thrust out proudly. He wouldn't be there long though. Soon the regiment would be leaving for France. She must make the most of his presence while she could.

'Hey, come on, stop your day dreaming,' Lily said. 'It's dinner time.' She led Daisy through into the canteen. It was almost empty, just a couple of soldiers seated at the other end of the room and some sailors queuing up at the counter.

On the wall behind the counter a board listed the menu for the day.

'Steak and kidney today, my favourite,' Lily said, picking up a tray.

When they had been served, she led Daisy to a table at the other end of the room, where a girl was already tucking into her pie. 'Mind if we join you?' She turned to Daisy. 'This is June.'

'We met – briefly.' Daisy smiled. 'Pleased to meet you.'

'Lily tells me you live in the town,' June said.

'Born and bred like Lily. What about you?'

'I'm a Londoner. Didn't have much say in where they sent me. I'm lodging in Marine Parade. Big house, proper bathroom and all.'

'Sounds nice,' Lily said. 'Room to yourself as well, you lucky thing. I have to share with my two sisters.'

'My sister's in the WAAFs so I've got a room to myself until she comes home,' Daisy offered.

'Well, how do you like working here then?' June asked.

'OK, I suppose. Too soon to tell really.'

'Just watch out for Mr Browning. He's a real tartar. Doesn't stand any nonsense.'

'Who's he then?'

'Manager. Luckily, we don't see too much of him. He keeps to his office, leaves all the work to Mrs Green, lazy b….'

Lily chimed in. 'He gives me the creeps, always coming up behind you and checking what you're doing.' She turned to June and asked if she had enjoyed the film last night. Soon the two girls were chatting and laughing and Daisy felt a bit left out.

She concentrated on her food, enjoying the tasty steak and kidney. Much better than what Mum makes, she thought. Still, her mother didn't have much time to cook since she'd joined the WVS, her contribution to the war effort, not to mention coping with the rationing which everyone said would get worse as time went on.

Lily and June kept up a stream of chatter, but Daisy hardly heard a word. Her attention was on the entrance and every time the door opened, she looked up from her plate, hoping that Bob had come in. She was disappointed that there was no sign of him by the time they had finished their meal and she reluctantly stood up and followed Lily back to the kitchen.

'More washing up, I suppose,' she said.

'Spuds, more like,' Lily said with a groan.

She was right. Sergeant Shiner called them over and indicated a sack full of potatoes. 'Get on with that lot,' he said. 'I need them done ready for the evening shift.'

'At least we can sit down to do 'em,' Lily whispered. 'My feet are killing me.'

Daisy's feet were aching too. She wasn't used to standing so long after sitting at a sewing machine in the shirt factory. Her relief was short-lived as her back started to ache bending over the tub of potatoes which steadily filled up only to be whisked away by the chef's assistant and replaced by another.

'Why did I leave the factory?' she murmured. 'Have I made a mistake coming to work here?'

'Why did you then?' Lily asked.

'I told you – got fed up. Well, I really wanted to join the WAAF's like my sister. But I'm too young. I'll sign on after my next birthday.'

Lily looked disappointed. 'I'd be sorry if you left. It's nice having someone to work with.'

'Well, it won't be for a while. And I might not get in.'

'Of course you will. Where's your sister stationed then?'

‘Somewhere in Norfolk but she wrote that she’s getting some leave. I’m looking forward to seeing her – want to find out about the WAAFs, what it’s like and that.’

Lily dropped the last potato into the tub and rubbed her hands on her overall. ‘I don’t blame you for wanting something better. And that WAAF uniform is so glamorous.’

Daisy smiled. It wasn’t so much the glamour that was the attraction. It was the hope of being able to match her sister’s achievements for once. Sylvia was clever as well as beautiful and, although Daisy wasn’t exactly jealous, she did sometimes wish that she wasn’t so much in her shadow.

Private Harold Tompkins, the chef’s assistant, came over and removed the last tub of potatoes, giving Daisy another wink. ‘That’s it for today,’ he said.

‘Thanks, Private.’

‘You can call me Harold,’ he said.

‘What now, Lily?’ Daisy asked, ignoring him.

‘Nearly home time,’ her friend said.

Mrs Green appeared from the little cubbyhole off the kitchen which she used as an office. ‘I’ve been keeping an eye on you, Daisy Bishop,’ she said sternly.

Daisy bit her lip. Had she been talking too much? Had the supervisor noticed Private Tompkins winking at her? But they had still got on with their work. She was about to say so, but Mrs Green allowed herself the vestige of a smile. ‘Well done. Keep up the good work and I’ll think about swapping you with June to clear tables.’

Not exactly a promotion, Daisy thought, but she smiled and said thank you. At least she’d be out of this kitchen and seeing a bit of life – and a chance to see more of Bob.

***

Daisy shivered as she left the warm NAAFI kitchen and went out into the cold. A bitter wind blew off the sea and she pulled her collar up, shoving her hands into her pockets as she hurried out to the garrison’s main gate. She paused and looked down the road towards the parade ground. Bob was taking her out tonight and she'd hoped he could get away early. There was no sign of him and she shrugged. She'd be seeing him soon.

Almost spring, but it still felt like winter, she thought, deciding not to take her usual route home along the sea front. She liked walking along the prom instead of the High Street, but she didn't fancy braving that icy gale. She spared a thought for those at sea - many of the lads she'd been at school with had joined the Royal or Merchant Navy. Thank goodness Bob had ignored the lure of the sea.

She pushed open the back gate and went in through the scullery calling out, 'It's me, Mum. I'm home.'

'In here, Daisy, love.' Dora Bishop called from the front room.

What were they doing in there? They must have visitors, Daisy thought, hanging her coat up behind the door and going up the passage to the room they only used on special occasions.

Dora and Sylvia were sitting on the sofa and her father was standing with his back to the fire where a good blaze was roaring up the chimney. 'Hello, lass. Had a good day?' he asked.

'Yes, love. How was it?' Dora asked.

Before she could reply Sylvia stood up, smoothing down the skirt of her air force blue uniform. 'Hello, Sis. I was hoping you'd get home before we went out. I want you to meet Roland.'

Only then did Daisy become aware that there was someone else in the room as the tall man in RAF uniform turned from the window.

He stepped towards her, holding out his hand. 'Pilot Officer Hargreaves. Pleased to meet you.' He held on to her hand a fraction longer than necessary and smiled. 'So you're the little sister I've heard so much about.'

Sylvia moved towards them, hooking her arm into his and smiling up at him. 'So now you've met the family, it's time to go. We don't want to miss the start of the film, do we?'

‘No rush, darling,’ he said. ‘Since your father was kind enough to offer me a drink, I should at least finish it before rushing off.’ He picked up a glass from the window sill and took a sip. ‘Good beer, Mr Bishop.’ He turned to Daisy. ‘Sylvia tells me you’re working in the NAAFI. Must pop in some time.’

His smile embarrassed her and she knew Sylvia was looking daggers at her. ‘Sorry, it’s other ranks only,’ she said, finding her voice. She turned to her sister. ‘Only two years to go and I’ll be wearing a uniform like that,’ she said.

‘I don’t think so,’ Sylvia smirked.

‘I don’t see why not.’

‘Haven’t you heard? You won’t be allowed to leave. Wartime regulations. You’ve signed on for the duration.’

‘No, that can’t be right. Dad, what do you think?’

‘She might be right. You should have stayed at the shirt factory. I told you, didn’t I?’

Daisy was lost for words. She scarcely noticed when Sylvia and Roland left to go to the cinema. Her mother saw she was upset and tried to comfort her. ‘At least you’ll be at home love,’ she said. ‘What with young Jimmy evacuated to Wales and Sylvia stationed in Norfolk, I’d be lost if you went away too.’

‘I know, Mum. It’s just...’ She couldn’t explain. It seemed so petty to be envious of Sylvia. She should be thankful she had a loving home and a boyfriend who thought the world of her. Thinking of him, she gasped. ‘Oh dear. Bob’ll be here soon. I must get ready.’

‘You haven’t had any tea,’ Dora protested.

‘Don’t worry. I had a good dinner in the canteen. We’ll get some chips.’ She rushed upstairs and sat at the dressing table. It was littered with pots of make-up and creams. In the mirror she caught sight of Sylvia’s suitcase open on the other bed, lacy lingerie spilling out of it and stockings draped over the chair.

No time to get changed, just to tidy her hair and put on some lipstick. ‘Wonder how long she’s staying,’ she muttered as she rummaged among her sister’s things to find her own lipstick. Since Sylvia had joined the WAAF she'd enjoyed having a bedroom to herself.

Why couldn't her sister use Jimmy's room, she asked herself.

Later, as she sat in the cinema, snuggled up with Bob's arm round her, she tried to forget Sylvia's sniping and enjoy being with the man she loved. But occasionally her thoughts strayed to Roland Hargreaves and the way he had held on to her hand and gazed into her eyes.

Sylvia might think she had him hooked round her little finger, but Daisy couldn't help thinking that he wasn't the sort of man to be tied down to one woman. She squeezed Bob's hand. How lucky she was to have a nice steady boyfriend who loved her.

Chapter Three

Daisy scarcely noticed the cold wind stinging her cheeks as she walked home in a daze, her hand in Bob's. She had no recollection of the film they had seen, her mind full of their kisses in the back row of the Rio Cinema. When they stopped at her back gate, he pulled her towards him and kissed her again, holding her close.

When he finally released her, he muttered, 'I don't want to go,' his lips close to her ear.

'Me neither. I could stay here all night, never mind the cold,' Daisy said with a smile.

'No. France – I mean – I don't want to go to France.'

'No need to worry about that just yet. You've only just finished your training,' Daisy said, but a lump settled in her throat as she realised what he meant. 'No, when?' she gasped.

'First thing tomorrow. Crack of dawn. Down to Dover and then over the water.'

Daisy choked back her tears. 'Why didn't you tell me before?'

'Didn't want to spoil our last night together.' He pulled her close to him and stroked her hair. 'Oh, Daisy love, I'll miss you so. You will write to me, won't you?'

She nodded, unable to speak.

'And I'll write to you - every day if I can.'

Daisy was about to reply when she heard the back door open. 'That you, Daisy? Time to come in, love,' her father called.

Bob pushed the gate open. 'Better go in, sweetheart.' He kept hold of her hand. 'Don't forget me, will you, what with all those blokes in and out of the NAAFI giving you the eye.'

'Don't talk daft, Bob Gardner.' Daisy attempted a laugh, but her voice choked on a sob. 'I'll miss you.'

'One last kiss then.'

Daisy hurried up the path, her lips still burning from that last passionate embrace. She turned at the back door to see Bob still there. He raised his hand in a wave and then he was gone.

As she entered the kitchen her mother glanced at the clock. 'Have a nice time, love?'

Daisy nodded, hoping Mum wouldn't notice her tear-stained face. 'I'm off to bed, early start in the morning.'

'Goodnight then. Sylvia's not in yet. I'll tell her to be careful not to wake you.'

'I thought she'd be back by now,' her father said. 'I'm not going up till she's back.'

'Stan, she's a grown woman. She can take care of herself,' Mum protested.

'She said they were going to the pictures. I thought she'd come back with Daisy when the film finished. I don't like my girls being out late at night, especially in the blackout with all these soldiers and sailors about.'

Daisy turned at the bottom of the stairs and smiled as her mother shrugged as if to say, you know your father.

'You worry too much. Sylvia's with that nice airman. What harm can she come to?'

Stan banged his pipe out on the side of the fireplace and snorted. 'Him! Bit too smooth for my liking.'

***

Daisy had just drifted off to sleep when she was awoken by the door opening. She sat up rubbing her eyes. 'That you, Sylvia?' She blinked as her sister switched on the light. Good job she'd remembered to fix the blackout curtain before getting into bed.

'Who else would it be?' Sylvia threw her handbag down on the dressing table, knocking one of Daisy's scent bottles onto the floor.

Daisy didn't comment. She didn't want to quarrel with her sister who was only home for a short time. Still, she couldn't help thinking she'd be glad to have her bedroom to herself again. 'Have a good time?' she asked.

'Ooh, it was lovely.' A dreamy smile crept across Sylvia's face.

'You enjoyed the film then?'

'What about you? Was it fun sitting in the back row with the boy next door? I bet you and little Bobby didn't see much of the film.'

Daisy blushed and Sylvia laughed. 'Actually, we didn't go to the pictures,' she said. 'Roland's staying at the Britannia Hotel and we had a meal there. A bit better than eating a bag of chips on the way home.'

Why does she have to sneer all the time, Daisy wondered. Why does she have to be so toffee-nosed? 'Well, I enjoyed my chips. Could you put the light out please? I need to sleep, I've got an early start in the morning.'

'Don't you want to hear about the rest of my evening?'

Daisy shook her head and pulled the covers over her head, but Sylvia wasn't deterred. 'We went up to his room,' she whispered.

Daisy sat up abruptly. 'You didn't...?'

'That'd be telling.' Sylvia laughed and switched off the light. As she got into bed she pleaded. 'You won't tell Mum, will you?'

'Of course not.' Daisy had always covered for her even when she was annoyed with her. Despite their differences she had always admired and looked up to her clever beautiful sister.

As she settled down to sleep, she tried not to think of what Sylvia and Roland might have got up to in his hotel room. For a few minutes she had managed not to think about Bob and his news. Now, despair swept over her. Would she ever see him again, would he keep his promise to write? It had been bad enough those weeks he was away at training camp. Now he was off to France and who knew what awaited him over there?

She could not imagine life without the boy next door. He had always been there, defending her from school bullies, taking the blame when she got into trouble for some mischief. They were grown-up now and their feelings for each other had changed, she couldn't remember quite how or when.

She turned over and buried her face in her pillow. 'Oh, Bob,' she murmured trying to stifle her tears. She didn't want Sylvia to hear her crying and start teasing.

***

When Daisy woke the next morning, Sylvia was still asleep. She got up quietly, not wanting to disturb her sister and continue their conversation of the night before. She didn't want to believe what Sylvia had hinted, although she wasn't really shocked. Hadn't she often wondered what it would be like with Bob and been tempted to go a bit further than kisses and cuddles in the seafront shelters? No, she was worried. Suppose Sylvia got pregnant. Their dad would go mad, not to mention she would be drummed out of the WAAFs.

Downstairs, Dora Bishop was pouring water into the teapot. 'Got time for breakfast, love? Dad's had his – gone over the allotment already. Don't know what he finds to do in this weather.'

'He's always over there.' Daisy said.

'I know, but he has to keep busy. It's frustrating for him not being able to work. He feels he's doing his bit, putting food on the table. Now then, what about breakfast?'

'Just toast please, Mum.' Daisy poured herself a cup of tea. 'Sylvia still asleep?'

Daisy nodded. 'She got in quite late.'

Dora's lips tightened. 'Can't say much to her. She has a life of her own now. Still, I wish...' Her voice tailed off as the kitchen door opened and Sylvia came into the kitchen, still in her dressing gown, her hair tousled.

Not so glamorous now, Daisy thought, inwardly chiding herself for her unkind thought. 'Morning, Sylvia. Shall I pour you a cuppa?'

Sylvia yawned and nodded.

Dora turned to Daisy. 'Here's your toast, love. Better get it down you if you don't want to be late for work.'

Daisy sat at the table and bit into her toast. 'When do you go back, Sylvia?' she asked, her mouth full.

'Later today.'

'So soon?' Dora said, sitting at the table.

'I told you it was a flying visit.'

'What about Roland?' Daisy asked.

'Didn't I say? He's been posted to Eastchurch, just up the Island. I said goodbye to him yesterday. He can't get away today.'

She didn't sound very upset but then, Daisy thought. Sylvia had never been one for showing her real feelings.

'I expect you'll miss him,' she said.

'Plenty more where he came from.' Sylvia said, busying herself with buttering her toast. 'I'm not like you, Daisy, settling for the first man who comes along. I intend to have fun before I settle down.'

'I thought Roland was special. You seemed very close last night.'

Dora came in with a fresh pot of tea, putting an end to the conversation.

Sylvia shot Daisy a warning look. 'Just because we went to the pictures...We travelled down from Norfolk on the same train, that's all,' she snapped.

Daisy finished her breakfast and stood up. 'I'm off. Safe journey, Sylvia. And don't forget to write to Mum and Dad.'

She hurried off in the direction of the barracks, thinking about Sylvia and the fib she'd told about going to the pictures. She just hoped her sister wasn't going to be hurt, that's all.

The wind wasn't so cold today and she looked forward to signs of spring. She wondered if Dad was right when he'd said the long severe winter had held up the progress of the war. That was probably why Bob's regiment was only now embarking for the continent. Most of them had gone as soon as war was declared and were already over there trying to hold back the Germans' advance on France.

As she hurried over the moat, she saw a line of Army lorries pouring out of the garrison gate. They turned right and roared through Blue Town, past the Dockyard wall and on to the coast road. As she reached the gate, she saw soldiers hanging over the backs of the lorries, waving. She stopped and waved back, hoping for a glimpse of Bob. And there he was, leaning out as far as he could, waving until the lorry turned the bend.

She stood there for a few moments, wiping away a tear. When would she see him again? A tap on her shoulder startled her.

It was Lily. 'Come on, we'll be late. Don't want Mrs G after us.'

June was already there when they entered the kitchen. She smiled a good morning as Muriel Green came out of her office.

'You, Lily Scott. Potatoes, this morning,' the supervisor snapped.

She turned to Daisy and handed her a white overall instead of the horrible beige one. 'Tables to be laid. June will show you.'

As Daisy pulled on the overall and followed June out of the room, Mrs Green's voice followed her. 'And cover that hair.' She sighed and fetched the hated cap from where she'd left it the night before.

She remembered where the cutlery was stored at the end of the counter and went to fetch a handful of forks, but June stopped her. 'We don't lay the tables – they fetch their own cutlery when they go up for their food. We have to put out the sauce bottles, salt and pepper on each table. First we have to wipe them all down.'

She showed Daisy where the cloths were kept and fetched an enamel bowl of hot water. It didn't take long and she wondered what to do next.

'Come on, Daisy. Stop mooning about. We have to get the plates now, stack them up at the end of the counter. Then fill up the cutlery trays.'

They'd scarcely finished when the doors opened and their customers started to trickle in.

'I didn't think there'd be anyone in today. Haven't they all gone off? I saw the lorries.'

'Some of them stay behind – for maintenance and that. And then there's the navy blokes.'

Mrs Green appeared and took her place behind the counter. 'No time for idle chatter, girls,' she said.

'Sorry, Mrs G. I was just showing Daisy what to do.'

They were kept busy for the rest of the morning fetching cigarettes, sweets and other goods from the stores to replenish the shelves behind the counter. Then it was clearing the tables and carrying the used crockery out to the kitchen.

When she went through with the next lot Daisy saw that Lily had finished peeling the potatoes and was now chopping carrots. The pile of dirty dishes on the draining boards was growing and Daisy guessed what her next job would be. But first they were allowed a short break and she was glad of a chance to rest her aching feet as well as a chat with her new friends.

She sipped her tea and gave a contented sigh. She was surprised how much she had enjoyed the morning's work, bustling in and out. Keeping busy helped the time fly, too.

Even the thought of that pile of greasy dishes didn't bother her, especially if she had Lily to chat to. She liked June, too. It was nice working with girls her own age. Most of the women at the factory had been old – well middle aged she supposed. And they'd been bossy too. She had more in common with these girls and she hoped they'd become real friends in time. And at least Mrs Green left them alone to get on with it - most of the time.

Lily took her cup back to the counter. 'Come on. Time to get stuck in again.'

'What about you, June?' Daisy asked.

'I'm off home – back again this evening.'

'I hate those split shifts,' Lily said.

'I don't mind. Anyway, I'm hoping that tall bloke will come in again later. You must have noticed him – over six foot with dark curly hair.'

'Hasn't he been posted then?' Daisy asked.

'I hope not. He's gorgeous, just like a film star.' June sighed.

Lily laughed. 'You're always swooning over some bloke. It'll be someone else tomorrow.'

'Why do you think I took this job?' June grinned and went for her coat, waving goodbye at the door.

As Lily and Daisy tackled the mountain of washing up Lily said, 'That June – she's a regular flirt. No harm in her though.' She nudged Daisy's arm, flicking soapy suds over her. 'Was he really that good-looking?'

'I didn't notice.'

Lily gave a disbelieving snort.

'It's true. My boyfriend was with those who went off this morning and I've been thinking about him all day.'

'I'm sorry,' Lily said. 'I didn't realise.'

Daisy choked back a sob. 'Oh, Lily, what will I do if he doesn't come back?'

Lily put a comforting arm around her shoulder. 'You mustn't think like that.'

Daisy shook her off. 'You're right. No more moaning.' She picked up a tea towel and carried on drying dishes. But she couldn't shake off that image - her last glimpse of Bob as the lorry turned the corner. She decided to pop in and see his mum when she'd finished work. Mrs Gardner would be feeling sad, all alone in the house. Bob's father had died when he was small and there were no other children.

Chapter Four

Daisy had been working in the NAAFI for two months and she found she was starting to enjoy life. She had made two new friends and there were always the soldiers and sailors in and out teasing and making them laugh. Not that she took any of them seriously. She was saving herself for Bob.

But there had been no letters and she was getting worried. Mum said she shouldn't upset herself. Bob's mum hadn't heard from him either.

'You don't know what it's like over there, love. You've heard the news - I expect writing letters is the last thing on his mind.'

Daisy had burst into tears. 'Suppose something's happened to him, Mum. He might be wounded or...' She couldn't bear to think the worst.

Then a few days later, June said she'd heard from her brother who was in the same regiment as Bob and on the same day, Mrs Gardner had a letter and came round to say Bob was all right. So why hasn't he written to me? Daisy asked herself.

As more time passed, she began to be annoyed. All that talk about waiting for him and staying true to him and he couldn't even be bothered to write. Deep down she knew she was being unreasonable, but it helped to hold on to her anger. No use sitting in a corner and crying.

When Lily and June asked her to go to the pictures with them she went along, trying not to think of the last time she had been to the Rio, sitting in the back row with Bob and hardly seeing anything of the film at all. To her surprise she enjoyed herself although she wasn't really a fan of Spencer Tracy. Lily and June were good company and helped to take her mind off worrying about Bob.

It was still bitterly cold and starting to rain when they came out of the cinema. They ran down the Broadway but instead of turning left to go home, Daisy stayed with her friends and went along the High Street, tumbling through the door of Jacobs' fish and chip shop and shaking the raindrops from their hair.

'You're lucky to get any fish, girls,' Mr Jacobs said. 'Real shortage now. The lads can't get out on the boats so much nowadays.' He shovelled chips into the newspaper. 'Bloody u-boats,' he muttered. 'There - at least there's plenty of chips.'

The girls thanked him and walked back along the High Street, eating out of the paper and giggling. 'Bloody u-boats,' June said, laughing.

'It's not funny,' Daisy protested.

'I know. It's just the way he said it.'

They sobered up and walked on eating their chips in silence, each busy with their thoughts, until they reached the Clock Tower. The war was becoming more real to them now. For so long the papers had been calling it the 'phony war' and nothing much seemed to be happening, but just lately the wireless news bulletins were becoming more sombre. Each of them had someone to worry about – June's brother, Lily's cousin and Bob. However hard she tried he was never far from her thoughts.

When she'd said goodnight to her friends and let herself in the back door, the light was still on in the kitchen. Mum always waited up for her however late she got in.

'Good film, love?' Nora asked.

'Not bad. Spencer Tracy.'

'My favourite, I should have come with you,' Nora said with a smile, turning to the dresser and picking up an envelope.

Daisy's heart leapt for a moment and then she sighed as her mother said, 'From Jimmy. Poor lad. He sounds really fed up. Wants to come home.'

'Well, Mum, I don't see why you don't let him. There's been no bombs. And if he's unhappy...'

'But they say we must keep them out of harm's way, just in case...' Nora sighed. 'I've seen a poster about it.'

Daisy didn't know what to say. She gave her mother a hug and said, 'I'm going up. Early start tomorrow.'

As she lay in bed, she said a prayer for Bob's safety as she did every night. But her last thought as she drifted off to sleep was 'why is everyone getting letters except me?'

***

The next morning she had just hung her coat up and was tugging on the dreaded cap when Mrs Green called her into the office.

'I've been keeping my eye on you,' the supervisor said.

Daisy trembled. Had she done something wrong?

But Mrs Green was smiling. 'You're a good worker. I think you're cut out for more than washing up and peeling spuds. How do you fancy going on the till?'

'Really? Yes, I'd like that,' she stammered. 'Yes please.'

'Well, I'll give you a trial period. See how you get on.'

'Thank you, Mrs Green I won't let you down. When do I start?'

'Tomorrow, but it's time you had a proper uniform, although you'll be wearing your white overall behind the counter.' She stood up and said, 'Come with me. We'll get you measured up.'

As they made their way through the kitchen, Lily looked up from chopping cabbage and frowned. But Daisy gave her a reassuring smile.

Mrs Green strode across the parade ground to the stores and Daisy hurried to keep up with her. A proper uniform instead of that horrid brown overall, she thought, and a hat with a brim and a maroon badge, a belted jacket with epaulettes. Dressed in that she would really feel that she was ‘doing her bit’, a proper war worker. Of course, it couldn’t compare with her sister’s WAAF uniform – a uniform she’d hoped to be wearing herself one day until Sylvia crushed her hopes.

‘Come along girl. I haven’t got all day,’ Mrs Green chided. ‘And stop looking at the men.’

‘I’m not, I wasn’t,’ Daisy protested. She had been so lost in thought she hadn’t even been aware of the group of squaddies marching past. But as she looked up she couldn’t help noticing the one June had been raving about – the tall one they called Lofty. He stood head and shoulders above the rest of them and he was smiling at her.

She hastily looked away and followed Mrs Green into the stores. Half an hour later she was kitted out in her new uniform and marched proudly back to the NAAFI building. Only then did it occur to her that her new friends might be a bit put out by her promotion. After all, they had been there longer than she had.

***

Back in the kitchen, Daisy had to finish her shift and would start her new job the following morning. She could hardly face her friends but to her relief, Lily congratulated her on her promotion. June, however, was obviously upset.

‘I’ve been here over a year and you come in and take over,’ she said.

Daisy didn’t know what to say. It wasn’t her fault.

Lily came to her rescue. ‘She had no say in it. You know what Mrs G’s like, she makes her own rules. If you don’t like it, complain to Sid Browning. He’s the one in charge.’

‘Oh, yes, and then Mrs G will take it out on me. You know she hates us going over her head.’

‘Well then, just put up with it. And don’t go being nasty to Daisy. I thought she was your friend,’ Lily said indignantly.

June sniffed and gave a tentative smile. 'Sorry, Daisy. I know it's not your fault. It's just Mrs G has been promising me...'

Daisy felt uncomfortable. She didn't want to fall out with her new friend. She smiled back and went to fetch her overall, leaving the new jacket on the peg behind the door. That morning she worked twice as hard and took on some of June's duties as well, hoping to mollify her a little.

It seemed to work but when they stopped for their break, June was very quiet.

At the end of their shift, Mrs Green asked Daisy to stay behind to be instructed in the use of the till. 'It'll give you a start in the morning,' she said. 'Don't worry. You're a bright girl. You'll soon pick it up.'

Daisy said goodbye to her friends and followed the supervisor into her office.

After explaining that as well as taking money on the counter, she would be responsible for cashing up at the end of the shift, Mrs Green led her through to the canteen. They spent a few minutes practising until Daisy felt confident she could manage.

'Well done. Now, I'll be with you for the first half hour and then I expect you to manage alone. I've too much paperwork to do to spend more time with you.'

Daisy still felt a bit nervous, but she smiled and nodded, hoping she looked confident.

She said goodnight and went to fetch her coat. As she buttoned it up, the door opened and Private Tompkins came in.

He started and said, 'Oh, you're still here. I thought everyone had gone now the canteen's closed.'

'I'm just off,' Daisy said, edging past him. What was he doing here so late?

'I've been doing some overtime. Mr Browning asked me to stay late,' he said, hastily stepping aside.

Daisy hurried out, glancing behind to make sure he wasn't following. She remembered Lily's remark and that cheeky wink he'd given on her first day, the way he'd flirted with her. There was something about him that made her shiver and yet he hadn't really said or done anything untoward. But why had he felt it necessary to explain why he was there? It was none of her business after all.

She had just reached the main gate when she heard footsteps behind her. She wasn't nervous. After all there were always two soldiers on guard at the entrance to the garrison so she felt safe enough – most of them knew her now and she was seldom asked to show her pass.

She called out a cheery goodnight to them, slowing down so that whoever was behind her would overtake her. She was used to walking home in the dark on her own despite the blackout, but she didn't fancy it with someone following.

She sighed when someone called, 'Daisy, wait. I'll walk you home.'

It was Harold Tompkins hurrying to catch up with her. 'I thought you were working late,' she said.

'I was just finishing up. You shouldn't be on your own this late.'

'Don't you have to be back in barracks?' she asked.

'Got a late pass,' he said. He walked alongside her, whistling under his breath. It was a habit she found extremely irritating. Still, it was better than him trying to chat to her. He'd hardly spoken two words to her since she'd started working in the NAAFI and she was happy to keep it that way. When they reached the Clock in the town centre, she stopped and said, 'I'll be OK from here. See you tomorrow.'

As she made to walk away he grabbed her arm. 'Daisy, I've got something for you.' He thrust a package at her.

'What...?'

'It's fruit cake – left over. Mr Browning said I could take it. He lets me have a few things – extras, when I work late.'

Daisy didn't like to say no, but she didn't want to upset him. 'Why give it to me?'

'I've got plenty,' he said. 'Anyway, I know how hard it must be for your mum – with the rationing and that.' He hurried away and she stood for a moment staring after him, then down at the package in her hand. She was tempted to throw it away, feeling a little sick at the thought of him trying to get round her that way. But she couldn't. Food was food and there were strict rules nowadays about wastage. Besides, Mum hadn't been able to make any cakes lately due to the shortages. Daisy just hoped she wouldn't ask too many questions about where it came from.

Chapter Five

Still no letter from Bob and Daisy was feeling really fed up. She had written to him again last night, filling pages with stories of the NAAFI and her new friends, although she didn't mention Harold or the cake. As usual, she'd ended by telling him how much she loved and missed him. She would post it on her way to work. Perhaps there would be something in the second post. It was a hope to hold on to during the long working day.

When she came downstairs, her father was finishing his breakfast and he grinned at her as he wiped his plate with a piece of bread. 'Mum tells me there's a nice slice of fruit cake in my dinner tin today. Any more where that came from?'

'I don't think so, Dad. I'm a bit worried actually. I think Harold gave it to me to keep me quiet.'

'What do you mean, love? You said it was left over.'

'That's what Harold told me, but I'm not so sure. He looked a bit shook up when he came out of the store and saw me. I had a feeling he shouldn't have been there.'

Dora turned from the sink, the teapot in her hand. 'Oh, no. Do you think he pinched it?'

'I don't know, Mum. It's just a feeling I had.'

'Well, you'd better steer clear of him, my girl. I don't want you bringing stolen goods into this house.' She banged the teapot down on the table, causing the lid to rattle.

Daisy wished she hadn't mentioned her suspicions. 'Don't worry, Mum. I don't like him and I have no intention of accepting any more gifts from him. Besides, I might have got it wrong.'

Stan pushed his chair back. 'Perhaps you're making too much of it, love. It's not unheard of for a bit of pilfering to go on. I saw it when I worked in the Dockyard. The bosses turn a blind eye most of the time, unless it gets out of hand.'

'Well, Stan Bishop, I hope you never get involved in any of that. We're a respectable family.' Dora's face was red with indignation.

'Don't worry, old love. Too scared of getting caught, me.' Stan took his coat off the back of the door and kissed Dora's cheek. He turned to Daisy. 'Still, as your mum says, best keep out of his way. If he is up to no good, you don't want to get caught up in it.'

Daisy nodded and sat down at the table, while her mother poured tea and placed two slices of toast in front of her. 'Thanks, Mum. I'm sorry to have caused an upset. I didn't think.'

'I know you wouldn't do anything wrong, love. Now, get on with your breakfast, you don't want to be late for work.'

Thoughts of Bob were banished as Daisy walked to work, going over the previous evening's encounter with Harold. Had she been too hasty in suspecting him? She resolved to put the incident out of her mind and to avoid him as much as possible. It would be hard, given they worked in the same place, but from now on she would make sure she walked home with one of her workmates.

As usual they were so busy she didn't have time to think about anything but getting the order right and giving the customer the right change.

It was nearly dinner time and she was looking forward to resting her aching feet when the tall soldier they called Lofty came in and asked for a packet of ten Woodbines. 'I'm sorry, we've run out. Will Senior Service do?'

'I'm not sure. I'm getting them for a mate. I don't smoke myself.'

The dinner time rush hadn't started and there were only a few customers so Daisy said, 'If you're not in a hurry I could go and see if there's any in the store.'

'All right. I'll have a cup of tea while I'm waiting.'

Daisy served his tea and asked June to keep an eye on things while she went to the store.

Mr Browning was there checking the shelves and ticking items off on a clipboard. He glared at her as she reached up to the shelf where the cigarettes were kept. 'Don't forget to make a note how many you take,' he snapped. 'You girls are too lax. How can I be expected to keep track of what's needed and order more if you don't keep proper records?'

'Yes, Mr Browning.' She grabbed a pack containing twenty-four packets of Woodbines and ticked it off on the list by the door, scribbling her initials beside it. She hurried outside, glad to get away from the grumpy manager. His attitude made her wonder once again if he could really have given permission for Harold to take home the leftover food. It seemed out of character to her.

Back in the canteen she found that a queue had formed and June was looking flustered. 'I'll take over now,' she said, handing her a packet of Woodbines and asking her to take them over to Lofty, who was sitting at a table with one of his mates.

She turned to the next customer, a sailor who gave her a cheeky grin and ordered a cup of tea and sausage and mash. She served him and then went on to the next one in the queue, and the next. She didn't have time to respond to the flirty remarks and suggestive grins.

When the crowd thinned out, she looked across to where Lofty had been sitting but he had gone. She was a little disappointed that he hadn't stayed for a chat as he usually did. She wasn't being disloyal to Bob, she told herself. It just made a change to talk to someone who didn't tease or make suggestive remarks when she served him.

At last it was time for her break and she joined June at their usual table. Her friend lit up a cigarette and offered the pack to Daisy, who shook her head.

'Sorry, I forgot,' June said. 'Your friend doesn't smoke either. So, what's he doing buying Woodbines?' She grinned slyly as she emphasised the word friend.

'He's not my friend. Anyway, he said they were for a mate.'

June winked. 'Just an excuse to come in and see you,' she said.

'Don't talk daft.' Daisy could feel herself blushing and June giggled.

'Well, he did look a bit put out when I went over instead of you and he kept looking across at you.'

'I've already got a boy friend as you well know,' Daisy protested.

'But he hasn't written, has he? I'd give him the elbow. Plenty more fish in the sea.' That was June all over; "love 'em and leave 'em" was her philosophy.

Daisy didn't reply, drained her teacup and stood up. 'Better get back to work,' she said.

She took over from Mrs Green at the till and was soon inundated with customers, most of whom were buying cigarettes. They were the most popular item as they were cheaper to buy in the NAAFI.

It seemed no time at all before her shift ended and she paused, rubbing her back which ached from standing so long. She couldn't wait to get her coat and be on her way home. As she lifted the flap on the counter, Mrs Green called out. 'Before you go, would you mind just re-filling the shelves for me? Those fags are going like hot cakes today. I think Mr Browning's in the office, so you need to ask him for the key.'

Daisy hated speaking to the grumpy manager, but she nodded and hurried away. He was sitting at his desk writing in a notebook and he started as she came in after getting no rcply to hcr knock.

'Don't you knock?' he snapped

'I did,' Daisy said indignantly. 'Sorry to disturb you. I need the store key.'

'Why? You already got more fags earlier on.'

'We've nearly run out and Mrs Green wants the shelves filled ready for the evening shift.'

He threw the key across the desk and Daisy grabbed it, anxious to get away.

As she opened the door he called after her, '...and don't forget...'

'To sign the sheet,' she muttered, as she hurried across the yard to the store.

Making sure the blackout curtain over the door was in place, she switched on the light and went to where the cigarettes were kept. She found an empty cardboard box and put in three packs of Woodbines. She decided to take only two of Senior Service as, due to their higher price, they didn't sell so many but as she reached up to the shelf, she noticed that there were not as many packs as there were when she'd come in earlier. As far as she knew, no other staff member had been in the store and the shelves behind the counter in the canteen were almost empty.

She shrugged and put the box down by the door while she signed the inventory list. There were no other signatures below her own initials that she'd written earlier. Something wasn't right. She knew that they sometimes sent stuff to the NAAFI at RAF Eastchurch if they ran low on supplies. Perhaps that's what had happened and Sid Browning had forgotten to record it. As she staggered over to the NAAFI with the heavy box she couldn't help smiling. The manager was so strict about keeping records but he wasn't infallible.

She hastily filled the shelves, said goodbye to Mrs Green who was cashing up the till, and hurried out into the balmy April evening. It wasn't full dark and there was a feeling of spring in the air. Not before time, Daisy thought, after the long hard winter they'd just gone through. She enjoyed the walk home after being indoors all day, taking the long way round up Beach Street to the seafront.

This time she had no fear of Harold following her. It had been his day off and she was glad that she hadn't had to speak to him as she was almost convinced that he hadn't come by that cake honestly. She certainly wouldn't be accepting any more gifts from him. Although she hated herself for her suspicions, there *had* been something furtive about his expression when she came upon him in the kitchen after everyone had gone home. So what had he been up to?

She was more worried about the missing cigarettes and resolved to mention it to Mrs Green the next day. Surely there must be an explanation. Sid Browning had simply forgotten to sign the inventory, she told herself.

Chapter Six

When she got home, the first thing she did before taking her coat off was to look at the mantelpiece to see if there was a letter, not that she expected anything. It had been weeks since she'd heard from Bob. Her heart leapt when she saw an envelope peeking out from behind the china dog, but disappointment swept over her when she picked it up and saw it was from Sylvia. It was addressed to her mother but had been opened. As she went to put it back, Dora came in from the kitchen.

'You can read it if you like,' she said. 'Not much news really. I suppose she can't tell us about her work, but she seems to be having a good time going to dances and that.'

Daisy smiled. 'Typical Sylvia. I wonder if she still keeps in touch with that Roland who came here.'

Dora handed her the letter. 'See for yourself. She says she hasn't heard from him, but she doesn't seem really serious about him. I think some of the glamour's worn off now he's based here. Still she's good at hiding her feelings. She puts up a front.'

After reading her sister's letter Daisy understood what her mother meant. It was obvious Sylvia was missing Roland and wished he was still stationed near her. At least he's not in danger like my Bob, she thought. Eastchurch was not operational but was being used as a Polish training centre.

Thinking about it made her realise she shouldn't be annoyed that Bob hadn't written. She had stopped really listening to the wireless news – it was too upsetting. But over their evening meal, Dad would go on and on, saying that the Germans were gaining ground and predicting an invasion any day. Daisy was glad he'd gone to the pub and they wouldn't be forced to listen quietly while he sat close to the wireless drinking in every word. She swallowed a lump in her throat. Bob was all right – he must be. His mother would have heard if anything had happened and Mrs Gardner would come straight round to tell her.

She would write to Bob tonight, and just hope that he got the letter. She finished her meal and, after helping her mother to clear up, she went upstairs and got out her writing pad and pencil. She hated writing in pencil but the nib had broken on her pen and she hadn't been able to buy a new one. Everything was getting harder to come by as the war went on. More food was being rationed but it wasn't just food. Her mother was always complaining that the shops were almost empty.

It was cold in the bedroom, but she pulled a cardigan around her shoulders and put a blanket over her knees. Her dad would be home soon, and she didn't want to go downstairs in the warm and brave his teasing about love letters.

She had filled two pages with little anecdotes about her job in the NAAFI and her fellow workers and then she stopped and bit the end of her pencil. She had to tell Bob how she felt, let him know that she longed for him to come home, that she would wait for him forever. She covered another page with words of love and longing, trying to stem the tears that rolled down her cheeks. 'Please, Bob. Write back to me,' she whispered.

She brushed her hand across her eyes and signed her name, adding a row of crosses as kisses. As she started to address the envelope, she heard a knock at the front door and a commotion in the front passage. She glanced at her bedside clock. It was just gone nine o'clock. Who could it be at this time of night?

Heart thumping, she ran down the stairs to see her mother embracing a young lad, tears running down her face. She was laughing and crying at the same time. She turned to Daisy. 'Look who it is. Our Jimmy.'

'Jimmy! What...?'

'I've come home. I hated it there. I ran away.' Jimmy looked defiant. 'You can't make me go back.'

'Never mind, love. Come into the warm. Oh, let me look at you. How you've grown,' Dora urged him into the kitchen where the range was still throwing out a little heat. 'Now, sit down and I'll get you something to eat.' She bustled around cutting bread, taking butter and cheese from the pantry.

Daisy sat at the kitchen table beside her brother. 'How did you get here? It's a long way from Wales.'

'Leave the boy alone, Daisy. Let him have something to eat and drink, then he can tell us the story.' She placed a plate of sandwiches in front of him and then filled the teapot. She poured tea for all three of them and sat at the table watching fondly as Jimmy wolfed the food down.

When he had finished she said, 'Now then, son. What's all this about? Why did you run away?'

'They wasn't nice people, Mum.' A sob caught in his throat. 'Please don't send me back. They made me work all hours and there wasn't enough food. And when I moaned about being hungry, he beat me – the farmer. Used a stick, he did. Look.' He stood up and pulled his shirt out of the waistband of his trousers.

Daisy gasped at the sight of the weals across his back. The beatings must have been going on for some time as fresh cuts overlaid those which had almost healed. Dora pulled the boy to her and hugged him, stroking his hair. The old Jimmy would have shrugged her off with an embarrassed grin. But tonight he clung to his mother and wept. 'Please don't make me go back,' he begged.

'Mum, you won't will you – send him back, I mean? You can't,' Daisy said.

'Of course not. Besides, there's been no bombs. We shouldn't have sent him in the first place, but they said it was for the best...' She looked down at the boy's tear-stained face. 'You'd best get up to bed, son.' She turned to her daughter. 'Daisy, put a hot water bottle in for him. It's still cold at nights.'

'All right, Mum.' She poured water from the kettle into the stone bottle and left the room, giving Jimmy another stricken look before going upstairs to make up his bed and put the hot water bottle under the covers. Despite so often being impatient with her annoying little brother, she only felt compassion for him now. What must he have endured to dare the long journey across the country to get home?

When he came upstairs, he got into bed without completely undressing and smiled sleepily up at Daisy. 'Thanks, sis,' he said. His face changed and, with a look of apprehension he said, 'What will Dad say? Will he be mad at me?'

'Don't you worry about that now. Have a good sleep. We can talk in the morning.'

When Daisy came downstairs the next morning her father was still in bed. 'Does Dad know Jimmy's home?'

Dora nodded. 'We agreed to let him sleep. Poor lad was exhausted.'

'Is he mad at Jimmy?'

'He wants to send him back, says the news is bad and the bombing could start any day.'

'He can't do that,' Daisy protested. 'Has he seen the state of Jimmy's back?'

Dora shook her head. 'Said we'll talk about it later.'

'Poor Jimmy. How did he manage to travel all that way?'

'He'll tell us when he wakes up. Now, love, sit down and have some breakfast. You don't want to be late for work.'

'Plenty of time. I'm on late shift today, start at two and won't finish till ten.'

Dora placed two slices of toast in front of her. 'Go easy on the butter. Ration's nearly finished. It'll have to be marge till the end of the week.'

Daisy ate her toast slowly, thinking that if she was on the early shift she would have had a more sustaining breakfast in the canteen. One thing about working in the NAAFI, there was always plenty to eat. Still, it was nice not to have to rush. She'd go to the post office later and send her letter.

There was the sound of movement from upstairs and she decided to wait until she'd heard about Jimmy's adventures.

He came downstairs rubbing his eyes, his face still tear-stained, his hair on end. Daisy smiled. He looked much younger than his almost thirteen years and she was reminded of the times she'd looked after him while Mum was busy and how much she had resented it.

Now, she felt only sympathy, especially when Dora turned from the stove and said roughly, 'Look at the state of you. Go and wash your face and while you're at it, put a comb through your hair.'

Jimmy shuffled through to the scullery and Daisy looked at her mother in surprise. But Dora flapped a hand at her and said, 'Don't mind me, love. I'm so glad to have him home but I daren't show my feelings. Your dad is determined to send him back to Wales and I'm afraid he's right. There's bound to be bombs even if the rumours of invasion are wrong. And with the dockyard just up the road, as well as the airfield up the Island, we'll be in the firing line.'

'Mum, you can't send Jimmy back to the same place. Look what they did to him,' Daisy protested.

They didn't notice that Jimmy had come back into the room until he spoke. 'I ain't going back, you can't make me. And if you do, I'll just run away again.' His voice choked on the words and Daisy put her arms around him.

'We won't make you go. We'll talk to Dad, make him understand.' She turned to her mother. 'We'll persuade him, won't we Mum?'

'Of course we will. Wait till he sees how those people treated him.' Dora bustled around making breakfast for him and topping up the teapot. 'Take a cup up to your dad, will you?' Dora asked. 'Time he was up.'

Before she could do so, the door opened and Stan came in. 'Now then, son. What've you been up to then?'

'Dad, he was horrible, that farmer. Locked me in the barn, he did. Said he'd deal with me later. I knew what that meant and I wasn't going to hang around to get beaten again.' A note of defiance entered Jimmy's voice. 'I just ran, didn't know where I was but I had to get away.'

'And you managed to get home – all that way?'

Jimmy nodded. 'Please don't send me back, Dad.' He was almost in tears.

'We'll see. Now tell us what happened.'

'How did you get out of the barn?'

'Why did he lock you up?'

They all spoke at once and Stan waved them to be quiet. 'Let the boy tell us in his own time.'

'He called me a thief – but I didn't steal anything. I pulled up a carrot from the garden and ate it and he saw me. Said I should wait till his missus called us in for dinner.' He turned to Dora. 'I was hungry, Mum.'

'And he locked you up for that?' Daisy's eyes widened incredulously.

Jimmy nodded. 'But I got out, kicked the door until the lock broke - and then I just ran.'

Gradually the story came out, punctuated occasionally with sobs and pleas for understanding. He had walked for miles, hiding in hedgerows and farm buildings, helping himself to the occasional loaf of bread from a baker's van or fruit from a vegetable cart. 'I know I shouldn't have, Mum, but I was so hungry,' he sobbed.

'Never mind that, love,' Dora said, ruffling his hair.

'How did you find your way?' Daisy asked.

'I don't know. I just kept walking. There's no signposts or anything and I couldn't ask in case someone made me go back.'

Finally, someone had given him a lift. He had meant to hide until the lorry had passed by but he was too late and the man had stopped and shouted at him. When he tried to run, the man jumped down and grabbed him by the collar. 'I was so scared,' Jimmy said. 'But he was kind. And he drove me to the next town and gave me some money. Told me to get the train home.'

'So you didn't walk all the way then,' Daisy said.

'No, but I didn't have enough for the fare to Sheerness. I walked from Sittingbourne.'

'How did you get on to the Island? They've got guards near the bridge and you have to show your identity card,' Stan said.

'An army lorry stopped at the checkpoint and I crept up and hung on underneath until we got over the bridge. Then I jumped down and walked the rest of the way.'

'You were lucky to get away with it. They could have arrested you as a spy,' Daisy said with a laugh.

'It's no laughing matter,' Dora snapped. 'He could have got into real trouble.'

Jimmy looked worried. 'I won't, will I Dad?'

'No, son. We'll just say you hitch-hiked.'

'What about the stealing?'

Before Stan could reply, Dora gave him an impulsive hug. 'Don't worry about that. I'm just so glad you're home.' She shot a warning glance at her husband.

'Will I have to go back to school?' Jimmy asked.

'We'll see.'

'They didn't send me to school in Wales. They said it was too far. We were right out in the country. Besides, I had to work on the farm to earn my keep, they said.'

'If only I'd known, I would never have sent you away.' Dora sighed. She got up and started to clear the dishes.

'I'm inclined to agree with you,' Stan said.

Daisy helped with the washing up and then went out to post her letter. As she walked up to the Post Office, she thought about how scared her little brother had looked, and how frail he was. Obviously under-nourished and weak from the beatings he'd received, he had lost his old perky spirit. She hurried home, anxious to add her pleas to her father to let him stay home. Who cared what the government said about keeping children out of harm's way? He'd endured far more harm in the months he'd been away.

Stan was sitting at the kitchen table eating his dinner when she entered the house but there was no sign of Jimmy or Dora.

Daisy's heart sank as her father looked up from his plate and frowned. 'Not at work then?' he asked.

'Late shift,' Daisy answered.

Just at that moment Dora came in. 'Got time to eat before you go to work, love?' she asked.

'Yes, please, Mum. Don't worry, I'll get it.'

'Sit yourself down. You'll be on your feet soon enough. Rest while you can.' She turned to Stan. 'Want some rice pudding?'

He pushed his plate away and nodded. So far he hadn't said a word about Jimmy. Daisy wanted to ask but didn't want to provoke a row. Stan Bishop was usually fairly easy going, but he was capable of losing his temper if things didn't go his way. And it had been at his insistence that Jimmy had been evacuated with the other boys from his school, despite Dora's pleading to let him stay.

Stan had accused her of being too soft. 'You gotta cut the apron strings some time,' he'd said. 'He'll be starting work in a year or two, nearly a man.'

When Dora had served Daisy's meal she said, 'I've saved some for Jimmy. Poor lad's still sleeping, half-starved and exhausted he was.'

Daisy glanced at her father to see his reaction. To her surprise he nodded and his lips tightened, but instead of berating Dora for mollycoddling the boy he said, 'If I could get my hands on those b....'

'Now then, Stan. No need to swear,' Dora interrupted.

'He should have written and told us. I would've been up there and dragged him home like a shot.'

'He said he did write but we never got a letter after that first one saying what a good place it was and how he liked being in the country.' Dora choked back a sob. 'He said he begged us to fetch him home.'

'They must have read the letters and not sent them.' Daisy turned to her father. 'You're going to let him stay then, Dad?'

'Course I am. What do you think? And if that WVS woman comes round here saying he'll be safer in the country, I'll give her a piece of my mind.' He finished his food and stood up. 'I'm off to the allotment.'

Daisy got her coat. 'I'm off too.'

When they reached the High Street, they joined the human tide of dockyard workers going back for the afternoon shift. Many were on bicycles, others walking, a familiar sight for Daisy ever since she was a child.

Some of the men waved and called out greetings to Stan and Daisy wondered if he missed the work, although he seemed to have adapted well to his enforced retirement. Only a slight limp now betrayed the accident that had caused it. He had recovered well but was no longer strong enough for the heavy work that his job had entailed.

In the past, when Dad had been on a long shift with no time to come home for dinner, Daisy and Jimmy would often take him a packet of sandwiches. She had always loved going into the Dockyard and seeing the huge ships in the dry dock, the clanging of hammers and the smells of hot tar and paint as the men swarmed over the hulls repairing and painting. Nowadays, no one could get near the place without a pass.

At the entrance to the allotments, Daisy said goodbye to her father.

'I'll come and meet you from work,' he said. 'Don't want you walking home on your own late at night.'

'I'll be all right, Dad. You worry too much.' As she turned away, she said, 'I'm glad Jimmy's staying.'

Stan grinned. 'I didn't think you missed him, always saying how annoying he was, pestering you.'

'I did actually,' Daisy said with a laugh. But the laugh turned to a sob. 'I feel sick at the thought of...'

Stan patted her arm. 'Don't fret, love. He's home now. Your mum will feed him up. He'll be all right – soon be back to being your annoying little brother. Now, get along to work.' He laughed. 'And I wouldn't say no to more of that cake now we've an extra mouth to feed.'

'Shsh, Dad, you'll get me into trouble,' she whispered

But he just grinned and she hurried away, her stomach churning. Dad's jokey words had revived her worries about the goings on in the NAAFI. Were her work mates stealing food and other goods? Since rationing had started earlier in the year a thriving black market had sprung up. Her mother wouldn't have anything to do with it but she knew others were not so scrupulous.

Daisy showed her pass at the garrison gate and dismissed the thought from her mind. She just hoped that neither June nor Lily were involved anything dodgy. But who could she trust?

Chapter Seven

Daisy's shift passed without incident – at least she wasn't aware of anything untoward. Besides, she was too busy to worry about what her colleagues were up to.

When there was a lull in the never-ending queue of soldiers and sailors all jostling for her attention, she managed to grab a cup of tea and a brief sit-down. Lily joined her and she told her friend about Jimmy's adventures.

'I don't blame him for wanting to come home,' she said. 'My mum missed the little ones so much when they were evacuated, she went down and fetched them home. They tried to make her send them back, but she wasn't having none of it. No bombs, she told them, so why should I send them away. They need their mum, that's what she said.' Lily took a swig of her tea and banged the cup down on the table, showing her annoyance at those people in authority.

Daisy nodded agreement. But she couldn't help thinking it was a bit hard on Lily, who often spent her free time looking after the little ones when her mother was at work in a local pub while Mr Scott had shift work at the gas works. Still, after what happened to Jimmy she wouldn't blame anyone for wanting to keep their children at home. She might feel differently if enemy bombers started to come over but until then...

She finished her tea and left Lily to finish her break. Back behind the counter, she tried not to worry about Jimmy and how the abuse he had suffered would affect him. Still, he was home safe now. But there were other things on her mind. Aside from her concerns about Jimmy, there was her suspicion of wrongdoing at work. And then there was Bob. What was happening to him?

Her sombre mood lightened a little when Lofty, the despatch rider, came in. He took his motorcycle helmet off and leaned on the counter, watching as she filled his cup from the tea urn and put one of the rock buns the assistant chef had made earlier on a plate.

'Thanks sweetheart,' he said with a grin.

'I'm not your sweetheart,' she retorted.

'Ah, but wouldn't you like to be?'

She shook her head, but she couldn't help smiling. It wasn't like Lofty to be so cheeky. He was usually so quiet. Perhaps he felt braver with none of his pals around. Still, why not have a laugh and a joke with him, even flirt a little?

'How do you know I haven't already got a boy friend?' A picture of Bob flashed through her mind. But he was far away – and he hadn't written.

'Well, I saw you at the pictures with your work mates,' Lofty said. 'Girls don't go out with other girls if there's a lad to take them.'

She tilted her head. 'Are you offering?'

He was about to answer when the door burst open and three soldiers came in, laughing and pushing each other. 'Hey, Lofty,' one of them called out. 'What're you up to, sweet talking the ladies?'

He flushed bright red and picked up his tea and cake, pushing past the newcomers to find a table.

They continued to tease him. 'Dark horse, that one. Thought he was too shy to talk to the girls,' another one said.

Daisy felt sorry for him. She had noticed that he didn't often join in the banter with the others. He was always the quiet one and she thought he was just shy. She had been surprised that he seemed to be flirting with her today. She didn't really mind. In fact, she'd been on the point of agreeing to go out with him – if he'd had the chance to ask her.

She liked his polite reserve, although she had enjoyed the banter. He was a different person when he was on his own. And he wasn't bad looking either, with his mop of dark curls which even the severe Army haircut had failed to tame.

She glanced across at him but he dropped his gaze and she busied herself with the tea urn and giving change. She laughed at the teasing of the lads who crowded the counter – Jock and Taffy and one they called Swede. They all had nicknames and she was getting to know them. She joined in with their banter, giving as good as she got. But she couldn't stop thinking about Lofty, wondering if he'd really been on the verge of asking her out. Would she accept if he did? Don't be daft, she told herself. You don't even know his real name.

Towards the end of her shift her feet were hurting and she kept glancing at the clock. Although she usually enjoyed her work, tonight she just wanted to get home. She was concerned about Jimmy and still wasn't sure if her father would let him stay or insist that he went back to Wales. Mum'll talk him round though, she thought.

At last the hands of the clock moved round to ten o'clock and she closed the till. There were only three customers left and she shooed them out with a laugh. Lofty must have left earlier. She had been so busy she hadn't seen him go. She locked the door and took the money drawer out, carried it through to the office. Mrs Green was there going through the accounts.

'Off home then?' she said. 'Got your torch?'

'Yes. And my dad's coming to meet me. He doesn't like me going home on my own.'

'Good. I was going to ask Mr Browning to give you a lift. He's just leaving.'

'I didn't realise he was working late.'

'Stock-taking,' Mrs Green said.

Thank goodness Dad's coming, Daisy thought. She didn't fancy walking home in the dark with the manager, still less sitting beside him in the van. She said goodnight to the supervisor and got her coat, hurried out into the mild spring night.

When she reached the garrison gatehouse she paused, looking up the road. No sign of her father. Should she start walking alone? As she hesitated, a figure loomed out of the darkness.

She gasped, a hand on her chest as she struggled to catch her breath. 'Oh, it's you. You scared me.'

Lofty was leaning against his motorcycle which was propped up against the kerb. 'Sorry, I didn't mean to frighten you. I was worried about you going home in the dark on your own. Fancy a ride?' He indicated the bike.

'On that? No thanks.'

'You might enjoy it. Thrill a minute, like a fairground ride.'

She was tempted but just at that moment she saw the glimmer of a torch and her father appeared out of the darkness. 'Here's my dad. I'd better go.'

'Some other time then?' He swung his leg over the bike, kick-started it and turned into the garrison and roared away across the parade ground.

'Was that bloke bothering you?' Stan asked.

'No. It's all right, Dad.' She linked her arm in his and they set off towards town, Stan pointing his dimmed torch towards the ground.

'Been busy, love?' he asked.

'Yes, as usual.' Daisy paused and asked hesitantly, 'How's Jimmy?'

'Not too good to tell the truth. God knows what the lad's been through. I was all for sending him away again until your mum showed me his back.' Stan muttered a string of swear words. 'Sorry, love. I don't often use language but...'

Daisy squeezed his arm. 'I won't tell, Mum. I know how you feel though. Still, he's home safe now.'

'Let's hope he stays safe, that's all. Things aren't going too well over there.'

Daisy didn't want to think about 'over there' where Bob was, fighting for his country. And here she was, toying with the idea of going out with another man. How could she? Just because Bob hadn't written. A wave of guilt swept over her and she resolved that the next time Lofty came into the NAAFI she would ignore him.

'Here we are, love,' Stan said, opening the back gate and dispelling her thoughts. 'Nice cup of cocoa and then bed.'

As Daisy followed him into the house, Dora put her knitting down and got up. 'I've got the milk on for your cocoa.'

For once, Daisy's gaze did not go immediately to the mantelpiece in search of a letter. 'Thanks, Mum. How's Jimmy?'

'He's fine now. Good food and a long sleep's done him the world of good. He won't talk much about what went on. He wants to put it behind him, just glad to be home and happy not to be sent back.'

'I'm glad. Any news from Sylvia? We ought to let her know Jimmy's safe.'

'Nothing.' Dora gasped. 'But, oh dear, I almost forgot. There's a letter for you.' She pointed to the clock where the corner of an envelope poked out.

A wide smile split Daisy's face and she grabbed the letter, tearing it open, tears running down her faced. 'Oh, it's from Bob. He's written.'

She sat down at the kitchen table and devoured the single sheet of paper, ignoring the cup of cocoa which Dora placed beside her.

His note, for that was all it was, not a proper letter, said that he was sorry for not writing before. 'Thing's pretty hairy here. Can't tell you much – not allowed,' he wrote. 'But I think of you all the time, picturing you back home and doing your bit for the war.'

'Oh, Mum, He's all right.'

'I knew it, love. And look at the date. He wrote it weeks ago. And we know from the news they're fighting hard, no time for love letters.'

'I know. I've been silly, being cross with him.'

She tucked the letter into her handbag to read again later and drank her lukewarm cocoa. She kissed her parents goodnight and went up to bed, first looking in on Jimmy, who was fast asleep, the blankets all in a tangle. Perhaps he'd been having a nightmare. She straightened the blankets, tucking them round him and, in an unusual gesture for her, stooped to kiss his cheek.

My annoying little brother, she thought with a fond smile.

***

Christopher Jameson stretched out on his bunk and sighed. Trust her dad to come along and spoil things, he thought. He'd been just about to ask her out. He knew she already had a boyfriend. But Bob was overseas and who knew when, if ever, he'd be back. It was wrong to think that way, he knew, but he couldn't stop thinking about her.

He'd noticed her straight away the first time he'd seen her telling Taffy Jones off for his cheek – but in a nice way. All the lads liked her and treated her with respect. He had started going in to the NAAFI more often now, always hoping for a chance to see the girl with the laughing brown eyes, not to talk to her but just to sit and watch as she deftly poured tea and dished up plates of egg and bacon. He liked to sit there with his cup of tea watching her dashing around, so quick and efficient, not slapdash like Lily.

Until now, he'd preferred to stay in his billet reading up on motorbikes, or tinkering with his Matchless motorcycle. He'd always loved motor bikes and saved up to buy a BSA Bantam, the only one he could afford. He'd joined the Royal Corps of Signals solely for the chance to become a despatch rider. His application had been granted and he had been promoted to Corporal. It set him apart from the other lads who were Royal Artillery and teased him about his obsession with bikes, but he didn't care. He'd never been one for going down the pub and getting drunk like some of them. Not that there was much chance of that these days. Riding the bike or working on keeping it in tiptop condition was like heaven to him. That was, until he met Daisy, giving his mates more reason to tease. They were always on at him to ask her out.

As he lay on his bunk brooding and wondering if he dare ask her, three of the lads burst into the billet and threw themselves down on their bunks.

'Still mooning over the fair Daisy?' Jim asked.

Christopher ignored him.

'Go on, Lofty, you know you like her,' Jim said.

'She's got a boy friend.'

His friend laughed. 'Out of sight, mate...'

'She's not the sort to cheat on him,' Christopher snapped. He picked up one of his bike magazines and tried to concentrate on it, pushing all thoughts of Daisy Bishop out of his mind.

After a while the lads gave up and talked among themselves, reliving the fun they'd had on their evening off duty after a day's anti-aircraft training. All too soon, it would be morning and the training would start once more.

Chapter Eight

Over in France, everything seemed to have come to a halt. No one seemed to know what was happening, even the officers. There had been some fighting near the Belgian border and then Bob's unit fell back. They were now camped out in a deserted village with an unpronounceable name awaiting further orders.

Bob and his mate Tom had been sent out by their sergeant to forage for food, their rations having almost run out. On their long march they ate whatever they could scrounge - produce from farms, food from deserted shops.

Now, there was little to find, another troop had obviously been through here before them, although they once found a couple of hams hanging in a cellar. They'd eaten well that night.

They turned down a narrow lane on the outskirts of the village and Tom stared around him. 'Nothing here, mate. Everyone's gone – probably taken everything with them.'

'Let's take one more look,' Bob said opening a gate. They found themselves in a dusty yard where a few scrawny looking chickens scratched in the dirt. It was quiet, only the wind stirring in the trees along the lane.

'These'll do,' Bob said, creeping up and diving on one of the hens. He missed, and it scuttled off with a squawk and flurry of feathers.

'Damn and blast,' he muttered, while Tom looked on laughing.

He stood up, dusting the knees of his trousers and was about to swear again when he caught sight of a young woman peeping round the edge of a barn door.

'*S'il vous plait. Non. Les poulets,*' she said, a sob in her voice.

'We thought there was no one here.' Bob walked towards her, holding out a placating hand. 'I'm not going to hurt you. Do you speak English?'

She shook her head. 'A little only.' She pointed to the chickens. 'Not kill. We need eggs.'

'Oh, sorry,' Bob muttered.

Tom pushed him aside. 'We need eggs too. Soldiers hungry.'

'Leave her alone,' Bob said, turning to the girl. 'Can we buy some from you?'

'I will ask Maman.'

'We should just take them,' Tom protested.

'That's OK if the owners have gone. But we can't just steal from them. We're not savages.'

The girl ran across the yard towards the house calling for her mother and the two men followed. An older woman came to the door, letting loose a torrent of words and waving her hands at them.

'Non, Maman. English, not German.' The girl took her mother's arm and beckoned the men into the house. 'She is afraid,' she said. 'So many strangers in our land.'

'We are here to help you against the Germans,' Bob said. 'We will be moving on tomorrow.'

'But first you need food.' She turned to her mother and spoke rapidly, all the while opening cupboard doors and filling a basket – not just eggs, but a large piece of cheese, freshly-baked bread, and onions. She placed the basket on the table and smiled at their expressions of surprise.

'This is too much,' Bob said, 'but thank you.' He felt in his pocket for some money.

But she shook her head. 'No need money, you keep,' she said.

'You shouldn't have offered it,' Tom said, picking up the basket and turning towards the door.

Bob hung back and put a few coins on the table. 'We must pay,' he said, then, blushing a little, he asked, 'What is your name?'

'Francoise – Francoise Lebrun.'

He noticed she was blushing too but, greatly daring, he took her hand and said, 'I'm Bob Gardner. Very pleased to meet you, Francoise.' He turned to her mother. 'And you, Madame Lebrun. I hope we meet again.'

'I too,' she whispered.

Outside, Tom leaned on a wall, smoking. He grinned. 'Made a conquest there, mate. And you know what these French lassies are like.'

'She struck me as a nice girl - not like in those places in Cherbourg.'

Tom chuckled. 'What would you know? You steered clear back then – too busy writing love letters to that girl back home.'

Bob ignored him and started walking back to the village hall.

***

Bob moved closer to the window to catch the last of the light. He chewed the end of his pencil and peered at what he had already written. – 'My dearest Daisy...' He hadn't written for weeks but now that he had the chance he just couldn't think what to say. A picture of that petite French lass with the golden hair and lovely blue eyes would keep intruding on his thoughts, despite his efforts to push them away.

They had received orders to move up towards the river and he and the remnants of his unit were holed up in a farmhouse, not far from the Belgian border. The occupants had fled. 'They must have thought we were Krauts,' Tom said as they explored the deserted building.

'Well, they're not far behind,' Bob said. But so far there had been no sign of the enemy.

Tom was sure they had been held back on the far side of the river. The British blew up the bridge and Bob's unit had been ordered to hold steady for further orders. Two days later those orders still hadn't come. But that's how it had been since they'd landed. No one seemed to know what was happening; their officers had disappeared and here they were, waiting for orders that never came. It had been like this for weeks, two steps forward and one back. The rumour was that they were pulling out altogether, but their sergeant told them not to listen to rumours.

In this period of unaccustomed quiet, Bob decided that he must write to Daisy, although there was little chance that she'd ever get the letter. Before he could continue with it, a rattle of gunfire followed by the crump of shells made him leap up, dropping his pencil and paper, the letter forgotten.

Tom peered through the broken window. 'I think we should get out of here,' he said, grabbing Bob's arm.

Sergeant Williams shouted at them to get their kit together and Bob's letter was forgotten.

A week later they were back in the village where Bob had met the Lebruns – only the sergeant and five of them left. The place had been bombed and smoke still drifted up from the ruins. Bob thought about Francoise and her mother. Were they safe? She had never been far from his thoughts since that first brief encounter.

The church was still standing and Sergeant Williams pushed open the heavy oak door. 'Come on men. This'll do for tonight. We'll move on in the morning.'

In the shaft of light from the open door they saw a group of villagers huddled in the front pews, the priest kneeling at the altar. Anxious faces turned towards them and the priest stood.

'Carry on,' Sergeant Williams said. 'We won't disturb you. Just need a place to rest.'

'You are welcome, my sons. Please, sit.'

Bob and his mates shuffled off their packs, dropped their rifles and sank wearily into the pews.

The priest completed his prayers and came up the aisle to speak to Sergeant Williams. Bob listened to the murmur of their voices but couldn't make out what was being said. Exhaustion claimed him and he sank into a deep sleep.

He was woken suddenly by someone shaking his arm. 'Bob, Bob. Is it really you?'

He looked up into the face of Francoise Lebrun and for a moment he thought he must be dreaming. He struggled to sit up and became aware of his grinning mates and the priest's disapproving frown. He ignored them and clasped the girl's hand. 'Are you all right? What happened? Is your mother OK?'

She shook her head and put a finger to his lips. 'Speak slowly so I understand. OK – I know that word. Yes, we are OK but the farm is gone, the house bombed.'

'Not our people?'

'Germans.' She almost spat the word.

Bob turned to Sergeant Williams. 'Did you hear that Sarge?'

'The priest told me. Well, lads, looks like we'd better not hang around here. We need to go north, try and meet up with our lot.'

Amid groans and protests, the men got to their feet, shrugging on their packs. Another long night of marching lay ahead.

'What about the villagers, Sarge?' Bob hated leaving Francoise and her mother.

'Nothing we can do, son. If we had transport, we could take them. But most of them are old, can't expect them to march with us. Besides, who knows where we'll end up?'

'S'pose you're right, Sarge.' Bob turned to Francoise, who was anxiously watching their exchange. He took her hand. 'We have to leave. But I'll come back for you - I promise.'

She shook her head. 'No, we will not be here. My mother and I will try to get to the village where my aunt lives. It is near Amiens.' She thrust a small piece of paper at him. 'This is her address. Maybe – when the war is over...?'

'Come on, lads. Get fell in.' Sergeant Williams bawled.

The men stumbled out of the church and lined up in the street. Francoise stood in the doorway. She gave a tearful smile and raised a hand in farewell.

When they reached the edge of the village Bob looked back. She was still standing there.

'Forget her, mate.' Tom's voice penetrated Bob's misery. 'No future in it. She's just another pretty girl.'

Bob sighed. 'You're right, Tom. I'm being daft. It's just – the thought of her – all of them – left there and the Krauts marching in any day.'

'Well, we can't do anything about it. I don't care what Sarge says about rumours, I reckon we'll be on our way home soon. And you've got your Daisy waiting for you, haven't you?'

Bob didn't answer. Since meeting the French girl he had hardly given Daisy a thought and Tom's words started a little niggle of guilt in his head.

They trudged on through the night, ears alert for the rumble of tanks and gunfire behind them. As dawn broke, they saw ahead of them streams of people walking, some pushing carts and prams, some bowed down under heavy bundles.

'My God, look at that. Where are they all going?' Tom said.

'They probably don't even know, just want to get away,' Bob replied.

'I don't believe it. Looks like they've just given up. I thought we were falling back to another defensive position,' one of the other men said.

'No lad,' Sergeant Williams said. 'I'm pretty sure we're retreating. God knows what happens when we get to the coast.'

It was the first time Bob had heard the sergeant sound so tired and defeated. Usually he was gungho, jollying them along. Now, Bob began to realise their true position.

He looked up at the sound of a motorcycle coming towards them. The despatch rider skidded to a halt and hailed them. 'There's transport up ahead. Taking you to Dunkirk on the coast.'

The men sent up a faint cheer and marched on with more vigour in their flagging footsteps, until, a few miles on, they spotted a column of smoke up ahead. The lorry they hoped would take them on to Dunkirk was completely gutted. There was no time to bewail the fact that they had to keep on walking as a scream and whistle from overhead had them diving into the roadside ditch. Machine gun bullets kicked up the dust as the Stukas dived over them and headed off into the distance, only to wheel round and come back at them.

When it was quiet again, Bob picked himself up from the ditch and looked round for his mates. Tom was all right, but Sergeant Williams clutched his arm, blood dripping down from his sleeve.

The others escaped injury but several of the civilians who had been trudging along the road ahead of them were dead. Most of them had made it into the cover of the ditch and were now crawling out, looking dazed but resigned. 'They'll be back,' one old man muttered.

Bob tore a strip off his shirt tail and bound it round the sergeant's arm. 'That'll do for the moment, Sarge.'

'Thanks, lad. Let's get on, shall we?'

They trudged along – you couldn't call it marching - their steps slower now, shoulders hunched. Now and then a lorry or van would pass them, all crowded to overflowing with soldiers from other units. No chance of being picked up but they all shouted encouraging words which did little to revive their flagging spirits.

Several times they were forced to dive for cover as more Stukas screamed overhead, raking the crowded roads with machine gun fire. The third time it happened, Tom leapt to his feet, waving his arms and shouting obscenities. Bob tried to calm him down and they plodded on, Tom still muttering what he'd like to do with the buggers if only he hadn't run out of ammunition.

It was boiling hot and they were all desperate for a drink. Just as Bob was beginning to think he could walk no further, Sergeant Williams called a halt. He pointed to a small wood on the other side of the field which ran alongside the road. 'We'll take a breather,' he said.

'Thank God,' Tom muttered.

The others threw themselves down in the shade of the trees while Bob filled his water bottle from a nearby pond.

'Don't drink that,' Sergeant Williams snapped. 'Boil it first.'

They lit a small fire and propped a billycan over it. They had little food, but Bob produced a few tea leaves and they drank the weak liquid thirstily.

Bob leaned back against a tree trunk and sighed. He fished in his pocket for the photo he always carried. Daisy's cheeky smile looked out at him. She was perched on a railing on Sheerness seafront, her head thrown back, her curls flying in the wind. He tried to picture what she would be doing now – serving some handsome sailor with his Senior Service he supposed, giving him that sexy smile, being cheeky, like as not. He shouldn't be jealous, given the way his thoughts leaned these past weeks. He made a conscious effort to dismiss Francoise from his mind. It was Daisy he loved. And he knew that, despite her flirty ways, it was all just a front. She had promised to stay to true to him and he believed her. Would he ever see either of them again? He put the photo back in his battledress pocket as Sarge gave the order to pack up and resume their march.

Chapter Nine

Stan Bishop listened to the wireless, leaning close to the set, his expression grim. They had moved it into the kitchen as they spent more time in there these days and Stan spent every spare moment listening to the news.

When Daisy came home from work on the evening of May 30th she crept in quietly. It had been a boiling hot day and her only thought was to get out of her uncomfortable uniform, have a cooling wash and put on a light summer dress.

She had just put one foot on the bottom stair when her father called, 'Here, Daisy, listen to this.'

With a sigh she entered the kitchen. She was in no mood to listen to Dad ranting about the incompetence of those running the war, but it didn't do to ignore him. She knew from the gossip in the NAAFI that things weren't going well and she was worried enough about Bob without Dad going on about it. She had stopped being angry with Bob for not writing, realising that she was being selfish putting her own feelings first. Not only that, she was worried about Lofty too. He'd told her that he might soon be posted, along with several others she'd got to know over the past months.

The measured tones of newsreader, Alvar Liddell, filled the little kitchen as Stan turned the volume up. 'The little ships are gathering at Dover to bring our brave lads home – so far several thousand have been rescued. Many more crowd the beaches of Dunkirk, waiting their turn.'

'Does that mean Bob might be coming home?' Daisy asked.

'How do I know? Shut up and listen will you.'

Daisy bit her lip. It wasn't like Dad to snap but she knew he hated interruptions when he was listening to the wireless. Poor Jimmy had often been sent to his room for chattering when the news was on.

She kept quiet until the announcer finished, going on to read out more information about rations and other restrictions. Stan turned the wireless off and sighed.

'Well, looks like this is it. We've been run out of France; they'll have to fend for themselves now.'

'Does this mean we've lost the war, Dad?'

'What do you think? Old Hitler will be here any day now. We'll fight on, of course but...' He sighed again. 'I've been thinking about this LDV I've joined. I can't see we'll do much good – no guns or equipment.'

Daisy felt a churning in her stomach. Would there really be an invasion? But we've still got the air force and the navy, she thought, and if the Germans do invade, there's still lots of soldiers here to defend us. They wouldn't have to rely on volunteers like her dad.

Before she could reply, the back door banged open and Jimmy came in, his face red with excitement. 'Just been up on the seafront. Lots of ships out there, little boats too. Someone said they're full of troops.'

'It was just on the wireless,' Daisy said.

Jimmy started to badger their father with questions and Daisy couldn't bear listening to his chatter. She went upstairs and sat on the edge of her bed, wondering what it all meant, her brain awhirl with conflicting emotions. She hardly dared hope that Bob would be among those rescued; he could have been taken prisoner – or worse. And if it was true that the army had given in and accepted defeat what did that mean? Would German paratroopers be descending on them any day?

She heard her mother come home and knew she should go down and help prepare the evening meal. Slowly, she changed out of her uniform, putting off the moment when she would have to re-join her family. Their talk would all be about the war and what was happening over in France.

There would be another news bulletin later in the evening and they would have to listen to it all over again. Things were probably a lot worse than they said. Everyone knew that the BBC was not allowed to report everything for fear of spreading 'alarm and despondency' as they called it.

Daisy sat at her dressing table and covered her face with her hands. 'Please, God, let Bob be all right,' she sobbed.

She sat up straight when she heard Jimmy thundering up the stairs. He barged in without knocking but she didn't have the heart to tell him off.

'Mum said tea's ready,' he said, peering at her. 'You've been crying. Nothing to cry about. Dad says they're bringing our troops home.'

Daisy wiped her eyes and stood up. 'I'm all right now. Tell Mum I'll be down in a minute.' She straightened her dress, patted her hair into place and followed her brother downstairs.

Dora still had her WVS uniform on and was dishing up the shepherds pie she had left in the oven earlier. 'Come and eat, love,' she said.

Daisy and Jimmy sat at the table but Stan hadn't moved from his place by the wireless where he fiddled with the knobs.

'Leave that,' Dora said. 'Let's eat our meal in peace. And no war talk, please. There's nothing we can do about it, so let's just enjoy this pie.'

'All right, all right,' Stan grumbled, pulling his chair up to the table.

Soon they were all tucking into the pie, which was more potato than meat. But Dora had added some vegetables and plenty of seasoning and Stan nodded appreciatively. 'Don't know how you do it, love. I'll have some more if there's any left.'

Daisy smiled. She had better food when she was on duty in the NAAFI but she wouldn't say anything. It was just so good to be sitting here with her family, especially as, for once, Dad heeded his wife's words and wasn't going on about the war and the possibility of invasion. But she couldn't ignore the news for long and she found herself trying to imagine what was happening to Bob at this moment. Was he on one of those ships Jimmy saw out in the estuary, or was he still fighting his way through France to escape the German advance?

***

It took three days for Bob and the meagre remnants of his unit to reach the coast. Stumbling along bomb pitted roads, hiding in woods and barns, diving into ditches as yet another wave of Stukas came over leaving death and devastation in their wake, the sergeant, with Bob, Tom and two privates had managed to escape further injury. A few days earlier, Sergeant Williams's arm had begun to fester and he was in great pain. Bob and his mates had taken turns helping the wounded man along, despite repeated pleas to leave him behind.

At last they caught a glimpse of the sea between smoke blackened buildings and they pushed their way through the crowds thronging the little harbour.

Bob gasped as they reached the harbour wall and looked out to sea. He could hardly believe what he was seeing – lines of men wading out waist high into the sea, stretching hands out to the boats that waited to take them on board. They queued silently, patiently, except for a few who tried to push their way to the front.

Tom helped the sergeant to sit with his back against the wall and straightened, running a hand through his hair. 'Strewth, mate. What a sight.'

Bob nodded. He bent to speak to Sergeant Williams. 'We can't stay here, must get you into one of those queues. The sooner you're on board a ship the better.'

'Don't worry about me. Get yourselves down on the beach. I'll be OK.' The sergeant's voice was faint and he closed his eyes.

'Come on, Bob. You heard him.'

'No Tom. You and the others go. I'll try and get help for him.'

Tom looked round frantically. 'What help? Don't talk daft, man. Come on.'

'I won't leave him.'

Tom shrugged and beckoned to the other two. They didn't need telling twice and in a moment they had disappeared, swallowed up in the throng making its way down to the beach.

Bob sat down beside the sergeant and leaned against the wall. What hope of finding a medic in all this chaos, he thought. But he had to help Williams, who'd been a good leader when they'd been deserted by their officers. He'd got them this far and Bob would not leave him now.

'We can't stay here,' he muttered. He could hear guns in the distance and the rumble of tanks. Was it more of their own troops or the advancing enemy? Better not wait to find out and probably end up a prisoner of war. He stood up and scanned the crowds, his heart leaping as he spotted a red cross painted on the side of a half-ruined building. He helped Sergeant Williams to stand up and, holding on to his good arm, led him towards the first aid post.

A medic rushed forward and helped the injured man on to a stretcher. Inside was chaos but Bob felt relieved that at least Sarge stood a chance now, even if taken prisoner.

The medic, after ascertaining that Bob was not injured, waved him away. 'Get going, while there's still time,' he said. 'Your man will be all right. We'll look after him.'

Bob hurried away, scanning the crowds for a sight of Tom and the others.

***

Daisy was on early shift and they were extra busy, but she couldn't avoid the buzz of conversation as sailors crowded in to the NAAFI. They had no ship's name on their caps, but she overheard one of them saying that HMS *Ross* had returned the night before. 'Loose lips sink ships', she thought. They weren't supposed to talk about what went on in the dockyard. As she bustled around making up piles of sandwiches and re-filling the tea urn, she was dying to ask how many troops they had rescued. Was Bob among them? She sighed. It was too much to hope that even if he had been taken off the beach, he would have ended back here.

'Come along, girl. Stop day-dreaming.' Mrs Green's sharp voice startled her and she almost dropped the can of corned beef she was struggling to open.

She heard a laugh and turned to see Harold smirking behind her back. The smile left his face as Mrs Green glared at him. 'And you, Private Tompkins. Haven't you got anything better to do?'

Daisy hastily finished opening the can and started slicing the corned beef. Soon she had another pile of sandwiches and she was about to take them through to the canteen when Mrs Green said. 'I've got a job for you. Wrap those up and take them down to dockyard gate.' Her voice softened. 'Those poor lads are exhausted and starving.'

'Yes, Mrs Green.' Daisy found some greaseproof paper and wrapped the food, placing the packages into a cardboard box. Her heart quickened as she hurried past the parade ground towards the dockyard entrance. Would she get the chance to ask about Bob? Daft idea really. Hundreds, even thousands, of men had been rescued. What chance to find one among so many? But she had always been an optimist and she smiled up at the guard on the gate, asking if she could take the food to the ship.

'Sorry, love. No one past the gate without authorisation. I'll take that.' He held out his hand for the box.

Daisy handed it over but hesitated before turning away. 'My fiancé might be on that ship. Is there any way...?'

'No, love. There's hundreds of the poor buggers. They'll be sent on to other units once they've been debriefed. Sorry, love, I don't know any more than you do.'

Daisy bit her lip, holding back tears. Where was he? It had been foolish to hope, she knew.

The guard took pity on her. 'You're Stan Bishop's lass, aren't you?'

She nodded.

'And it's young Bob Gardner you're asking about?'

She nodded again.

'Well, I'll see what I can find out but don't hold your breath. It's a right muddle as far as I can tell.'

She smiled and thanked him. 'Better get back to work,' she said.

Back in the NAAFI Mrs Green was behind the counter serving a long queue of sailors and soldiers, while June scurried around clearing tables.

'You took your time,' she snapped as Daisy hurried in. 'Take over here. I need to go and check the stores.'

June stuck her tongue out behind the supervisor's back and Daisy struggled to hide a smile. 'Sorry Mrs Green,' she said, donning her overall and going behind the counter.

As she poured tea, gave out cigarettes and gave change, she tried to put Bob out of her mind. Maybe there would be news when she got home this evening. The crowd thinned and she checked the shelves behind her to make sure there were sufficient cigarettes for the next lot of customers.

Mrs Green's remark about checking the stores reminded her of her suspicions some time ago when she had been sent to get stock. She had been so busy and her mind so full of worry about Bob that she had almost forgotten Mr Browning's telling her off about not signing stuff out. Not that she had neglected to do so. She was sure it had been his mistake – or was it a mistake? She resolved to pay more attention to the number of goods sold, compared to what was in the store. And if there was any funny business, she would report it. But who to, she wondered.

A tap on the counter brought her thoughts back to her job and she smiled as Lofty said, 'A penny for them?'

'What?'

'Your thoughts. You were miles away.'

'Sorry. What can I get you?'

‘A cuppa and one of those rock buns,’ he said, pointing to the glass case.

He passed over the money and teased, ‘Dreaming of your boy friend, were you?’

‘He’s over there – in France,’ she said, a sob catching her throat. ‘Suppose he doesn’t get back?’

Lofty’s face reddened and he spoke abruptly. ‘Sorry. I didn’t mean to upset you.’ He picked up his cup and plate and went over to a table in the corner.

All her worries flooded back and Daisy thought no more about Mr Browning and any possible wrong-doing. There were more important things on her mind.

At last her shift ended and she threw off her overall and grabbed her uniform jacket off the peg behind the door. She didn’t wait for June and Lily but hurried out into the warm May evening.

She was home in ten minutes and, as usual, her eyes went to the mantelpiece in search of a letter. Of course, there was nothing there and she threw herself down on one of the kitchen chairs, covering her face with her hands. She wouldn’t cry, she told herself fiercely. Bob was safe, on his way home – he must be.

She sat up as the back door opened, wiping her hands over her face and turning to smile at her mother, who was still wearing her WVS uniform. ‘Just got back from the station’ she said. ‘We’ve been handing out tea and sandwiches to the lads. Poor souls. After all they’ve been through, they’re sending them back to their units. So many of them...’ She sighed.

‘We’ve been busy at work too,’ Daisy said. ‘I kept looking for Bob every time the door opened. And they sent me down to the dock gate to hand over a pile of sandwiches.’ She sighed. ‘They wouldn’t let me in though.’

‘Of course they wouldn’t. Don’t be daft, girl,’ said Stan.

Before Daisy could say anything, Dora said, ‘Oh, I nearly forgot. Mrs Gardner popped round this morning...’

‘She’s had news?’ Daisy jumped up. ‘He’s home?’

'No, dear. I'm sorry, I didn't mean... It's one of Bob's mates. He came to see her. He got back on one of those destroyers. My goodness, what a time they've had.'

'But, Mum. What about Bob? Is he safe?' Daisy could hardly contain her impatience. She dashed to the back door. 'I must go and see her.'

'Daisy, wait...'

But Daisy couldn't wait. She pushed through the gap in the fence that had been there since they were children and, without knocking, pushed open the back door to the Gardners' house. She could tell at once that Bob's mother had been crying and her heart sank.

She rushed across the room and, kneeling in front of her chair, took the older woman's hands. 'What's happened?' she looked round to see a soldier standing by the window, twisting his cap in his hands.

'I'm Tom,' he said. 'Bob's mate. We were together till...' He coughed and paused. 'Sorry. It's hard. I don't know what to say.'

'They left him behind,' Mrs Gardner wailed. 'My boy...'

'We didn't want to leave him,' Tom protested. 'He insisted. You see, our sergeant was wounded and Bob stayed with him. He was very brave.'

Daisy patted Mrs Gardner's hands. 'Don't worry. He's probably safe. They're still bringing people off. I heard it in the NAAFI today.' She didn't really believe it, but she needed to comfort Bob's mother.

Tom looked embarrassed. 'I hope so but it's crazy over there and the Germans were right behind us.'

'Maybe he's been taken prisoner,' Daisy said, clinging on to a little bit of hope. 'That must be it.' She turned to Bob's mother. 'We mustn't give up hope yet.'

Tom shifted his feet. 'I shouldn't really be here. I was on my way to the station. I just felt I had to come and give you what news I could.'

Mrs Gardner straightened her shoulders. 'Thank you, young man. I'm grateful. And, as Daisy says, we mustn't give up hope.'

Daisy followed him to the door and thanked him. But as he turned away he said, ‘I’m sorry to say, from what I saw there was precious little chance he got away. I just hope he’s taken prisoner, not...’

She didn’t reply, just closed the door and went back to try and offer Bob’s mother some comfort.

Chapter Ten

Bob waded out into the sea, holding his rifle above his head. A small boat bobbed alongside him and willing hands pulled him on board.

'That's it, mate, soon have you home.'

Bob was so exhausted he scarcely heard, gazing back at the sand dunes pitted with craters and littered with dead or dying men. The little boat came alongside a destroyer and he managed to climb the ladder onto the deck. The ship was crowded and he looked around, bewildered. There was nowhere to sit and when he moved towards the companionway, hoping to find somewhere to rest, an able seaman stopped him. 'Full up down below, mate.'

Bob stumbled away and managed to squeeze into a corner where exhaustion claimed him. He slept so deeply that he was oblivious to the noise of bombs dropping all around them.

He was awoken by a hand on his shoulder and he opened bleary eyes. 'What you doing here, mate?'

'Where are we? Is this Dover?'

The man laughed. 'Dover? You joking? Listen to that.'

Bob could hear machine gun fire and he stood up groggily, gazing around in bewilderment. 'I thought we'd be home by now,' he said.

'Mate, you *were* home. We offloaded everyone and turned back to pick up another lot. Don't know how we missed you.'

Bob groaned. Back in Dunkirk, just when he thought his troubles were over. He stumbled towards the rail and looked down at a scene from hell. His thoughts turned to Sergeant Williams and guilt assailed him. He shouldn't have left him behind. He turned to the sailor who had woken him.

'I want to get off,' he said.

'Go back there? You mad?'

'I left a mate behind. I need to see if he's OK.'

The sailor shrugged. 'Better get a move on then. We won't hang about too long.'

Bob was still shaky but the sailor helped him to the rail and lowered him into one the small boats that had just unloaded another cargo of shocked and wounded men. He looked across to the beach, dismayed at how many men were still there, all hoping to be picked up.

The boat reached the shore and he jumped into the shallows and waded towards the beach, pushing his way through the crowds to the causeway. He tried to remember where the first aid post was where he had left the sergeant. But the buildings he passed only a few hours ago were now a blackened smoking ruin. He groaned. Too late. He'd better get back to the boats.

As he turned away and joined a group of men making their way to the beach, he heard a sound that turned his blood to ice. The rumble of tanks approaching - German tanks. He stopped, turned and, following the advice of the officer in charge, held up his hands. Some of the men tried to run but were mown down. Bob felt sick but he held his head high.

A long march inland began, prodded from behind by German soldiers. Bob stumbled along, eyes on the ground cursing his bad luck. Where would they end up? Would he ever see Daisy again? His own fault. He had almost been home. Why hadn't someone woken him? Too late now.

***

It was a week after Tom's visit to Mrs Gardner and there was still no news. Daisy still prayed that Bob had somehow survived, that even now he was on his way home. But it was becoming harder to cling on to hope.

There was very little in the newspapers or on the wireless news about the evacuation from Dunkirk, but Prime Minister Churchill made a speech in the House of Commons a few days ago and an extract from that had been read out on the nine o-clock news.

'Trying to keep our spirits up,' Stan Bishop said, as the family sat round the table eating their tea. 'A miracle of deliverance,' he says, but we all know what's coming.' He went over and turned the wireless up. 'Let's hear what J B has to say.'

They ate in silence for a while, listening to J B Priestley's 'Postscript', the talk he gave after the evening news. He too was talking about the 'miracle of Dunkirk'.

'Propaganda,' Stan exclaimed through a mouthful of shepherd's pie. 'It's defeat, not victory however they try to dress it up.'

'Oh, Dad,' Daisy said, a sob in her voice. She pushed her plate away. 'I can't eat any more, Mum. I just keep thinking about Bob.'

'Sorry, love. Didn't mean to upset you.' Stan put on a more cheerful voice. 'Well, Mr Churchill said, 'we will never surrender' and I for one will carry on doing my bit,' Stan said. 'You too, Daisy love, don't give way. I'm sure, wherever Bob is now, he's trying to do his bit too. That's why he joined up.'

Daisy didn't care what the Prime Minister said. Everyone knew the Germans were almost on their doorstep just waiting to invade. 'What good can *we* do, Dad?'

'I don't know, love. But we're trying. The LDV are getting proper training and they've promised us guns, proper equipment.'

'Not much use against tanks and...' She choked on a sob, pushed her chair back and rushed upstairs before she could give way to the threatening tears. She threw herself down on the bed but after a few minutes she sat up and wiped her eyes. No use crying, she told herself. She must be brave, like Dad. Face whatever happened when – if – it happened.

If only she could write to Bob, pour out her hopes and fears, tell him how much she loved and missed him.

She must do something to take her mind off this all-consuming worry though. She decided to write to Sylvia. They hadn't heard from her since her brief visit earlier in the year.

Writing to her sister helped to calm her down and she even managed to make a few jokey references to the lads who came into the NAAFI. She told Sylvia about creepy Private Tompkins, about grumpy Mr Browning and Cook Sergeant Shiner who acted as if he was a chef at the Ritz.

She didn't ask if Sylvia had heard from Roland, the handsome RAF officer she had brought home with her. She was sure that, despite her offhand comments, her sister had been really smitten with him but he didn't seem the sort to stick to one girl friend, especially one who was so far away. And she didn't mention Bob either.

She felt a bit better after writing and she sealed the envelope and went downstairs to ask her mother for a stamp.

Stan was still hunched over the wireless while Dora was in the scullery washing up. Daisy picked up a tea towel and began to dry the dishes.

'Where's Jimmy?' she asked.

'He's gone up to Barton's Point,' Dora replied. 'He can't keep away – says he's helping the gun crews, running errands for them and that. I don't like it but what can I do?'

'You worry too much,' Stan called from the other room. 'There's been no raids as yet. Time enough to worry when old Hitler gets here.'

Dora tipped the water away and dried her hands, then marched into the other room. 'Don't talk like that, Stan.' Her voice trembled and Daisy put her arm round her mother and gave her a hug.

'No use getting upset, Mum. We just have to get on with it and do what we have to do.'

The back door banged open and Jimmy came in, his hair on end and his eyes alight with excitement. 'Just saw another destroyer making its way to the Dockyard. Perhaps Bob's on board,' he said.

Hope flared in Daisy's breast again and despair fled. Jimmy could be right. She mustn't give up hope yet.

***

Bob felt as if he'd been walking for days. His boots were falling to pieces and he had lost his tin hat, left behind in the scramble to get to his feet after one of their brief stops. The sun beat down on his head, sweat dripping into his eyes so that he could hardly see where he was going. Not that he wanted to look around him, nauseated by the sight of the dead and dying by the roadside. Soldiers and civilians had been mown down by Stukas in their desperate attempt to reach the coast. Why had he and the small group with him been spared?

He wondered where they were and glanced up as they reached a crossroads. They were ordered to go straight on, but Bob caught a glimpse of a signpost pointing off to the right. 'Amiens'. Hadn't Francoise said her aunt lived near there? He couldn't remember the name of the village, but she had told him about the Cathedral of Our Lady in the city. Had she managed to reach there? Bob prayed she was safe.

He stumbled as his foot caught in one of the potholes made by the bombing and a German soldier gave him a shove. He glared at the man, only to receive a harder blow. He managed to keep walking, eyes on the ground.

Dusk was falling when their captors ordered them to halt. They sank to the ground where they stood. Two Germans patrolled the line of exhausted men, almost daring them to try and run away. As if they could, the state they were in. Besides, where could they run to? The rest of the German unit gathered round a hastily lit fire and opened their rations. No food or drink for the prisoners who stretched out on the grass verge and within minutes were asleep. Bob lay down too, but he couldn't sleep. He kept seeing that signpost in his mind's eye. How far away was

Amiens? He hadn't had time to see a number on the sign, just the word. It made him think of Francoise and her pretty accent as she said it.

It was almost dark, and he glanced around him. The road stretched into the distance, leading who knew where. Behind him a field of early wheat, less than a foot high. No hiding place there. But at the far side, a small wood. If he waited till full dark and moved slowly, he might be able to reach its shelter. A faint chance but worth a try. Better than staying here to be shot or incarcerated in a prison camp. He debated waking the man next to him to share his plan but decided against it.

The guards reached the end of the line and were walking back towards him. When they passed, he turned over onto his stomach and inched his way across the grass and into the field. He crawled away, expecting a bullet in his back at any moment. After several minutes, he looked back, seeing only the shadowy figures of his captors by the light of the campfire. He was almost halfway across the field. He crawled on, his progress slowing as he tired, but at last he reached the furthest edge and tumbled into a ditch. Stagnant water lay in the bottom, but Bob didn't care. He was well hidden and, so long as his absence wasn't discovered, he would be safe – for the time being anyway.

***

Despite her father's gloomy predictions, Daisy hadn't believed that there would really be an invasion. They still had the Navy didn't they? And those thousands of soldiers who'd made it back home could defend them, couldn't they? They wouldn't just have to rely on men like her father in the LDV. So she tried to comfort herself.

But, a few days later, as she walked over the moat bridge towards the garrison, she was amazed to see a roadblock in position. She had got so used to walking through the gate and waving jauntily to whoever was on guard duty. But this morning, before she even reached the entrance, she was stopped and asked to show her pass.

She smiled cheekily and said, 'You know me, don't you?'

He looked at her, not a flicker of a smile in reply. 'Orders, miss.'

She shrugged and got her pass out of her bag, then walked through the gate, past the guard room towards the NAAFI.

Inside, June was hanging up her cardigan and putting on her overall. 'What's going on?' she asked.

'Invasion alert, so Harold Tompkins said.' June looked scared. 'Do you think it's going to happen?'

Although she felt butterflies in her stomach, Daisy smiled reassuringly and said airily. 'What does *he* know – a private in the Catering Corps! He's trying to scare you, June.'

Still, the increased security was worrying. She got ready for work and tried to stifle her concerns in keeping busy. There were more soldiers than sailors in today, many of them looking drawn and tired. Survivors from Dunkirk, Daisy surmised, but she didn't ask questions, tempting as it was to ask if any of them knew Bob. What chance was there among the thousands who were taken off the beaches? Don't think about it, keep busy, she kept telling herself.

She was run off her feet for the whole morning and looking forward to a break when Mrs Green asked her to go over to the stores for some razor blades. They were selling like hot cakes to the dishevelled and weary soldiers. Daisy sighed and rubbed her aching back but she nodded and grabbed the chit Mrs Green held out to her. Her feet hurt too – she hadn't sat down all morning. She stumbled as she hurried across to the stores, imagining a hot bath and a cup of tea when she got home.

She pushed open the door and tried to remember where the razor blades were kept. She passed rows of boxes of cigarettes, reminded of her last visit here and her concerns about possible missing goods.

Everything seemed to be in order today and she quickly found a box of blades, ticked them off on the list by the door and hurried back to the canteen.

'Take the chit through to Mr Browning,' the supervisor said. 'He's doing a stock check.'

Daisy couldn't help thinking that if he was the one responsible for things going missing, he could easily cover it up when stock taking. But she nodded and reluctantly went through to the manager's office, telling herself that she had no proof. It was just her dislike of the man making her suspicious.

She knocked on the office door, hoping he wasn't there. She would just leave the paper on his desk and get away. When he shouted at her to come in, she took a deep breath and opened the door.

'Chitty for razor blades, sir,' she said. 'Mrs Green asked me to bring it.'

'Put it down there,' he snapped. 'I'm busy.'

He was examining the contents of a box on his desk and as she sidled past to put the paper in the tray, he turned to her and said, 'Do you know anything about this?' He pointed to the box.

'No, sir. What do you mean?'

'Someone's been tampering with the stores. This box should be full.'

'I don't know anything about it. This is the first time Mrs Green's sent me to the stores for ages.'

'Well, girl, I've seen you flirting with the men. You sure you don't slip them the odd free packet of fags now and then?'

'Mr Browning - I wouldn't dream of...' Daisy almost choked as tears threatened. How dare he accuse her?

'All right, all right, don't start blubbing. I'm not accusing you. But watch it. I've got my eye on you.'

Daisy fumbled for the door handle and rushed out. His accusation of flirting hurt almost as much as the implication that she was a thief. She paused outside to compose herself before resuming her duties.

She wanted to confide in June or Lily but didn't get the chance as Mrs Green called her in to the office. 'I've got a job for you. Take those baskets of food down to the Dockyard station and hand them out to the lads on the train. Lily can take the tea urn. There's a cart outside. Harold will help you.'

It was chaos at the station. As each train pulled in, soldiers scrambled for seats. Handing out the sandwiches while Lily filled their tin mugs with tea from the urn presided over by the WVS, Daisy scarcely had a chance to look at the men.

Sometimes there was a slight lull between one train and another and she scanned the crowd, hoping for a glimpse of Bob. He must be here, although how would she recognise him among these unshaven and dirty soldiers, their uniforms bedraggled and their eyes hollow with fatigue?

As the last train pulled out, she heard someone call her name and she turned round to see someone waving to her over the heads of the crowd. She pushed her way through to the group of WVS women by the tea urn.

'Mum, I didn't expect to see you.'

'Doing my bit, love.'

'Me too.' Daisy sighed. 'It's awful, Mum. Those poor lads.' Her eyes filled with tears.

Dora put a comforting arm around her. 'No sign of Bob then?'

Daisy shook her head.

'He probably landed at Dover. You're sure to have word soon. Don't give up, Daisy.'

Daisy didn't reply. It was the thought that Bob could have been among those thousands of weary men that upset her. She could have missed him in the crowds but, surely, he would have seen her? 'I just want to know he's all right' she sobbed.

Lily tapped her on the shoulder. 'Come on, Daisy. Better get back or we'll be in trouble.'

Daisy dried her eyes and said goodbye to her mother.

She was glad that Harold had already gone, leaving them to haul the empty cart back to the NAAFI. She didn't want anyone to see how close she'd come to breaking down.

Lily tactfully didn't say anything on their way back.

For once Mrs Green was in a good mood and didn't comment on how long they'd been gone. 'You've done well, girls,' she said. 'Off you go. You too, June. Have a nice evening and be back here bright and early tomorrow.'

The three girls didn't need telling twice. They threw off their caps and overalls and went out into the May sunshine.

Lily said, 'It's a lovely evening. Let's walk along the seafront.' On these early summer evenings, they had got into the habit of taking a look at the sea instead of going straight home.

Daisy was still thinking about those poor men. What must they have been through? Still, at least they'd been rescued and managed to get home. What about those who'd been left behind? Oh, Bob, where are you, she thought.

'Come on, Daisy, cheer up.' She took her friend's arm and whispered. 'Try not to worry. Like your mum said, he's probably landed at Dover. You'll hear from him soon.'

Daisy wasn't convinced but she summoned a smile and said. 'Let's hope so.'

The three girls linked arms and started up towards the promenade, past the entrance to the fairground. It had been a favourite haunt of the local kids before the war. Now the gates were locked, the big wheel dismantled, and the rides all boarded up. Beyond the fairground site on the seawall, two guns were mounted.

They hurried past and up towards the beach.

'What's going on,' Lily asked, pointing to a group of soldiers on the promenade.

As they got nearer, they stopped, staring. Barbed wire was stretched across the gap in the wall and huge pyramid-shaped concrete blocks also barred the way onto the beach.

'Clear off. You can't come this way,' one of the men shouted.

Lily wasn't deterred and she marched up to the men. 'Why not?' she demanded. 'We always walk home this way.'

'Orders,' he said.

'Orders,' she muttered. 'That's their answer for everything these days.'

Daisy pulled at her arm. 'Come away, Lily. They've got guns,' she whispered.

Lily pushed her off reluctantly and followed her and June as they started off across the grass by the boating lake.

They stopped when one of the men hailed them and Daisy turned to see Lofty coming towards them. 'Hang on a minute, girls,' he called.

'Is all that because of the invasion?' Daisy asked.

'Yes, although we're not supposed to say. They're giving out that it's flood defences.'

Daisy scoffed. 'That won't fool anybody. Barbed wire won't keep out a flood.'

Lofty laughed. 'Too right. Anyway, I just wanted to apologise for my mate. He didn't have to be so rude.'

'That's OK. Anyway, we'd better get home. My mum doesn't like me being late for tea.'

'You're not staying in after, are you? It's a lovely evening. Care to meet up later?'

Lily grinned. 'We're going to the pictures, the three of us. You can join us if you want.'

'All right. Which one?'

'The Rio, seven o'clock.'

The girls walked off giggling, leaving Lofty staring after them.

'I told you he's taken a shine to you, Daisy,' Lily said. 'I think he'd prefer it if you went on your own to meet him.'

'Not on your life,' Daisy said. 'I don't want him getting ideas.'

'You shouldn't flirt with him then,' June said.

Was she flirting? Was Mr Browning right to accuse her? It was harmless enough really. If any of them got too cheeky, she reminded them that she had a boyfriend serving abroad and they usually backed off.

They reached the Clock Tower in the town centre and went their separate ways, arranging to meet later. Daisy made her way up the High Street still thinking about the soldiers rescued from Dunkirk.

Indoors, she automatically glanced towards the mantelpiece for a letter. Disappointed, she went upstairs to change into a summer dress for her evening out. Surely if Bob had managed to get back to England he would have written. As she tidied her hair, she made up her mind to stop worrying and enjoy her evening out with her friends. She would put it all out of her mind - the worry about Bob, the forthcoming invasion, as well as her concerns about possible thieving from the stores. She went downstairs and laid the table for their meal while her mother dished up.

'Going out tonight?' Dora asked as she put a plate of sausage and mash in front of her.

'Pictures, with June and Lily.' She didn't mention that Lofty was joining them. She didn't want Dad to start on about her being flighty or young Jimmy to start teasing. Not that there was anything in it, she told herself. He was just a friend. But she couldn't deny that she was looking forward to seeing him outside the working environment.

She finished her meal and asked to be excused from the table, put her jacket on and picked up her handbag from the sideboard.

'Don't be late, love,' Stan said. 'You know how your mother worries.'

Daisy smiled. Dad worried more than Mum, but he tried to hide it. 'I'll come straight home,' she said, kissing his cheek.

June and Lily were already waiting outside the cinema. 'Come on, we don't want to miss the start of the film,' June called.

'No sign of lover boy,' Lily teased. 'Disappointed are you?'

'Course not,' Daisy protested but she felt herself blushing when he hurried up to them, apologising for being late. She would make sure that she sat between her friends, didn't want him getting ideas. But as they made their way along the row, Lily pushed past her to sit between her and June, so she found herself next to Lofty after all.

She didn't mind though, but she kept her eyes on the screen where the Pathé news was just finishing. She wondered what it would mean for them now that Italy had declared war. It seemed to be all bad news lately.

She sighed and settled down to watch the film, hoping it would take her mind off things. *'The Four Feathers'* told a good story, although John Clements wasn't one of her favourite actors. And it was quite upsetting in parts, the war scenes making her think of Bob and all those others fighting for their country.

It had a satisfying ending though and she found herself sniffing a bit and fumbling for a hanky. Lofty handed his to her without a word and none of the teasing comments she usually got when she became emotional over a film.

Outside, June and Lily chattered about the film, but Daisy didn't join in. Lofty walked beside her and, as her friends turned the corner and waved goodbye, he took her hand and guided her across the road. Confused, she felt she should pull away. But she had to admit she liked the feel of his hand in hers. She wasn't being untrue to Bob; it didn't mean anything. Besides, Bob hadn't written for ages, even before all the confusion of the Dunkirk evacuation. He'd written to his mother, and June told her she'd heard from her brother who was in the same regiment. So why hadn't he written to her? And why shouldn't she go out and enjoy herself while he was away?

'You're very quiet,' Lofty said as they reached the turning to her street. 'Didn't you enjoy the film?'

'I did, but I couldn't really concentrate on it. I felt guilty for enjoying myself, thinking of those poor men, the ones left behind in France.'

'Bob, you mean? I know you're worried about him, but you can't sit at home brooding. I hoped I could help you take your mind off things.'

'Easier said than done,' she said.

He kept hold of her hand and bent towards her from his greater height. 'I don't like to see you unhappy. I would change that, if I could,' he said. 'I know you don't think of me that way, but I'm fond of you, Daisy.'

'Please, don't talk like that,' she begged. 'I like you, but I promised Bob...' her voice trailed off and she pulled her hand away. As she pushed open her back gate, she looked over her shoulder and said with a half laugh, 'Besides, I don't even know your real name.'

She left him staring after her. But she heard him say, 'It's Christopher – Chris.'

***

Chris strode down the road, scarcely looking where he was going, his thoughts in turmoil. He shouldn't have told Daisy how he felt. Now, she would probably avoid him, and he wouldn't even have the chance to join her and her friends at the cinema or chat to her as she served him at work.

That's it, he told himself, I'll stop going in the NAAFI, keep out of her way. Now he wished he had been sent abroad with the rest of the regiment. Despite what was happening over in France, at least he wouldn't have met Daisy in the first place.

Unbidden, the treacherous thought wormed its way into his head. Perhaps Bob won't make it back. No! That wasn't right. Oh, why hadn't he been sent over there away from temptation?

Chapter Eleven

Daisy woke early next morning and lay for a while in the dark before switching on her bedside lamp. She had been dreaming – a pleasant dream of walking along the cliffs at Minster hand in hand with someone who made her feel warm and loved. As the dream faded, she couldn't be sure if it had been Bob or Lofty but as she sat up, a faint smile twitched at her lips. 'Christopher – Chris,' she murmured.

Shaking her head and telling herself not to be so silly, she got out of bed and started to dress. It was just a dream after all.

She and Lily were on late shift today and had arranged to meet by the Clock Tower and have a wander round the shops during the morning - not that there was much to buy these days what with the rationing as well as shortages even of stuff that wasn't rationed.

She took her time getting ready, nice not to have to rush. When she came downstairs, Mum was just leaving for her shift at the WVS shop in the High Street.

'Where's Dad,' she asked.

'Special meeting of the LDV – preparing for invasion,' Dora replied.

'They really think it's going to happen then?'

'Don't worry, we'll smash 'em,' Jimmy said, stuffing toast into his mouth.

'Don't talk rubbish,' Dora snapped. 'Anyway, time you was off to school.' She turned to Daisy. 'Make sure he's not late.'

'Not going to school,' Jimmy said after the door had closed. 'Don't tell Mum or Dad.'

'You must go. You'll get into trouble.'

'Don't care. Besides, I've got a job.' Jimmy stood up, shoving the last mouthful of toast into his mouth. 'Gotta go.'

'What job?'

But she was talking to empty air. He had gone, slamming the door behind him. Daisy sighed and shrugged. She couldn't stop him. Mum and Dad were sure to find out anyway. Besides, she had too much on her mind to worry about what her brother got up to. He was probably up at Barton's Point making a nuisance of himself around the gun crews. Although with the invasion scare, they would probably chase him off. Knowing Jimmy, he would soon find some other mischief to get up to.

Daisy finished her tea and cleared the breakfast things away. After a little hesitation, she washed the dishes. It wasn't fair to leave it all to Mum. She dried her hands, noticing how rough they were. She'd have to go to Boots and get some Pond's cream – that's if they had any left.

Lily was waiting for her by the Clock Tower and they carried on up the High Street, looking in the shop windows although there was very little to catch their eye.

'What's the use of earning good wages when there's nothing to spend it on? 'Lily complained.

'Well, at least I managed to get my cream,' Daisy said.

'Let's go back to Woolworth's,' Lily suggested.

After looking round the store they went across to the Neptune Cafe for a cup of tea and a bun. Usually, on a fine day like today, they would have gone for a walk along the prom or wandered round the Fairground. But that was all closed now, locked and boarded up.

'I suppose that's it for the duration,' Daisy said, 'unless the Germans come.'

Lily shivered. 'What will happen if they do?' she asked.

'How do I know?' Daisy snapped, then immediately regretted her sharpness. 'Sorry. Don't let's talk about it.'

Lily took a sip of her tea. 'Changing the subject, what about you and lanky Lofty?'

'His name's Christopher,' Daisy said, and then wished she hadn't as Lily's eyes widened.

'Ooh, really. So, have you given up on Bob then?'

'Certainly not. I promised to stay true to him, didn't I?'

'But Lofty walked you home. Did he kiss you goodnight?'

Daisy's face flamed and when Lily giggled, she gave her friend a little push. 'Don't be silly.' She finished her tea in silence, while Lily apologised and turned her attention to her rock bun which, she said, was more rock than bun.

Daisy gave a vague smile, lost in thought. Lily's teasing recalled last night when Lofty became so serious. And for one moment she'd thought he was going to kiss her. How would she have responded if that had happened? Being honest with herself, she admitted that she might have found it very pleasant.

She became aware that Lily was trying to attract her attention and she turned to her friend with a smile. 'What have you been up to? You've been dying to tell me, haven't you?' she asked

'I've met someone,' Lily said, her pale face flushing and her eyes lighting up.

'Who? When? Not one of the customers,' Daisy said.

'Not on your life. He's a bit more exciting than that. An RAF officer, would you believe?'

'You're a dark horse.' Daisy leaned forward. 'Is it serious, Lily?'

'I think so. Oh, Daisy, he's ever so handsome. I can't believe he asked me out.'

'How did you meet him?'

'It was on my last day off. I was on the bus going up to Eastchurch to see my auntie and he came and sat next to me. He's stationed up at the aerodrome, training the Polish airmen.'

'And he asked you out?'

'We went to the pictures last week and then the other evening we went for a lovely walk along the cliffs.' Lily blushed.

‘I knew there was something going on. Why didn’t you tell us before?’

‘I don’t know really, wanted to keep it to myself for a while. Besides, you were worried about Bob and I didn’t want to rub it in that I had someone.’

‘Don’t be silly. I’m pleased for you.’ She was reminded of Sylvia’s young man - Roland. ‘My sister brought an officer home a few months back when she was on leave,’ she said. ‘He was being posted to Eastchurch and they travelled down on the same train.’

‘A boyfriend?’ Lily asked.

‘I’m not sure. She seemed keen but she had to go back to Norfolk.’ Daisy realised Lily hadn’t told her the new boyfriend’s name. She grinned. ‘I wonder if they know each other,’ she said.

Lily didn’t reply. She looked at the clock on the wall behind the counter and gasped. ‘Goodness, I must go. I promised Mum I’d look after the little ones for an hour.’ She grabbed her bag and rushed off, turning at the door. ‘See you at work later on.’

Daisy gazed after her, wondering what the hurry was. She hadn’t mentioned having to look after her little brother and sisters before. Perhaps she was just a bit shy about this new boyfriend and didn’t want to talk about him. Daisy shrugged. She was in no hurry and she ordered another cup of tea. Fancy Lily going out with an officer though. Could it be the same person? Of course not. There were hundreds of RAF personnel based at Eastchurch.

Her sister hadn’t answered her letter yet. Knowing Sylvia, she had probably found someone else to take her out dining and dancing. She was never short of admirers and often teased Daisy for ‘settling for the boy next door’ as she put it.

***

Sylvia was not out dancing, in fact she had not gone out at all since returning to Norfolk. She was off duty this evening and lay fully dressed on her bed in the Nissen hut that served as a billet for seven other girls. They had all gone off to the nearby town, but she'd stayed behind. She looked at the clock, wishing now that she had gone with them. No use moping around feeling sorry for herself. She sat up and shook her blonde curls, pushing her hair back behind her ears. She straightened her clothing and went over to the wash basin, peering into the mirror behind it and rubbing her eyes, red and swollen from crying when once more there had been no letter from Roland.

She'd watched for the post every day, convinced that Roland would keep his promise to write often. Despite what she had told Daisy, she was desperately in love with him and had been devastated when he was posted away. Of course she was grateful that he was not flying, although she knew how frustrated he was when he had been grounded and sent down to Kent. At least he wasn't in any real danger, not like so many of the young men on this base who never returned from their mission.

She sighed. At least there was one thing she didn't need to worry about now, as she'd discovered this morning. When she had first suspected she might be pregnant she'd almost dashed off a letter to Roland straight away. Now she was glad she hadn't. She still longed for him to contact her, although she vowed she'd never even hint at what might have happened. She was furious with him for persuading her to go up to his hotel room that night – not that she'd needed much persuading. But she had trusted him when he said you couldn't get pregnant the first time. Even so, she still treasured tender thoughts of that magical evening. She would forgive him – if only he would write.

She splashed water on her face - she didn't want her friends to see her tear-stained face when they came back. Joyce especially would tease her unmercifully.

'You've got the pick of the bods in the officers' mess,' she'd said. 'Don't waste your time crying over the one who's not here.'

It was the sort of thing Sylvia would have said herself in the past. But Roland was different. No other man made her feel like this. She thought once more of that wonderful night. And then she'd had to come back here, leaving him behind.

She smiled wryly. She had been so desperate to leave home, to get away from the Island. Now, she would give anything to be back there. She almost envied Daisy and her humdrum job, her simple carefree life and love for the boy next door.

Thinking of her sister reminded her that she had not answered Daisy's last letter. She hadn't written to her parents either. Perhaps it would take her mind off Roland. She made up her mind not to write to him again. It was up to him to get in touch, she thought, shaking her blonde locks and painting a smile on her face. It was easy to pretend she didn't care.

She would write home though. It wasn't fair to Mum, not keeping in touch. She knew Dora worried about her. But she would try to sound cheerful and say how much she was enjoying herself in the WAAFs. She couldn't say too much about her work; letters were censored in case they fell into the wrong hands. If only they knew how boring it was though – just typing and filing. And Daisy thought it was so glamorous. She wrote a short letter and put a note in for her sister asking if there was news of Bob. But she resisted the urge to mention Roland.

***

The next day Daisy and her friends were on duty together and during a lull in the flow of customers they seized the opportunity for a rest and a cup of tea. Daisy was dying to tell June about Lily's new beau but it wasn't up to her. Lily wouldn't be able to keep it to herself though. Her flushed cheeks and sparkling eyes gave the game away anyway, and June soon wheedled it out of her.

'An officer,' she squealed. 'How did you manage that?' Most of the girls in their circle only went out with private soldiers or ordinary seamen. Officers were out of their league. Besides, working here in the NAAFI there wasn't much opportunity to meet the higher ranks in their job.

Lily recounted the story she'd told Daisy about meeting him on the bus and as they chattered excitedly, Daisy stopped listening. She found her gaze turning towards the door every time it opened and realised she was watching for Lofty – Christopher as she now thought of him. She hadn't really given up on Bob, but it was hard to stay true to a dream. Just a note, or a telegram to his mother saying he was safe, or a prisoner would be enough, she told herself.

Her thoughts wandered until she heard Lily say, 'Roland – Roland Hargreaves.'

June giggled. 'Ooh, posh name.'

Lily slapped her wrist. 'He's not that posh.' She sighed. 'I don't know what he sees in me though.'

'Don't be daft. You're as good as anyone,' June replied.

So it *was* the same man, Daisy thought. Should she say something? No, she decided. Lily looked so happy. Besides, Sylvia had said in no uncertain terms that she wasn't serious about Roland. Still, she couldn't help feeling a bit worried on Lily's behalf. She hadn't really taken to Roland herself, charming as he was. She remembered the way he'd held on to her hand for too long – until Sylvia took his arm possessively. She'd thought at the time he was a bit of a ladies' man, not the sort to stay true to one woman, and she worried about Sylvia. She didn't want her sister to get hurt – or Lily.

***

Her concern for Sylvia was put to rest when she got home and her mother said her sister had written.

'She sounds as if she's having a good time. You wouldn't think there was a war on,' Dora said.

Daisy quickly read the short note Sylvia enclosed with Mum's letter. No mention of Roland, she saw with a sigh of relief. She seemed to have forgotten him already; dances with Tim, the pictures with Jumbo, and others. No mention of the war or what work she was doing.

'I'll answer this straight away,' she said. 'What about you, Mum? Shall we put them in the same envelope?'

'All right. I'll try to find time later this evening. I suppose I ought to tell her about Jimmy.' Dora sighed. 'I don't know what to do about that boy. I know he's not been to school. Goodness knows what he gets up to while we're all at work.'

'I think he needs to feel useful. He thinks school's a waste of time. He told me he's got a job but he's too young for proper work.'

'A job,' Dora exclaimed. 'Who'd take on a lad of his age?'

'Don't worry, Mum. I'll have a chat with him. He might tell me things he wouldn't tell you or Dad.'

'I just don't want him getting into trouble.'

'He'll be all right. He's a sensible lad deep down. And look how he managed to get home all the way from Wales, on his own too. That took guts.' Daisy took a pen and writing pad out of the dresser drawer and sat at the kitchen table to write to Sylvia.

It was a hard letter to write. She didn't want to mention Lily's new boyfriend or to ask if Sylvia had heard from Roland. It would help if she knew what her sister really felt about the man. She mentioned that there was no news of Bob but what else could she say? She daren't mention her growing friendship with Christopher and she didn't think Sylvia would be interested in anecdotes about her workmates and life in the NAAFI - pretty humdrum compared with the glamour of the WAAFs.

She finished up with a brief account of Jimmy's adventures as he made his way home. Mum would probably have more to say about that, she thought, as she signed off and folded the single sheet of paper. She addressed the envelope and left it unopened on the table, ready for her mother to enclose her letter.

She looked at the clock and said, 'Dad's late.'

'He's at another meeting in the council offices - the LDV.' Mum finished drying the dishes and joined Daisy at the table. 'It's all this invasion talk – quite worrying. They're going to have proper uniforms and guns.' Dora shuddered.

Daisy took her mother's hand. 'That's all it is – talk,' she said. 'You mustn't worry. I'm sure it won't come to that.' But her brave words were a cover for her own fear. Living on the coast and so near to London as well, she realised how vulnerable they were.

She stood up and switched on the wireless, fiddling with the knobs until she found some music. 'There, that's a bit more cheerful,' she said, tapping her feet as the strains of a swing band filled the little room. Then the tune changed, and the Andrews Sisters started to sing, *'Don't Sit Under the Apple Tree with Anyone Else but Me.'* A spasm of guilt washed over her as she remembered Bob's last words to her. She should be thinking about him, not day-dreaming about someone else. She switched the wireless off before the end of the song and sat at the table again, her thoughts churning. She still loved Bob, didn't she? So why did the tall soldier with the mop of dark curls and laughing blue eyes keep intruding on her thoughts? Of course she prayed nothing had happened to Bob and if she only had news of him, heard that he was safe or a prisoner, she would thank God and put all thoughts of Christopher out of her mind.

'Dad'll be home soon,' Dora said, interrupting her thoughts. 'I'd better start getting him some supper. Give us a hand, Daisy.'

Glad to have something to do to take her mind of the confusion churning in her head, Daisy got up and took plates and cups down from the dresser.

The back door flew open and Jimmy came in, hair on end, socks creased around his ankles, grinning with excitement. 'Look what I've got, mum,' he said, holding up a string bag.

Daisy spotted the gleaming scales of a fish through the holes. 'Where did you get that?' she asked.

‘It’s a plaice. I caught it off the jetty,’ Jimmy said.

‘I thought no one was allowed on the seafront,’ Dora said. ‘What have you been up to now?’ She grabbed Jimmy’s arm, snatching the bag from him, and turning to Daisy. ‘This boy will be the death of me, always up to some mischief.’

‘I wasn’t, Mum, honest. I was talking to the soldiers and one of them showed me how to catch fish on a hand line.’ His face fell. ‘I thought you’d be pleased. You can cook it, can’t you?’

Dora’s annoyance faded and she said, ‘Of course. It’ll help with the rations. But please, Jimmy, don’t go there again, promise me. It’s dangerous. You could get into real trouble.’

‘All right, Mum. I promise. But, don’t tell Dad, will you?’

‘He’ll want to know where the fish came from though.’

Jimmy kicked the table leg and hung his head. ‘I suppose so.’

‘Well, wash your hands and face and sit up to the table. We’ll see what he says when he gets in.’

Supper was on the table when Stan got back from his meeting and he was so full of his meeting and what they were planning that he didn’t seem to notice how quiet Jimmy was.

‘Guns? Did you say guns?’ Dora asked.

‘Not yet. But we’ve been promised them. We’ll give old Hitler a run for his money.’ Stan laughed.

‘Stan, it’s no joking matter,’ Dora protested but Daisy laughed too. It felt good to be sitting round the table with her family, and the anxieties which plagued her lately faded into the background. But, as Mum said, it was no joke. The war was coming uncomfortably close. Even if there was no invasion, there could be air raids. Those guns placed all along the seafront weren’t there for decoration.

‘Can I join, Dad?’ Jimmy’s voice interrupted the conversation.

Stan burst out laughing. ‘What? You’re too young, lad.’

‘I’m serious. I want to do something useful.’

‘You’d be better off going to school instead of skiving off,’ Stan said, the laughter fading.

Jimmy started to protest but his father interrupted. ‘Oh, yes. I know what you’ve been up to, young man. This is a small town and I hear what goes on.’

‘I just...’ Jimmy shook his head. ‘Everyone’s doing their bit. I thought I was helping, running errands for the men up on the guns but I’m not allowed now, Mum says.’

‘It’s dangerous, Jimmy,’ Dora said.

‘So why can’t I join the LDV then? I could be useful if the Germans come. They wouldn’t notice a kid...’ His voice tailed off and he looked down at his plate.

Daisy felt sorry for him but there was nothing she could do. Her parents were right. It was too dangerous.

Chapter Twelve

Bob woke suddenly, startled by voices nearby. He burrowed deep into the hedge, holding his breath until the two German soldiers passed by. He did not know where he was or how much time had passed since his escape. He had lain in the ditch for hours until it was full dark. Faint moonlight lit the surrounding countryside with a ghostly glow as he crawled out of the ditch. He had crossed the field and burrowed into the hedge, deciding to rest until it was full dark. It was quiet now, although he could still hear the guns and rumble of tanks in the distance.

He must get back to the coast. Perhaps there would still be a boat to take him off the beach. He couldn't stay here, risking re-capture by the Germans. Worse still, he could be taken for a deserter if he did not report back – although who he would report to, he had no idea. Supposing they had all been captured and he was alone in this strange country. Should he give himself up?

He tried to settle to sleep again but despite his exhaustion sleep would not come. At first light, he looked around cautiously, then stood up, stretching and rubbing his back. His throat was dry and his stomach rumbled, reminding him that he hadn't eaten or drunk anything for almost two days.

He forced himself on, crossing another field, all the while glancing round for signs of pursuit. But the landscape was deserted. He reached the little copse he'd spotted the night before, glad to lose himself among the trees. But he couldn't hide out here forever. There must be a farm nearby, surely. He didn't like the idea of stealing food and drink, but he was desperate. He remembered the kindness of Francoise and her mother, their generosity in sharing what little food they had. He could not expect such a miracle to happen again.

He stumbled out of the trees into a narrow lane and hesitated, not sure which direction to take. The sun was well up now and it was going to be another hot day but at least it gave him some idea of which way to turn. With the sun behind him he should be facing north towards the coast. He wasn't sure why he felt that was the right way and he was beginning to wish he'd paid more attention in geography classes.

He straightened his shoulders and stepped out, briskly at first, but as the sun rose higher his head began to spin and his steps faltered. Still he kept going, his spirits lifting as he approached the outskirts of a village. He didn't care if it was already occupied by the enemy.

His last thought as his knees buckled and he fell to the ground was that he must have water.

***

It was cool, so blessedly cool. Bob raised his head and looked around him. He was lying on a stone floor and someone was bathing his head. He struggled to sit up, confused. Had he been captured? But a hand gently pushed him back down. 'Rest, my son,' a voice murmured in English.

He looked up into the face of an elderly priest, who smiled at him. 'You are safe now,' he said.

Gradually Bob took in his surroundings, the beamed roof, the stone columns and the stained glass windows. It looked familiar. Surely he wasn't back in the church where he had last seen Francoise. He gasped and tried to sit up again. 'The Germans? They are here?'

'Not yet, but they are not far away,' the priest replied.

Bob's head cleared and he clutched the priest's arm as he recognised him. He couldn't believe it was the same man. Somehow, he had come full circle. 'How did I get here?' he asked.

'Don't worry about that now. We must hide you.'

'No. It is too dangerous for you. Besides, I must try to rejoin my mates.'

'There is no one left. We thought you had all been captured. You must hide while we decide what to do.' The priest helped Bob to stand, holding his arm and leading him towards a small door behind a column. Steps led down to a crypt. 'You will be safe here for a while. Stay quiet. I will return soon with food and drink.'

When the priest left, Bob stood for a moment taking in his surroundings. The only light came from a small window high up. He made out a mattress in one corner and he sat down, his head in his hands. How had he arrived back here? He'd thought to be miles away by now. Although he was too exhausted to worry about what might happen to him, he prayed that Francoise had managed to get away and was safely with her aunt. There was nothing to do but wait until the priest returned. He lay down and in minutes he was asleep, the first proper sleep in days, except for those few hours on the ship.

***

There was more than one thing troubling Daisy this morning. Last night she gave in and accepted Christopher's invitation to the cinema. She could hardly concentrate on the film, so conscious was she of his nearness, the warmth of his hand as he took hers, the feel of his breath on her cheek as he leaned towards her to whisper something about the film.

And then there was that kiss outside her back gate, so different from Bob's tender caresses. She had fallen into bed confused but happy and this morning hadn't even looked for the postman as she usually did.

She was on washing up duty this morning, which gave her time to brood. Should she feel guilty for enjoying a romantic interlude? For that was all it was, so she told herself.

But now there was another problem.

As she and Christopher scrambled along the row to their seats, they had squeezed past a couple so wrapped up in each other they hadn't moved. That was, until the man in RAF uniform looked up and Daisy recognised Roland. But the girl he was with wasn't Lily.

Should she tell her friend the man she was so smitten with was two-timing her? It would break Lily's heart but surely it was better to know. And what about Sylvia?

She scrubbed furiously at the dried-on egg yolk on the plate she was washing and sighed. At that moment Lily came through the swing doors with a tray full of dirty crockery.

'What's up with you, Dais? I thought you'd be all happy this morning after your evening out. What happened?'

'Nothing. I had a good time actually.'

'Feeling bad about Bob then?'

'A bit,' Daisy admitted. She took the tray from her friend and smiled. 'What about you? How's Roland?'

Lily giggled. 'Smashing, although I wish I could see more of him. He doesn't get much time away from the aerodrome. I miss him,' she said. 'Ooh, Daisy, I think this is it. I can't describe how he makes me feel.'

'So, it is serious then?'

'Of course. Never been more serious in my life.'

'Is it the same for him?'

'What're you talking about? Of course it is. You should hear the things he says.' Lily blushed.

Daisy turned away to hide her expression and concentrated on her washing up. 'I'm glad you're happy, Lily.' How could she shatter her friend's happiness? And who knew, perhaps there was nothing in it. Or so she tried to tell herself.

When they stopped for their break, June joined them and asked if they were going to the dance at the Wheatsheaf Hall that evening. 'There's going to be a band and I heard some of the Poles from Eastchurch will be there.'

'Sounds like fun,' Daisy said. 'What about you Lily?' She wondered if Roland would be there with the Polish airmen.

'Can't. Promised Mum I'd look after the little ones as she's working late tonight. Besides, my boy friend's on duty tonight and I don't want to dance with anyone else.'

'You should come though. I'm hoping I meet someone nice.' June did a little twirl. 'Haven't had a dance for ages. You're coming, aren't you, Daisy?'

'Well, I was going to stay in and wash my hair, but I might as well.'

'Not going out with Lofty again then – sorry I mean Christopher,' Lily asked.

'I've decided not to. It's not fair to Bob.' Daisy sniffed. 'I don't even know if he's still alive, but I must keep hoping.'

'Well, dancing will help take your mind off worrying. You can't sit at home brooding. I'll meet you outside. Better get back to work now.' June picked up her cup and stood up. Lily and Daisy followed.

There was little time to chat as the busy afternoon wore on but as they took off their overalls and donned their uniform jackets ready for home, Lily said, 'I wish I was coming dancing with you two tonight.'

They walked up the High Street, arms linked as usual, chatting about the coming evening. As they left Lily at the turning to Hope Street she said, 'Have fun and don't do anything I wouldn't do.'

'Fat chance,' June said with a laugh. They parted at the Clock Tower, June hurrying up the Broadway to her lodgings, leaving Daisy to walk the rest of the way deep in thought.

Later, as she sat at her dressing table brushing her hair she thought about her growing feelings for Christopher. Was it possible to love two people at the same time, she wondered. Maybe, but there were different kinds of love. Bob had just been the boy next door until their feelings changed into something more serious. It was that last kiss that had done it, she thought, tracing the outline of her lips with her fingertips. That, and his passionate entreaty to be true to him, to wait for his return. How could she have refused when he was going off to war? And she meant every word of it, she really had. How could she have anticipated that she would be bowled over by a tall, blue-eyed despatch rider?

She threw down her hairbrush and stood up. This would not do. She would put both of them out of her mind and go out and enjoy a carefree evening with her friend. She ran down the stairs and called out a goodbye to her mother, promising not be late home.

June was waiting outside the Wheatsheaf Hall, a magnificent building containing a row of shops with two community halls above. Like many of the shops in town they were owned by the Co-operative Society who not only provided goods for the townspeople, but ran community activities for everyone from the children's choir to the young wives' groups. Daisy's dad had often said Sheerness *was* the Co-op, the first one ever, years before Rochdale set theirs up, despite the Lancashire town's claim that they were the first.

The two girls entered the foyer and bought their tickets, then ran up the wide staircase into the hall. The room was already full and the band on its dais at the far end played a foxtrot.

They sat at a small table and looked around, sizing up the dancers. A group of airmen huddled near the bar which ran along one wall, and there were several sailors and soldiers dancing.

'Is that the Poles?' June asked, gesturing at the airmen.

'Stop staring,' Daisy said.

June giggled. 'We want a dance, don't we? I'll go and get us a drink. Maybe one of them will ask us.'

'Go on then. I'll have lemonade.' Daisy watched her friend cross the room, teetering on her high heels as she manoeuvred her way between the dancers. One of the airmen turned as June approached and Daisy gasped as she recognised Roland. But hadn't Lily said he was on duty?

'Oh, no,' she murmured. He was walking towards their table carrying the drinks and laughing at something June said. Another airman joined them, and they all sat at the table.

'This is Stefan. He's Polish,' June said, turning to the other young man. 'And Roly.'

'I'm English,' Roland said.

'I know, we've met,' Daisy said, looking him in the eye.

He stared at her for a moment and then broke into a laugh, showing his white teeth. 'Of course. The little sister,' he said.

June looked confused. 'How do you two know each other then?'

'I was stationed in Norfolk before I came here. Met Daisy's sister on the train on the way down.' He turned to her. 'Have you heard from Sylvia lately? How is she?' The words were polite, almost disinterested and Daisy seethed.

How could he speak so casually when she had seen for herself how close they appeared? He was lying, too. They hadn't met casually. Sylvia told her they'd been going out together ever since she arrived in Norfolk. She managed to answer politely and he nodded, then turned to June, asking her to dance.

Left alone at the table with Stefan, the Polish airman, she tried to contain her anger and, for want of something to say, politely asked, 'Do you speak English?'

He smiled. 'A little only. But I am learning. Lieutenant Hargreaves, he is a good teacher. We are also learning about the English planes and how to mend them. Soon I will go to a squadron.'

'Will Roland   Lieutenant Hargreaves go too?'

'I don't know.' He looked embarrassed. 'I think he does not like it here.'

'Why not?' Daisy understood that those not native to the Island might not enjoy the landscape of bleak marshes and the constant bitter wind from the North Sea. But it was a good posting. And he had Lily, who was madly in love with him.

Stefan took a swig from his glass and did not reply as the music ended and June and Roland returned to the table.

Roland held out his hand. 'Your turn now, Daisy,' he said, pulling her to her feet. She didn't want to dance with him, still annoyed at his casual talk about her sister. And what about Lily? How would she feel if she knew that while she was baby-sitting her younger siblings, he was flirting with her and June, for flirting he certainly was.

She tried to pull her hand away and shook her head. 'I haven't finished my drink,' she said.

'Plenty of time for that. You came here to dance, didn't you?'

She gave in and followed him onto the floor.

She loved dancing and with any other partner she would have given herself up to the music and the rhythm. If only it were Bob or Christopher holding her in their arms. Roland's hand was sliding down her back as he twirled her round. She stiffened and firmly pushed it back where it should have been.

'Relax,' he said, pulling her closer.

She wanted to push him away, stalk back to their table but she didn't want to cause a scene. It's only a dance, she told herself, trying to ignore him by concentrating on the dance steps.

He laughed and twirled her round again. 'That's better. You're a good dancer, Daisy.' He leaned closer and whispered, 'and a good deal prettier than your sister. I had no idea there would be so many lovely girls on this god-forsaken Island. I was dreading being posted here to a non-operational base. Not my idea of fun at all.'

'You're not here to have fun, are you?' Daisy retorted, her anger rising again. She pushed him away and re-joined her friends.

'You all right, Daisy?' June asked.

'He trod on my toe. Gotta sit down for a bit.' Daisy slipped off her shoe and massaged her foot.

Roland followed her and laughed. 'Sorry, love. An accident.' He turned to June and held out his hand. 'Looks like you're going to be my partner for the rest of the evening.'

She got up and followed him on to the dance floor, turning back to Daisy with a smug smile. Oh dear, Daisy thought, I hope she's not falling for his charm and good looks too. Didn't she realise that 'Roly' was Lily's boyfriend? To be fair, she probably hadn't made the connection. This evening wasn't turning out as she'd hoped. Instead of a carefree few hours dancing and forgetting her worries, she couldn't stop thinking about Lily and how hurt she would be if she discovered what sort of man Roland was.

She was so lost in thought she was startled when Stefan asked her if she'd like another drink. 'Yes, please' she said. 'But you don't have to wait on me. Why don't you ask one of the girls to dance?'

'I don't dance so good,' he said. 'I don't know the steps.'

'Come on, I'll teach you,' she said, holding out a hand.

'But you hurt your foot.'

She laughed. 'Not really. I just didn't want to dance with Roland anymore.'

He stood up reluctantly and she pulled him onto the floor, showing him where to hold her and explaining the steps of the foxtrot to him.

'Foxtrot? Why is this name?'

'I don't know. But it's a good dance. Now, come on, follow my steps. No, don't look down, just listen to the music.'

They managed one circuit of the dance floor before Daisy gave up. Stefan tried hard but he could not relax, and he stepped on her toes so often that, with a laugh, she led him back to their table. 'Now, I need that drink,' she said laughing.

While he was at the bar, she watched the dancers. There were several girls she'd gone to school with and a few of the men she'd served in the NAAFI. June was still dancing with Roland, smiling at something he was saying. She was wearing a blue dress and looked so pretty with her hair waved and a touch of lipstick, which she'd borrowed from Lily. She'd told Daisy her parents were old-fashioned and didn't like her wearing make-up. 'Still, what the eye doesn't see,' she'd laughed.

All the girls were wearing bright summer dresses and contrasted well with the servicemen in their uniforms. The music was jolly and there was a feeling of gaiety in the air as the dancers swirled round the room. You wouldn't think there was a war on, Daisy thought. But how many of them hid worry or heartbreak under a semblance of gaiety?

Stefan came back with the drinks and she tried to think of something to talk about. 'Why did you come to the dance if you don't like dancing?' she asked.

'Roly said we would meet girls.' He took a sip of his drink and shook his head. 'I don't want to meet girls. I have girl friend at home.' He fumbled in his pocket and drew out a photograph. 'This is Maryka. She is beautiful, no?'

'Oh, yes, lovely.' Daisy handed the photo back. She wondered if Bob still had the photo she'd given him before he left. Did he show it to his pals and tell them she was beautiful?

'You look sad,' Stefan said. 'You have someone?'

'He's in the Army – over there. I haven't heard from him for a long time.'

'Maryka also. I pray she is safe.'

Neither of them got up to dance again, Stefan becoming more animated as he told her of his life in his homeland and his longing to help free his country from the invaders. 'I join air force, learn to fly. Soon I leave here to go to squadron.'

He asked about Bob and her work in the NAAFI and she made him laugh with her impersonations of the cook and her supervisor.

June and Roland danced the whole evening, only coming back to the table for a quick drink. All too soon the band was playing the National Anthem and they all stood till the music died away. In the cloakroom, Daisy said, 'I suppose you're being escorted home then?'

June looked taken aback by her friend's sharp tone. 'What's it to you? Anyway, looks like you've got someone to walk you home.'

'Stefan? Not on your life. He's nice but...'

'Actually, Roly and his mate have gone. Got the chance of a lift back to the aerodrome.'

Daisy was relieved. 'You seemed to be having a good time.'

'You know I love dancing and Roly's a good dancer. But that's all.' She took Daisy's arm as they descended the stairs and went out into the balmy summer evening. 'To tell the truth, I don't like him very much. He thinks he's god's gift. And oh, those wandering hands.'

'I know. That's why I sat down. He didn't really tread on my toe. I just wanted to get off that dance floor and away from him.'

They both laughed, then June sighed. 'Oh, but he is good looking though. Film star looks.'

'Looks aren't everything though.'

'True.' She paused. 'Daisy, I've been thinking. We've had a good time and poor Lily's stuck at home baby-sitting. Let's not say too much about what fun it's been. Don't want to upset her.'

Daisy had worried how Lily would re-act if she discovered that Roland hadn't really been on duty that evening, so she was relieved that June wouldn't go in to work tomorrow gushing about the handsome airman she'd danced with all evening. She nodded. So June had twigged that Roly was the man Lily was in love with after all and didn't want to hurt her friend's feelings.

But as she undressed and got into bed, Daisy wondered if perhaps it would be better if Lily *did* find out. Surely it was better to discover that the man was a two-timing rat.

Chapter Thirteen

Daisy sat at the kitchen table peeling potatoes for the hotpot her mother was making.

'Not much meat I'm afraid. They only had a bit of scrag end when I went to the butcher's,' Dora said. 'Thank goodness for Dad's allotment.' She turned to Stan in his chair by the range. 'About time you caught another rabbit for us,' she said.

'I set a snare last night. I'll go over later and see if I've had any luck. Not many around now,' Stan said. 'Just as well meat's not rationed yet then,' Dora replied.

'Maybe, but it will be before long.' Stan folded his newspaper and stood up. 'They don't tell you everything in the paper but reading between the lines, we're losing a lot of ships.'

'Trying to starve us out, are they?' Dora said. 'Just let them try.'

Daisy smiled at her mother's belligerent tone. But what could they do? Just make the best of it, she supposed. She finished slicing the potatoes and passed them over to her mother. 'Smells good, Mum.'

'You'll be in for dinner, love?' Dora asked.

'Yes, I'm not going out. Got some mending to do and letters to write.'

'Not much fun for you on your day off, is it?'

'I can't think about having fun. Too much on my mind.'

'Worrying about that lad still?' Stan joined in the conversation.

'Can't help it, Dad. It would be easier if I knew for sure what had happened to him.'

'You should be out enjoying yourself. You can't do anything about it.'

A pang of guilt struck her. She *had* enjoyed herself the night of the dance. 'How can you think I should be enjoying myself when poor Bob...?' Daisy gulped back a sob.

'Oh, love, don't take on. It won't help to sit indoors moping. Come over the allotment with me, do some weeding. See if we've caught a rabbit.'

'I thought Jimmy was going to help today.'

Stan laughed. 'Some hopes. He was off out straight after breakfast.'

She didn't feel like it, but she gave in. 'All right. I'll give you a hand then. The mending can wait.'

When they reached the allotment, Stan looked round and sighed. 'We need some rain. Better get started on the watering.'

Daisy fetched a watering can and filled it from the water butt next to the shed. As she walked up and down the rows of carrots and swedes she found she was almost enjoying herself. It was easy to forget the war, out here in the sunshine, listening to the birds singing and watching the butterflies.

They worked in companionable silence for a while until Stan stopped and stretched. 'I'll just check the snares,' he said.

Daisy half hoped he wouldn't find anything. Much as she enjoyed her mum's rabbit pie, the sight of the limp bodies upset her.

Stan came back dangling a rabbit in his hands and she pulled a face. He laughed at her squeamishness. He put the animal in a sack and said, 'Come on, have a cup of tea and don't think about it.'

They sat on a box outside the shed and Stan poured tea from his flask. 'You' should go out dancing more often,' he said.

'Not much point. There's no one to dance with. There's only a few soldiers left behind in the garrison and they're always on duty.' She didn't mention having seen Roland. Dad hadn't taken to him when they'd met.

'I suppose they've got to man the guns night and day, just in case, but it's my guess there won't be an invasion now. Hitler's missed his chance.' Stan took a swig of tea and turned his face up to the sun. 'It won't be over yet though. It's this loss of shipping that's more worrying. Bloody u-boats.''That's what Mr Jacobs said.' Daisy couldn't help laughing. 'Don't let Mum hear you swearing though.''Well, Hitler's enough to make anyone swear.' He stood up. 'Better get on with it.' He looked along the rows of plants. 'I don't know about "Dig for Victory". It's more like "weed for victory". Let's do a bit more before dinner.'As she bent to her weeding again, Daisy let her mind wander. It was true, she still worried about Bob, but it had been so long. Christopher occupied her thoughts these days - guilty thoughts, she knew. With most of the soldiers deployed elsewhere, she half hoped that he had gone too. Out of sight, out of mind, she told herself. But then, when she was sure he must have left, he came into the NAAFI, all smiles.'I'm staying,' he said. 'They need a despatch rider to carry messages between the garrison and the RAF station.''What's wrong with the telephone?' she asked sharply, trying to hide the joy that flooded her heart. Despite what she tried to tell herself, she dreaded his departure.'Unreliable,' he'd replied. 'Communications are always breaking down. And sometimes I have to deliver important papers.'Since then he came into the NAAFI several times but hadn't asked her out again. Too busy, she thought, but she had to admit she was disappointed. It would be good to go to a film and have him walk her home afterwards like last time. Just as friends, she told herself.Her thoughts were interrupted when Stan threw a clod of earth at her. 'Stop day-dreaming, girl. It's time we got home for dinner. I'm ready for that hotpot.'Daisy carried the basket which Stan filled with early peas and a few sun-ripened tomatoes.As soon as they got indoors, Stan switched on the wireless.'Oh, no, Stan, not the news again. Don't we hear enough doom and gloom?' Dora complained.'I like to know what's going on.''They don't tell us everything anyway. Let's eat our dinner in peace.' She dished up generous portions of steaming hotpot, the potatoes on top brown and crisp, the meat and vegetables underneath swimming in a rich gravy.

Daisy sat down and tucked in with relish. Being out in the fresh air had sharpened her appetite and she ate with more enjoyment than usual. Dad was right; she should get out more.

She glanced across the table at her father who had paused with his fork to his mouth. He put it down and leaned across to turn the wireless up. 'Another ship gone down, bloody u-boats,' he muttered.

Daisy waited for her mother to reprimand him, but she just shook her head and carried on eating.

When the meal was finished, she helped Dora to clear away and wash up, then went up to her room to fetch her mending. She looked around the little room she had shared with her sister for so long and realised with a pang that she actually missed Sylvia, despite her bossiness and untidy ways. Would things ever go back to normal? They had been at war for less than a year, but it seemed like forever. It was hard to picture what life might be like after the war – if it ever finished.

Shaking off her gloomy thoughts, she decided to write to Sylvia. But she wouldn't tell her that Roland was going out with Lily as well as kissing another girl in the cinema, not to mention flirting with June. He certainly fancied himself as a ladies' man and Daisy could only hope that Sylvia hadn't been too serious about him.

After darning her stockings and sewing on a loose button, Daisy started her letter, but she couldn't think what to say. In the end she just wrote a short note saying that the family were all busy 'doing their bit' and telling her about her morning on the allotment with Dad. She finished by sending her love and urging her to write soon.

As she sealed the envelope, she wondered if Sylvia would agree that she was really doing her bit. Serving tea and cakes to servicemen surely didn't compare with being in the WAAFs. But it was what she chose to do, and she had to admit she was happy with her job. It was just her love life making her depressed. That and worry over her friend's and her sister's love lives.

She sighed and went downstairs. What a way to spend a day off, she thought. Back to work tomorrow and that brought another unwelcome thought. She had tried to put it out of her mind, but several small incidents convinced her that something wasn't right at work. But who could she confide in? And suppose she was wrong? She didn't like Harold Tompkins very much, but she didn't want to get him into trouble. Besides, he might not be the one to blame.

***

It was so hot in the NAAFI kitchen and Daisy was fed up. She was on washing up duty today and on top of that, Mrs Green was in a bad mood and kept finding fault with her and Lily. They couldn't seem to do anything right.

'What's up with her,' Lily whispered as she plonked a tray full of dirty dishes onto the draining board. 'She's just told me off for dropping a spoon.'

'I don't know. I try to keep out of her way when she's like this.' The door opened and Lily hurried back into the canteen while Daisy hastily resumed scrubbing at a saucepan with burnt on gravy.

Mrs Green slammed the door and Daisy watched out of the corner of her eye as she stalked across to the Cook Sergeant.

'Sergeant Shiner. I've been getting complaints,' she snapped.

'Not about my cooking you haven't,' he answered.

Daisy smiled. He was so proud of his chef status, always boasting that he had worked at the top hotels before joining the Army. Probably just a kitchen skivvy, she thought. But, she had to admit, he was a good cook. So what was the supervisor on about?

'That gravy was disgusting,' Mrs Green was saying. 'And I agree with the men. I tasted it myself.'

‘Oh, that Tompkins. I’ll have his hide - the little toerag.’ Sergeant Shiner was practically foaming at the mouth. ‘I told him to chuck it out and make a fresh batch. Lazy little sod.’

‘Where is he now? Skived off for a cigarette, I suppose.’

’My staff don’t skive off. I sent him over to the stores.’ The sergeant looked at the clock on the wall. ‘Still, he should’ve been back by now.’

Mrs Green turned to Daisy, who had finished her washing up but, not wishing to draw attention to herself, lingered over wiping down the draining boards. ‘You, girl, go over to the stores and tell Private Tompkins he’s wanted. I’ll have a word with him myself. It’s not good enough.’

Daisy nodded and rushed out the door. Poor Harold. She wouldn’t want to be in shoes.

She ran over to the stores and almost bumped into Harold as he pushed open the door, carrying a large box.

‘Oops, sorry, Daisy,’ he said hefting the box in one arm and opening the door of a van parked nearby.

‘What are you doing, Harold? Sergeant Shiner is in a real temper, so is Mrs Green. You’ve been gone ages and they sent me to fetch you.’

‘I’m just...’ Harold stammered.

‘Just what?’

‘Nothing to do with you, miss. Get back to your work.’ Sid Browning came out of the store room and glared at her. ‘You, Tompkins, put that in the van and get back to the kitchen. Tell Sergeant Shiner I detained you.’ He went back into the stores and Harold and Daisy started to walk away.

‘Is he really mad at me?’ Harold asked.

Daisy nodded. ‘So is Mrs Green.’

‘The gravy, I suppose. It wasn’t my fault.’

‘Tell that to them.’ Daisy started to walk away. He always tried to blame someone else when things went wrong. ‘Come on then, go and face the music,’ she said.

Harold stopped suddenly, his hand over his mouth. 'Oh, blast. I've forgotten what I came for.' He hurried back inside the stores and came out carrying a sack of carrots.

'What was Mr Browning doing?' Daisy was curious. She had spotted several boxes in the back of the van.

'Taking stuff up to the RAF place at Eastchurch. He asked me to help load up.'

It sounded plausible but, as Daisy went back to work, she couldn't help thinking about the other times she had seen the manager in the stores and remembered the discrepancy she had noticed in the number of cigarette cartons. Perhaps Harold was involved as well. Should she tell someone of her suspicions, she wondered once again. But the answer was the same – who could she tell? Who could she trust?

Chapter Fourteen

France had fallen and the place was swarming with Germans. How much longer could Bob stay hidden in the church crypt? He should have insisted on leaving. Better to be captured again and spend the rest of the war in a prison camp than skulk here, putting Father Etienne and others who were helping him in danger.

The priest had been very good to him, as had the few remaining villagers. The Germans were everywhere, and Bob knew they were risking their lives giving him shelter. He made up his mind that he would go that night. If he kept under cover, he might be able to make it back to the coast. He just hoped all the boats hadn't left.

He started up as the door to the crypt opened and Father Etienne came in, bringing water, bread and a small piece of cheese. 'It's all we can spare, my friend,' he said. 'The Germans have taken most of our food.'

'I'll go then. I can't expect you to keep feeding me. Besides, I'm putting all of you in danger.'

'It's too dangerous for you to leave. Where will you go?'

'I'll make my way to the coast, travel at night, keep under cover. I'll go tonight.'

'Don't go yet. I have a plan. I'll come back later and explain. I must go now. It's time for mass.'

Bob ate the food, and then lay back on his makeshift bed. He sighed, wondering what the priest had in mind. There was no way he could pass himself off as a Frenchman, although he had learned a few phrases over the past few weeks. He couldn't imagine how he'd get out of this hole. He just wanted to get back to Daisy, back to his unit. He was sure he'd have been posted as a deserter by now, especially as he'd had a chance to get on one of the boats like his mates.

When Father Etienne returned, Bob had made up his mind that he would go it alone and not involve the kindly priest and his parishioners. But before he could speak, he realised there was someone behind the priest.

The young man awkwardly made his way down the steps into the crypt and lowered himself on to the bed, gasping with pain. His leg was bandaged, his foot was bent at an angle.

'This is Albert.' Father Etienne gestured to the wounded leg. 'A farm accident - that is why he is still here. The Germans took all the other young men to labour camps.'

Bob shook the young man's hand. 'I'm sorry.'

'No need to be sorry. At least he's still here.' The priest sighed. 'Who knows what has happened to the others? They said they were being sent to Germany to work out....' He shrugged.

'Why's he here?' Bob asked. 'Is he in hiding too?'

'Oh, no. He is part of the plan.' Father Etienne laughed. 'We are going to Saint Simon; it is a village near Amiens.'

Bob's heart leapt. That was the place Francoise had mentioned. Had she managed to get there? Would he see her again? He thrust the thought from his mind. He shouldn't be thinking about her. 'How will we get there?' he asked.

'Tomorrow is the Feast of St Anne. I have permission to take some of my flock to the shrine there – to pray for healing and strength.'

'Will we get away with it?' Bob's heart was racing. He was elated yet scared.

'You will wear the robes of a priest. If we are questioned, I will say that you have taken a vow of silence. You will help Albert as we shall have to walk. All our vehicles have been commandeered.'

It seemed risky to Bob but anything was better than sitting in this dark crypt fearing discovery at any moment. He thanked both men and sprang up to help Albert to stand. The priest turned at the door and said, 'Sleep well, my son, and be up early tomorrow. God be with you.'

***

The church was ablaze with candles as each supplicant made their way to the shrine to light another and say a prayer. Bob shuffled forward, supporting Albert whose limp became more pronounced on the long journey. It had been uncomfortable walking in the hot sun wearing the cumbersome priest's robe.

They were stopped only once as they entered the town and the German guard had peered suspiciously at him. He bowed his head as Father Etienne showed his pass and spoke rapidly to the soldier, indicating Albert's bandaged foot. At last the guard nodded and let the small party through.

Bob took his turn to light a candle and said a small prayer for Daisy and his family. He had never been inside a Catholic church and he gazed in awe at the statues and ornate carvings. A nudge from Father Etienne made him quickly bow his head.

As the long service proceeded, Bob's mind began to wander again. The priest had told him he would have to stay in the town until arrangements could be made to move him on. So many people were willing to put themselves in danger to help him. How could he ever thank them?

Another nudge from Father Etienne and he stood for a hymn. The singing swelled around him and his heart swelled with it. All too soon the hymn ended and, after a last prayer, the congregation started to shuffle out of the church.

As they neared the door, he saw a young woman standing in the porch. Was it Francoise? He hadn't seen her in the church and he started forward. She recognised him and a smile crossed her face. A pull at his arm stopped him in his tracks. 'Careful,' Father Etienne whispered.

A German sergeant stood at the church door scrutinising each person as they left. Bob folded his hands in his sleeves and walked past with bent head. Out of the corner of his eye, he saw Francoise speaking to the sergeant. A cold finger of fear touched his spine. Was he about to be betrayed? He couldn't – wouldn't - believe it.

He took Albert's arm and hurried outside, passing the soldier and the girl without a glance.

When they were some distance from the church, the little party stopped and Albert sat on a low stone wall.

Bob was about to demand an explanation for Francoise's presence in the church, but the priest held up a hand. 'I should have warned you,' he said. 'Don't worry, Francoise is on our side. She was chatting to the soldier to distract him.'

Bob sighed with relief. She had helped him before and he was sure she wouldn't betray him now, but who knew what a conquered people could be driven to?

'Now then, Bob. Listen to me. We must leave you now and return to our village. Our prayers go with you. Take off the robe and give it to Pierre,' the priest said.

Bob felt a moment of panic. Were they just going to leave him here? But Father Etienne smiled. 'Two priests left the village and two must return.' He pointed down a narrow lane that led off the main street.

'Three doors down, the cottage with blue shutters. Knock twice. They will look after you.' He shook Bob's hand. 'God bless you, my son.'

Bob watched until they were out of sight and then started down the lane towards the house the priest indicated.

***

After the slight lull following the Dunkirk evacuation, the war began to impinge on the people of the Island when enemy planes were spotted making their way to London.

Sheppey lay right in the path of the bombers and the soldiers manning the anti-aircraft guns long the coast were on constant alert.

'Looks like they're trying to soften us up before they invade,' Daisy's father said.

'Don't, Stan. I don't want to hear you going on about it.' Dora picked up her knitting and did a few rows, her needles flying and her lips tight.

Daisy thought Dad was right, but like her mum she tried not to think about it too much.

'They're targeting merchant ships in the Channel now,' he said. The attacks had been going on for a month now.

Dora looked up from her knitting. 'I suppose that's why there's nothing in the shops. I went along to the grocer's this morning and they didn't have half what I wanted. I thought rationing meant we would at least have something.'

'It's not just ships. What about the airfields?' Stan went on.

Daisy couldn't help thinking about Roland and that Polish chap, Stefan, up at Eastchurch. Much as she disliked Roland, she hoped he was safe, if only for Lily's sake.

She kept quiet and concentrated on her mending. She wished now she'd gone to the pictures with Lily and June, but she hadn't been able to face an evening of Lily going on about how wonderful Roland was. It was becoming harder to hold her tongue and not let on what she knew about him.

She finished sewing on a button and stood up to put her things away. 'I'm off to bed, Mum. Early start in the morning. Night, Dad.'

As she went up the stairs, she thought about what they'd heard on the news. She wished her father didn't pay so much attention to it, not that they told you much, trying to put a good face on things. But he picked up a lot of information at the anti-aircraft gun emplacements on the sea wall and along the canal bank. The LDV, who had recently changed their name to the Home Guard, were supplementing the army lads, most of whom had now been sent abroad – Africa, Dad said, although what they were doing in Africa, Daisy had no idea. Wasn't it Italy who had now declared war?

Now that most of the soldiers had left the garrison, they weren't quite so busy in the NAAFI these days. Christopher was still here though, and Daisy looked forward to seeing him on the rare occasions he popped in. She wasn't being disloyal to Bob, she told herself. She still worried about him and prayed for his safety every night. But Chris cheered her up with his lovely smile and why shouldn't she enjoy his obvious admiration for her?

***

'Did you enjoy the film last night?' Daisy asked June during a lull between customers.

'It was smashing. I do love Anton Walbrook. He was good in this one. You should have come with us.'

'I had a lot to do at home. I have to help out now Mum spends so much time with the WVS.'

'Well, *Gaslight's* on till the end of the week.'

'Perhaps I'll go later on then.'

'Lily was supposed to be minding her little brother and sisters, but she had a row with her Mum and sloped off. She said she deserved a night off.' June laughed. 'She was hoping to see Roland but he was on duty, so she had to make do with me.'

'Is she all right? She's been a bit down lately.'

'Pining for her handsome officer,' June said. 'She hasn't seen him for a while.'

'I hope he's not messing her about,' Daisy said. 'She's so in love with him.'

'I don't think it's that. She hasn't seen him for ages. With these raids on the airfield, he's on duty most of the time. And she's terrified something will happen to him now that the Germans are over every day.'

'My dad says they're trying to wipe out the RAF to make it easier to invade.'

June shuddered. 'Doesn't bear thinking of – Germans marching up our High Street.'

Daisy didn't get a chance to reply as Mrs Green swept in, eyes blazing. 'What are you two doing, lazing around gossiping? There's tables to be cleared, dishes to wash and I've just sent Lily home. She's not well so you'll have to do her work as well. Come on, get to it.'

'She was OK last night and she didn't say anything this morning,' June whispered as they scurried to do the supervisor's bidding.

'I'll pop in on my way home,' Daisy said. 'See if she's OK.'

***

Daisy had only been to Lily's house once before and she hoped she could find her way through the maze of alleys and courts which made up the area of wooden cottages between Hope Street and Russell Street.

It was starting to get dark by the time she knocked on Lily's front door. When her friend opened it, she was shocked at the change in her. Her face was pale, her hair straggly, and there were dark rings under her eyes.

'Oh, Daisy, it's you. Did Mrs Green send you?'

'She said you weren't well. What's wrong, Lily?'

'I felt a bit faint that's all, the heat in the kitchen. Don't know why she sent me home. I'm all right now.'

'You don't look all right. Can I come in?'

Lily pulled the door wider and beckoned Daisy inside. 'Mum and Dad are out, kids are in bed.'

'Good – chance for us to have a chat.' Daisy sat down at the kitchen table which was still piled with the remains of a meal.

'I said I'm all right. It's just...'

Lily looked as if she was about to cry and Daisy took her hand. 'Tell me, please. Is it Roland?'

Her friend's shoulders shook and a sob escaped her. 'I don't know if he's all right. I haven't seen him or heard from him and there's been raids...' She sniffed and looked up at Daisy. 'I couldn't bear it if...'

Daisy didn't know what to say to comfort her friend. In the end she resorted to platitudes. 'I'm sure you'd have heard.' How could she tell Lily that he probably hadn't given her a thought? Hadn't she seen him at the pictures with another girl, seen him dancing and flirting with June and other girls in the Wheatsheaf Hall?

She stood up and began to clear the table. 'I'll help you with this,' she said, 'then I'll have to go home. Mum will be worrying – you know what she's like.'

Lily dried her eyes and helped with the washing up. 'Thanks for coming, Daisy. I'd better pull myself together – can't let Mum and Dad see me like this. They wouldn't understand.'

As she walked home, Daisy went over their conversation. She was sure it wasn't just worry about Roland's safety that had Lily in such a state. Daisy hoped it wasn't something more serious on her friend's mind.

She sighed. One more thing to add to the pile of troubles weighing her down.

Chapter Fifteen

Lily didn't come to work the next day. One of her little sisters came into the canteen with a note saying she still wasn't well.

'How was she when you went round?' June asked.

'She looked dreadful. But she said she'd be here today.'

'What's wrong with her?'

'Probably a touch of summer flu, I expect.' Daisy wasn't going to voice her suspicions in case Mrs Green overheard.

When she finished work that evening, she didn't feel like going straight home. She turned off the High Street and walked up Beach Street towards the seafront. She knew she wouldn't get very far before one of the guards stopped her and sent her back. But she longed for a glimpse of the sea.

Usually at this time of year she and her friends would be up on the beach, swimming in the sea if the tide was in. She missed those carefree days. But she had to admit that wasn't the only reason she wanted to walk that way this evening. Perhaps she would get a glimpse of Lofty – Chris, she amended. She must get used to calling him by his proper name, she thought with a smile. If he was on duty, he would be riding his motor cycle along the prom between the gun emplacements, making sure the telephones were working and that messages were getting through all right.

She had just reached the top of Beach Street when the air raid siren went off. 'Oh, no, not again,' she muttered. Where was the nearest shelter? It was too far to run home. She wasn't too nervous. After all no bombs had dropped on the town so far. They seemed to be concentrating on the airfield or going further up the Thames towards London. Still, she shouldn't take a chance.

As she hesitated, someone shouted at her above the wail of the siren. 'What the hell are you doing here?'

She turned to see Chris on his motorbike. 'Come on, get up behind me.' She climbed on the pillion and clung to him as he roared off, depositing her at the entrance to the public shelter in the Broadway a minute or two later. As she turned to thank him, he swung round and was gone in seconds leaving her open-mouthed. After his initial shout he hadn't said a word. Why had he been so short with her?

She sat in the shelter praying for the 'all clear' siren, wondering if she'd done something to upset him. She'd have it out with him next time she saw him. Then her common sense asserted itself. It had been impossible to hold a conversation over the noise of the motorbike, and he had obviously been in a hurry. A smile crept over her face as she savoured the memory of her arms around his waist for the short ride. It had been quite exciting. She had scarcely been aware of the sound of the bombers approaching.

A few people she knew were huddled together in the shelter, some gazing up at the ceiling as if they could see enemy planes overhead. Who was going to get it this time?

Daisy spotted her brother with one of his pals and went over to sit with them. 'Does Mum know where you are?' she asked.

Jimmy shook his head. 'She went out after tea down to the WVS place and Dad's on duty.'

'She'd be worried if she knew you'd been out in an air raid.'

'Don't care,' Jimmy said. 'She's never at home these days.'

'She still worries about you though. And she's got to do her bit for the war effort – we all have.'

'I know. Me and Fred want to as well but we're just kids. What can we do? We used to go up to the guns and run errands and that, but we're not allowed any more.' He kicked his heels against the wall.

'You could help Dad, couldn't you?'

'I don't like working on the allotment and I'm too young to join the Home Guard.'

'You could run errands for them though. Why don't you ask him?' Daisy hoped her brother could find something useful to do otherwise he'd be getting up to all sorts of mischief.

Just then the 'all clear' went and there were sighs of relief as people stepped out into the early dusk. It was a beautiful evening, the sky to the west streaked with pink, and Daisy breathed deeply of the fresh air after the mustiness inside the shelter.

She turned round to speak to Jimmy, but he and Fred had gone. She caught sight of them running round the corner and wondered what they were up to. She should have insisted on him coming home with her, not that he would have obeyed. She had little influence over him these days; he had changed since his experiences as an evacuee in Wales.

She walked home slowly, stopping to speak to a neighbour, who said how lucky they'd been not to 'cop a packet' this time. 'Poor old London,' he said.

Daisy nodded and the man went on. 'They're starting to call this part of Kent 'bomb alley' with all these raids. We're bound to get hit some time.' He shook his head gloomily and she muttered a reply and hurried away before he could say anything else. She felt depressed enough already.

What with Dad always reading out bits from the paper and everyone so miserable these days, it was a job to stay optimistic. But Daisy was determined not to let things get her down. Of course, there was Bob and so many of their old school friends to worry about. But being miserable didn't help. So, she decided, she would stop feeling guilty and go out and enjoy herself whenever she had the chance. After all, she was doing her bit as best she could, like everyone else.

There was a letter from Sylvia on the mantelpiece when she got in and she sat at the kitchen table to read it. Her sister seemed quite cheerful, describing the dress she'd worn to a dance and the films she'd seen. But, as she turned the paper over, Daisy's heart skipped a beat.

'I don't want you to worry – and please don't tell Mum,' she'd written. 'We had a bad raid the other day – broad daylight it was when they came over. We lost quite a few planes and there's craters everywhere. I was on duty but luckily our building was spared. We are all right so please don't worry. Love Sylvia.'

Daisy swallowed a lump in her throat. She had been so wrapped up in her own affairs she had hardly spared a thought for her sister. And everyone knew the airfields were getting a hammering. She re-read the letter and noticed Sylvia had written a 'PS', an afterthought. 'Do you see anything of Lieutenant Hargreaves? Remember me to him.'

A casual sounding inquiry but Daisy couldn't help wondering if Sylvia was more smitten with Roland than she'd thought. Should she write back and tell her about Lily? She shook her head. Best not to say anything, she decided.

***

Daisy was at work when the sirens went again two days later. 'Not another raid,' she muttered, as Mrs Green ushered them outside and into the shelter. Their few customers vacated the canteen quickly and rushed off to their posts.

'This is the worst one yet,' the supervisor said, although they hadn't heard any bombs drop nearby. But the guns up on the seafront were going nineteen to the dozen and there seemed to be no let up.

Sergeant Shiner nodded knowledgably. 'It's Eastchurch they're after. All those planes lined up like sitting ducks.'

‘I thought they’d go for the docks,’ Mrs Green said.

‘They’ll be next.’

Daisy tried to shut out their voices. Why did they have to be so pessimistic? She bent her head, muttering a silent prayer for Roland and Stefan. Most of the Poles had been posted away but she knew Stefan was still there as his job was maintaining the planes’ engines. Lily said she had seen him in the town the other day, but she hadn’t mentioned Roland.

The raid went on for hours and she, Lily, and June clung together. It was a relief when the all clear went. Peeling potatoes and washing up was much better than sitting in the dark worrying. At least being busy took her mind off things.

It wasn’t till she got home from work that she found out what had happened at the other end of the Island. She swallowed back her sobs as her father described the horrors he’d seen at the Eastchurch base. His face and clothes were streaked with smoke and he slumped in his chair by the range, looking exhausted.

He’d not long been home from his Home Guard shift when he got the call. ‘We went up there to do what we could, but it was chaos,’ he said. ‘We lost a lot of planes and the ops room was hit.’

‘I’ll make you a cup of tea, Dad.’ Daisy went into the scullery and filled the kettle. ‘Anyone hurt?’ she called out, not wanting to mention possible deaths. It was too horrible to contemplate.

‘Not sure. We were helping fight the fires. There were some ambulances toing and froing.’

Just then her mother came in, plonking her shopping bag on the kitchen table and sinking into a chair. ‘What a day. I thought the all clear would never go.’ She looked up as Daisy came back in with the tea tray. ‘Tea, oh good. I could do with a cuppa.’

‘Dad’s been up at Eastchurch,’ Daisy said, pouring the tea.

‘Oh, my goodness. Are you all right, Stan?’ Dora leapt from the chair and went over to him. ‘I didn’t think you were on duty today.’

‘It was all hands to the pump, love,’ Stan replied. He patted her hand reassuringly. ‘It was nearly all over by the time we got there. I don’t want you worrying.’

‘I can’t help worrying, can I?’ Dora said. ‘What with Sylvia up there in Norfolk and us being bombarded and frightened out of lives. And goodness knows what our Jimmy’s up to.’ She blew her nose fiercely and picked up her cup. ‘Oh, don’t take any notice of me. It’s just been a heck of a day, that’s all. And then I come home and...’ She almost started crying but sniffed and stood up. ‘No use carrying on. I’ll get the tea on.’

Stan grinned at Daisy as Dora started banging pans around in the scullery. ‘She’ll be all right now she’s let off a bit of steam.’ He stood up. ‘I’d better have a wash, get out of these clothes.’ He squeezed her shoulder as he passed and said, ‘You all right, gel?’

Daisy nodded and went to help her mother. She was pleased to see that Dora was back to her usual self after her little outburst.

‘What have you been up to today then?’ she asked as Daisy started chopping carrots.

‘Much the same as I’m doing now,’ she said with a laugh. ‘Of course, with the raid, we didn’t have any customers this afternoon.’

‘You did go to the shelter though?’

‘Of course. Mrs Green is a stickler for following the rules. To be honest though, Mum, I would rather carry on working than sit there doing nothing and imagining what’s going on outside.’

‘I know how you feel, love.’

They worked in silence for a while and when the food was ready called up to Stan to come down. He looked much better, having put on a clean shirt and combed his hair. ‘No Jimmy then?’ he asked as Dora dished up the sausage and mash.

‘Here he is,’ Daisy said as the back gate clanged open and her brother burst through the door.

‘Wash your hands and sit up to the table,’ Dora said.

‘And where have you been?’ Stan asked.

‘Out with me mates,’ the boy replied.

‘Not getting up to mischief, I hope.’

‘No, Dad, honest. Just mucking about.’

After tea, Daisy went up to her room to write to Sylvia. She wished there was some way of getting news of Roland. Despite him being a two – or three – timing rat, she felt her sister deserved to know if he was all right. She must be worried, knowing that all the airfields in the southeast were being bombed continuously.

It was a difficult letter to write, trying to sound cheerful and minimise the strain they were all under. She told her sister that Dad was revelling in his Home Guard work and Mum was always out at the WVS and how she had to help more at home. ‘As for Jimmy, he’s always up to mischief as usual. I think he’s the only one enjoying this war,’ she wrote, ending on a light-hearted note.

She pulled another sheet of note paper towards her thinking she might as well write to Bob as well. But what could she say? And where could she send it? She had an official address where all mail for those serving overseas went but would he ever get it, since no one knew where he was and whether he had been taken prisoner. Oh, what was the use, she thought, screwing up the piece of paper and resting her head on her hands. A tear rolled down her cheek.

Sighing, she pulled his photo towards her. Gazing at it, she realised she had almost forgotten what he looked like. What had happened to him? It was the not knowing, imagining all sorts of things, that hurt most. A couple of weeks ago, Mrs Gardner had received a letter – ‘missing’ it said. That’s all. But everyone knew what that really meant, Daisy thought. She shook her head. No. She would not accept it. He was a prisoner, he must be. But then, he surely would have written, or if he couldn’t, his parents would have been notified.

The thoughts went round and round in her head and a lump formed in her throat. But she did not cry. Instead, she picked up her hairbrush and vigorously swept it through her thick locks. A dash of lipstick followed.

Sitting here feeling sorry for myself won't do. I must get on with my life, she told herself as she got ready to go out, swallowing the rush of guilt. She almost decided to stay home that evening, but Chris was calling for her in ten minutes. How could she let him down? Besides, he knew she was promised to Bob. She had told him so often enough.

He'd just laughed. 'Nothing to stop us being friends,' he'd said.

It was more than that though, and she knew it deep down. Going to the pictures, eating fish and chips on the way home – all harmless enough on the surface. Would Bob understand when – if – he came home?

A shout up the stairs put a stop to her introspection. 'Your friend's here.'

She pasted a smile on her face and went down to greet him. He was waiting in the narrow passageway and as she appeared, he opened the front door and ushered her through.

'Why didn't you come in?' she asked.

'I didn't want your dad quizzing me,' he said with a laugh. 'I don't think he approves.'

'It's not you. He'd be the same with anyone.'

'Not true. I bet Bob would be welcome.' His voice was flat.

'Oh, Chris. That's different. He's known Bob forever. We're neighbours - our families are friends.'

'Let's drop it, eh? I know where I stand.' He grabbed her hand and hurried her along. 'Come on. We'll miss the start of the film.' He didn't speak again until the lights went up at the end of the newsreel.

'Sorry about earlier. I didn't mean to upset you. Still friends?'

She nodded. 'Friends,' she said and was rewarded with his lovely smile.

The lights dimmed and the curtain opened on the big feature. Her mind strayed from the film and she kept glancing towards Chris. He appeared to be engrossed in the screen and she sighed. He seemed determined to keep a distance between them. That kiss a few weeks ago had obviously meant nothing. She should be pleased that he respected her feelings for Bob. But, she thought miserably, it's all very well being friends, but I'm beginning to think it's not enough.

***

Chris, too, had found it hard to concentrate on the film. He had been attracted to Daisy right from the start, but his feelings had soon developed into something stronger. He wasn't like most of the other lads, looking for a bit of fun to relieve the strain of being at war.

Daisy was special and he wished with all his heart that he had never heard of Bob Gardner. Not that he wished him ill - of course not. The man was fighting for his country after all and of course he respected Daisy's promise to stay true to him. If only things had been different. He sighed.

The film came to an end and everyone stood for the National Anthem. As the lights went on, a burly man pushed past them and Daisy stumbled as he stood on her foot. Chris grasped her hand to stop her from falling and she smiled up at him – a smile to stop his heart. He kept hold of her hand until they were out in the street. She hadn't pulled away at least.

They walked along the High Street, stopping for a bag of chips at Curd's in Rose Street. There was a long queue – right out the door and round the corner. Chris didn't mind if it meant more time with Daisy. He was still holding her hand when someone else joined the queue.

'Hey up, Lofty. What you up to, mate? Found yourself a nice bit of fluff then?' The man nodded towards Daisy and laughed.

Chris reddened and he bit his lip. Much as he'd like to punch the bloke in the mouth, he managed to hold on to his anger. He didn't want to make a scene in front of Daisy. 'For your information, Norman, this lady is Miss Bishop who works in the NAAFI. The next time you go in for your tea and fags I hope you'll be more polite than you have been now.'

Norman had the grace to look a little abashed. 'Only joking, mate,' he muttered. He looked at Daisy and said, 'Beg your pardon, Miss Bishop.'

She nodded and replied. 'I accept your apology. But, as Chris said, if you aren't polite to me or my friends in future, your next cup of tea might accidentally end up in your lap.'

Chris felt like cheering as the other man stood with his mouth open. The queue moved forward, but Norman seemed to have lost his desire for chips and walked away.

When they'd been served, they walked up the road eating out of the newspaper. Daisy suddenly started to laugh. 'His face, Chris, did you see his face?'

Chris laughed too. 'Did you mean it about spilling his tea?'

'Not really. Mrs Green would have my guts for garters if I did anything like that. Still, it might be worth it. I must admit I've been tempted many times when your mates start hassling me.'

'They're not all my mates,' Chris protested. 'I get on well with most of them, but a few of them get on my nerves. Always having to say *something,* you know.'

'I can take it,' Daisy said.

'I know. I've seen you in action.'

They both laughed and then walked on in silence, eating their chips until they reached Daisy's back gate.

Chris opened it and took her hand again. 'Thanks for a lovely evening, Daisy.' He wanted to kiss her goodnight, but he kept to his promise. Just friends. He coughed and said, 'I'm on duty all the rest of this week so I won't be seeing you for a while.'

'They're not sending you away are they?'

‘Not just yet. Don’t worry, I’ll let you know.’ He let go of her hand reluctantly and strode away. On the walk back to barracks, he couldn’t stop thinking about her. In a way he hoped he would be posted abroad. He would be spared the agony of seeing her and knowing she loved someone else. He cheered up a little as he remembered her dismay at the thought he might be sent away. Perhaps she felt something for him after all. He could only hope.

Chapter Sixteen

Over the next few weeks there were several air raids but the town itself was spared, although there were attacks on the Dockyard and the Eastchurch airfield. The anti aircraft guns along the seafront and on the garrison defences were now manned by the Home Guard but the few soldiers left in the garrison were kept busy supplying ammunition and relaying orders. Daisy had seen nothing of Chris since their evening at the cinema and she missed him – more than she should, she knew. Her only thoughts should be of Bob and her prayers for his safety uppermost in her mind. But she found herself looking up every time the door to the NAAFI opened, swallowing the little niggle of disappointment when Chris did not appear.

She had been tempted to ask one of the lads about him, but after that encounter in the fish shop queue, she did not want to lay herself open to suggestive remarks about her relationship with him. And there was also the fear that he, like many of the battalion, had been posted abroad.

Surely he would come in to say goodbye though, even if he had been deliberately avoiding her lately.

She still enjoyed her work in the NAAFI and her time off with Lily and June. Going dancing or to the pictures with them helped to take her mind off worrying about Bob and confusion about her feelings for Chris.

To add to her worries, she was becoming more concerned about Lily, who hadn't seemed to recover from her bought of summer flu – if that's what it was. Several times she had turned down invitations to go out with her and June, saying she had to stay in to look after her younger brother and sisters. She hardly mentioned Roland these days and Daisy wondered if she had discovered he was seeing other girls. Perhaps she was just worried about him - the bombing raids on the Eastchurch airfield had increased and many aircraft had been lost.

Daisy determined to have another chat with her to try and find out what was really on her mind. Sometimes it helped to talk. What was it they said? 'A trouble shared was a trouble halved'

June had told her to leave well alone. 'Don't interfere. If she wants to stay home, let her.'

Daisy couldn't do that. She wanted to help her friend if she could. Lily wasn't at work again today but she would tackle her tomorrow.

Meanwhile there were customers to serve and tables to clear. She looked up as the door opened and forced a welcoming smile to her lips. No Chris though.

June started serving, leaving Daisy to clear the tables and take the used crockery through to the kitchen. Another girl had joined the NAAFI recently. Mavis was very quiet, hardly spoke and just got on with washing the dirty crockery and pans without complaint. Daisy tried to draw her out of her shell but she resisted attempts at friendship, hurrying off home as soon as her shift ended.

Daisy determined to try again. 'Morning, Mavis,' she said cheerfully, plonking the tray of crockery onto the draining board. 'Need a hand?'

The girl plunged her hands into the soapy water and shook her head. 'I can manage,' she muttered.

Daisy shrugged and went back to her counter. 'Don't know what's wrong with that girl,' she said to June.

'Just ignore her,' June replied.

'I can't. She looks so unhappy.'

'You can't solve everyone's troubles,' June told her.

'I suppose you're right.'

Several sailors came in just then and they were kept busy for another hour. When a lull came, they were able to take a break and took their tea to a quiet corner. It was a relief to sit down and rest their aching feet. Daisy slipped her shoes off under the table and wriggled her toes, keeping an eye out for Mrs Green. She wasn't in the mood for a telling off.

'Lily hasn't mentioned Roland lately, has she? Do you think they've fallen out?' she asked.

'I hope so,' June said. 'I never did like him. Too fond of the ladies.'

Daisy decided not to mention her own suspicions, as well as her sister's involvement with the handsome RAF officer. 'She hasn't said anything but I think he might have been posted. Perhaps that's why she's been looking so miserable.'

'Well, we've all got someone to worry about, haven't we? She's not the only one but we don't go on about it.'

Daisy knew that June had a cousin in the merchant navy and, although they weren't close, she must be concerned about him, especially as so many ships were being sunk lately.

'You're right,' she said, touching June's hand. 'Still, I wish we could cheer her up, persuade her to come out with us next time.'

June shrugged her hand away. 'You can try.' She finished her tea and stood to take her cup back.

Daisy put her shoes on and followed, deep in thought. She couldn't help worrying about Lily but June was right. Didn't she have enough problems of her own to keep her awake at night?

Another trip to the stores brought another worry to mind. She had almost forgotten her suspicion that Mr Browning was involved in something wrong. Were some of the stores 'going walkabout' or was it just a case of 'cooking the books'? Daisy was now convinced that the manager of the NAAFI was stealing from the stores. Several times she had noticed things missing when she went to the stores and she was sure they hadn't been used in the canteen. But everything seemed to be signed for and that day when she saw boxes being loaded up, it seemed plausible that they were destined for the NAAFI at Eastchurch.

She had told herself she was being unduly suspicious until today, when Mrs Green sent her over to fetch a carton of cigarettes and some tea, which was stored in large tins, not the usual packets she was used to from the grocers.

She lifted a tin down, staggering backwards as the tin was much lighter than she anticipated. She set it down on a bench and reached for another. This one seemed heavier. Then she lifted down a couple more tins which seemed the right weight. She looked carefully at the labels with their Ministry of Food seal. They didn't look as if they had been tampered with and she shrugged. Perhaps she was being unduly worried.

She put the lighter tin back on the shelf with the others, keeping one back. She turned to pick it up, almost dropping it as a voice behind her said, 'Don't forget to sign for it.'

'Oh, Mr Browning. You made me jump,' she gasped.

'What were you doing?' he asked, nodding towards the shelf of tea supplies.

'Just checking how many tins were left,' she said.

'Not your job, miss. Now, off with you.'

'I need cigarettes too.'

'Ciggies for the boy friend is it?'

'No, Mr Browning. Mrs Green sent me. We're running short and...'

He grinned and patted her arm. 'Just joking, girl,' he interrupted. 'I hope you've signed for everything.'

'Of course I have.'

He picked up the clipboard and checked the signatures, then opened the door and stood by it as she left.

Daisy ignored him and walked quickly away. How dare he? A thought struck her. Had his so-called joking and bluster been a cover for his own dealings? What was he doing there anyway?

She shrugged. She had enough to worry about, not least a telling off from the supervisor.

When she got back, Mrs Green was waiting by the door. 'Took you long enough,' she said, grabbing the box from her. 'We've got customers waiting, you know. And we're short-staffed with Lily away.'

‘Sorry, Mrs Green.’ She hurried behind the counter, leaving the supervisor to unpack the cigarettes and put them on the shelves.

She was kept busy for the next couple of hours. But as she poured tea and dispensed sandwiches, she couldn’t stop thinking about that tin, which she estimated must have been only half full.

She was sure someone was stealing and if it wasn’t Mr Browning, then who? Was it only her dislike of the man that made her suspect him?

She didn’t like Harold Tompkins either, but she didn’t think he had the brains to cover up the thefts. Then she remembered the time he had given her half a large fruit cake, which he’d told her was left over and likely to go stale if not used. And surely there was no harm in using stuff that might be thrown away.

No, it wasn’t Harold. And it surely couldn’t be the chef or Mrs Green, could it?

Daisy was so wrapped up in her thoughts that she filled the cup she was holding to overflowing, the hot tea splashing onto her hand.

As she jumped back, dropping the cup which smashed on the tiled floor, Mrs Green shouted across the room. ‘What’s wrong with you today, Daisy? Wake up – and get that mess cleared up.’

‘Sorry Mrs Green,’ Daisy muttered, bending to pick up the broken crockery.

‘I’ve a good mind to take that out of your wages,’ the supervisor said.

June fetched a cloth and began to wipe up the spilled tea. ‘Please don’t do that, Mrs Green. Daisy’s a bit on edge after last night’s raid,’ she said.

‘We’re all on edge, miss.’ The supervisor went back to manning the till and June whispered, ‘Daydreaming about that Lofty, were you?’

‘Don’t be silly. Just tired, that’s all.’ She ignored June’s knowing smile and carried the broken crockery out to the kitchen.

If only she could confide in someone.

As she served the queue of soldiers and sailors, trying to keep a smile on her face as she responded to their usual banter, the worry about Lily re-surfaced. She hoped it was just a touch of summer flu and that her friend would be back at work the next day, laughing and joking as she usually did.

***

When Daisy got home that evening, her mother was sitting at the sewing machine mending a long tear in the blackout curtain which usually hung at the kitchen window.

'Hello, love, just got to finish this before I get the tea on,' she said.

'I'll do it, Mum. What happened to the curtain?'

'Jimmy of course. Trying to help, he said. Pulled too hard and this material's so flimsy.' Dora sighed. 'It's only an old sheet I dyed black. They didn't have enough proper blackout stuff to do all the windows.'

'Well, it gets dark so late now. If we don't put the light on in here, we should be all right.'

'No. I must do it. That Alf Stokes will be knocking on the door if we show a chink of light.'

'Trust him to get made an ARP warden, nosy old devil. He was always finding something to tell us kids off for even before the war.'

Dora laughed. 'He's in his element now, strutting around, banging on people's doors.' She finished sewing and cut the cotton. 'There, that'll do.'

'I don't know why we bother with the blackout at the moment. That moon was so bright last night, you don't need a torch.'

'Bomber's moon they call it.' Dora sighed. 'They'll be over again tonight.'

Daisy shivered. 'It's the aerodrome they're after. That Polish chap I met told me they're not even operational. A lot of the planes there are being repaired. Still, I suppose if they smash them on the ground at least our pilots are spared.'

Dora looked up sharply. 'What are you doing talking to a Pole? Your dad won't like that.'

'Oh, Mum. He was at the dance I went to, a friend of Roland, Sylvia's boy friend. We were just talking.'

'I know, love. Don't mind me. I know you wouldn't get involved with anyone else, but with Bob...' Her voice trailed away and she busied herself putting the sewing machine away and putting a cloth on the table.

Daisy didn't reply. Her mother's words had hit home. When Chris called for her the other evening she had tried to give the impression she was going with a group of friends. However hard she tried to deny it, she *was* involved with someone else.

She went into the scullery and picked up a saucepan. 'What's for tea, Mum?' she called through.

'Dad's at the hall tonight, eating up there, so it's just you and me. Beans on toast all right?'

'Fine. I had sausage and mash at the canteen. What about Jimmy?'

'He's had his. Dashed off out as soon as he'd eaten.'

'Not more mischief, I hope.'

'You won't believe this.' Dora opened the tin of beans and poured them into a pan. 'He's joined the Scouts. One of his mates talked him into it and he's been helping with collecting salvage and all sorts of jobs.'

'I'm pleased he's found something useful to do.' Daisy stirred the beans to stop them sticking while her mother cut bread and sat to toast it in front of the kitchen range.

As they ate, Dora chatted about her day at the WVS hall but Daisy scarcely listened. She had too much on her mind. Her mother didn't seem to notice and she was tempted to stem the flow of talk and confide in her. Not about her feelings for Chris of course. But there was the problem of the missing stores, not to mention her concern for Lily.

Before she could say anything however, the wail of the air raid siren interrupted.

Dora sprung from the table. 'Come on, Daisy, leave the dishes,' she urged, going into her well-practiced routine, picking up her handbag with its precious identity cards and ration books, and her knitting, grabbing a torch off the shelf before hustling Daisy outside.

Their street was one of the few with back gardens and Stan had erected their Anderson shelter at the start of the war. Until recently it was little used but with the start of the raids Dora had set about making it more comfortable with cushions and blankets and a shelf for books.

They sat in silence for a few minutes, listening to the drone of aircraft overhead and the thump of the guns.

Daisy nervously bit her nails, watching Dora's knitting needles flying and wishing she had something to occupy her.

'Sounds bad,' Dora said, hunching her shoulders.

Daisy moved closer and put her arm around her mother's shoulders as much for her own comfort as for Dora's. How long could this go on, she wondered. But she knew, from the wireless news and what her father picked up at the Home Guard meeting hall, that this war was likely to go on for a long time if they were to stop Hitler's army invading.

***

The next day they discovered just how bad the raid had been. Two houses were badly hit at the end of their road although, fortunately, the occupants got to the shelter in time. But that wasn't all.

Stan came home just as Daisy was getting ready for work, his eyes red-rimmed with weariness, his hair streaked grey with dust. Dora threw her arms round him. 'Thank God, you're safe. I was so worried.'

'No need to worry about me, love,' he said, pushing her away. 'It's those poor buggers up at Eastchurch. I've never seen anything like it. Much worse than the last raid. They hit the fuel dump – bastards.' He ran a hand through his hair.

Dora didn't reprove him for swearing this time. Daisy, bag in hand ready to leave for work, hovered by the door.

She couldn't ask but Stan said, 'So many injured, dead too.'

Daisy gasped – Roland, Stefan, all those young men who had been at the dance. She couldn't do anything about it though: like everyone else she just had to carry on.

She kissed her father's cheek and went out of the door, brushing away a tear as she hurried up the High Street towards the Garrison.

***

Two days later there was another raid, this time in daylight. There was so much damage to buildings and aircraft that the base was unserviceable. But the squadron continued their reconnaissance duties. After helping with the clear up, Stan and his Home Guard battalion went back to normal duties in the town.

When he got home each evening though, he was able to tell his family the news he gathered from the Army despatch rider who carried messages after communications were damaged in the raids.

Daisy hesitated to ask for details – after all, Dad wouldn't know his name. But she was sure it must have been Chris, so to her delight, he must still be here. Perhaps he was too useful to be posted abroad.

She was still concerned about Roland, much as she disliked him. But her father hadn't been able to find out if he was all right. 'The RAF personnel are billeted in cottages in the village – too dangerous for them to stay on the base,' he told her.

Lily returned to work after a couple more days off, still looking pale and anxious. She brushed aside Daisy's concern that she was not fit to work. 'I'm all right,' she said. 'Just worried about Roland.'

'You haven't heard from him?' Daisy asked.

Lily shook her head and walked over to clear one of the tables.

Daisy looked after her, biting her lip. If Roland was all right, why hadn't he contacted Lily to reassure her? He must know how she would be feeling. Of course, he was probably busy and not able to write but he surely could have sent a message via one of the soldiers helping with the clear up.

Chapter Seventeen

Bob had not stayed in the Amiens region for long. The plan seemed to be to move him on every few days, although he never knew quite when someone would appear, usually at night, and hustle him outside. He would be pushed into a cart and covered with hay, or into a van hidden behind crates of vegetables. In this rural part of France there was always a market being held and villagers had permission to go to the nearest market town to sell their wares.

He lost count of the number of such journeys he made and had no idea where he was, or even if they were still in France. From the open farmland of the Somme region he had left, they were now among rolling hills and on one of their stops, as he got down from the van to stretch his legs, he saw snow-capped mountains in the distance.

The days merged into each other and he had no idea how long he had been on the run. Weeks, maybe even months had passed, and he was now hiding in the back of a van loaded with boxes of apples.

He was grateful to these strangers who were risking their lives for him. His only regret was that he couldn't stay in touch. He prayed that one day he would be able to return and thank them. As the van jolted along the uneven road to yet another unknown destination, his thoughts turned once more to the two women he loved.

When he knocked on the door of the house with blue shutters he had been trembling inside. Who would answer the door? Would it be friend or foe? He still found it hard to believe he would not be betrayed to the enemy.

To his unconcealed delight, Francoise had stood there, wearing a smile to match his.

'Bobbee, you are here. I prayed you were safe, that you got back to England, but I was so happy to see you in the church.' She looked up and down the narrow lane, then drew him into the house. 'You must stay here for a few days,' she said.

Bob wanted to say he would like to stay forever but he remained silent as he followed her into a low-beamed room. His heart pounded – not with fear as it had so often in the past weeks – but with joy at being once more with the girl who was never far from his thoughts since the first time he saw her. After a few minutes his heart slowed, and common sense prevailed.

'I can't stay. It is too dangerous – for you. I would never forgive myself if...'

She put a finger to his lips. 'I am not afraid. Besides, you are not the first we have helped. I have become used to the danger. But I - and my friends – we must do what we can. We are determined. One day France will be free once more.' She threw back her head and her eyes glowed with fervour.

Bob's heart swelled with pride and, he realised, love for this brave woman. 'I wish I could help,' he said. 'But the best way I can do that is to get home and rejoin my unit. We must fight on.'

Francoise nodded and smiled. 'Of course. But first, you must eat.' She took his arm and led him through to a large kitchen. A scrubbed table stood in the centre, laden with more food than Bob had seen in a long while. Pans simmered on the long range which took up most of the far wall, giving off an appetising smell that made him realise how hungry he was.

An old man sat at the table, his weather-beaten face creased with a smile as he looked up and waved a hand in welcome. *'Asseyez vous,'* he said.

Bob had learned a few French phrases during his time here and he sat at the table, saying, '*Merci, Monsieur.*'

'This is my Uncle Henri,' Francoise said, then turned to the plump woman standing at the stove. 'And my Aunt Alys.'

'Pleased to meet you,' Bob said, his meagre store of French deserting him for a moment. 'What about your mother?' he asked. 'Is she here?'

Francoise pointed a finger upwards. 'She is sick. She stays in her bed.'

'I'm sorry. I hope she gets well soon.'

Uncle Henri nodded. 'She will.' He indicated the food and said, 'Please, eat, eat.'

Bob needed no second telling. He grabbed a piece of the fresh crusty bread and waited while Aunt Alys filled his bowl with thick vegetable soup.

During the days he spent with Francoise's family he almost forgot about the war, helping in the vegetable garden and feeding the chickens, most of which had been taken by the Germans.

'They take what they want to feed themselves and leave just enough for us to survive,' Henri said bitterly. 'A sergeant comes by every week for their share.'

Bob protested that they did not have enough to feed him too. He should move on. Besides, there was a real risk that he would be caught. Someone in the village must realise that the Lebruns had someone staying there.

When he was working outside, he found himself constantly stopping to listen and look around. In this flat open countryside he felt vulnerable and exposed. But Henri assured him the terrain worked in their favour. An enemy approach would be seen and heard with enough time to hide him.

One day Francoise was working alongside him in the vegetable garden, hoeing the weeds between the rows of cabbages. The sun was hot on his back and he took his shirt off, wiping the sweat from his forehead with it. He looked round to find Francoise staring at him.

His face reddened and he felt a momentary embarrassment until she stepped towards him and hesitantly ran a finger down his chest. 'Bobbee, you are so handsome,' she said.

He started to laugh, thinking she was teasing. But she moved her finger up to his lips and whispered, 'Kiss me, Bobbee.'

He pulled her to him, crushing her against his chest, and their lips met. The kiss seemed to go on forever, arousing in him feelings such as he'd never experienced with Daisy. He let Francoise go abruptly and turned towards the house.

'Someone might see,' he said. He didn't really care but the thought of Daisy spoilt that precious moment and guilt flooded him. He had promised to stay true to Daisy and asked her to stay true to him. He meant it at the time but how could he have anticipated meeting this lovely French girl and falling hopelessly in love?

In the days that followed they managed to snatch a few moments alone and their feelings for each other deepened into a passionate, yet tender love. They made promises to each other that Bob knew might be impossible to keep.

When the time came to part, he felt as if his heart would break. He peered over the back of the cart, watching as she waved him out of sight. Then he burrowed deep into the pile of hay, wondering if he'd ever see her again but determined that one day he would return to France and find her. He would find a way to let Daisy down as gently as possible. He was fond of her and didn't want to hurt her. After all, they had been close friends since childhood. But that was all – friendship. The deep affection he felt for her was nothing like the feelings he had for Francoise. He must try to forget her.

The van halted suddenly, jerking him out of his introspection. Gutteral German voices caused his heartbeat to quicken. He heard the van driver getting out and he tensed as footsteps approached the back of the vehicle.

So this is how it ends, he thought, bracing himself for discovery.

***

The air raids continued unabated, giving Daisy yet more to worry about. When the siren went she spent the hours in the air raid shelter biting her nails and praying that Sylvia and her family were safe. The Luftwaffe seemed to be concentrating on the airfields and she hadn't heard anything from her sister since that last brief note. She knew Mum was worried too, although she didn't say much. And Dad wouldn't be skulking in a shelter. He would be with his fellow volunteers. The LDV had recently changed their name to the Home Guard - now a proper military unit fully kitted out with uniforms, arms and ammunition.

If only she could do something more, Daisy thought, buttering more slices of bread, careful not to be too generous with the butter. Serving tea and sandwiches seemed tame compared with what others were doing.

Her thoughts were interrupted by a tap on the shoulder. 'Mrs Green wants you in the office,' June said.

Lily rolled her eyes. 'What have you been up to?' she whispered.

Daisy shrugged and hurried away. She knocked on the office door and, hearing a muttered 'come in', she went in, her heart hammering. To her knowledge, she hadn't done anything wrong since breaking that cup and saucer.

For once, the supervisor was smiling. 'Well, Miss Bishop, how do you fancy a change of scene?' She looked down at some papers on her desk before continuing. 'They need someone in the NAAFI at the airfield,' she said.

'Eastchurch?' Daisy's stomach flipped. That part of the Island had been badly hit in the continuing air raids. She would do what she had to do though. Hadn't she just been wishing she could do more for the war effort? Still, she had to ask.

'Why me? Lily's worked here the longest.'

'Mr Browning suggested you. The girl who works there received injuries from flying glass and has been sent home. We have an extra pair of hands since Mavis joined us so we can spare you. Collect your things and make your way there without delay.'

‘Will I be able to come home each evening?’ Daisy asked.

‘No. There is a billet for you in the village. The buses are so unreliable at the moment. It makes more sense for you to stay there.’

‘I suppose so,’ Daisy said.

‘You’ve no choice, my girl.’

‘I’d better go home and pack then.’

‘Make haste while the buses are still running. Who knows if there’s going to be another raid?’

Daisy suppressed a shiver, remembering her father’s description of the devastation and loss of life he had witnessed. She straightened her shoulders and said, ‘Very well, Mrs Green.’ She turned at the door. ‘Before I go, there’s something I want to mention.’ She bit her lip, hesitating.

‘Out with it then, girl. I haven’t got all day and you should be on your way.’

She took the plunge. ‘I noticed the other day that some of the stores seem to be missing. I should have mentioned it before.’

Mrs Green sucked in her breath. ‘And what business is it of yours what’s in the stores? Last time I went over, I checked and everything’s been signed for.’ She flapped a hand at Daisy. ‘Go on. Be on your way. I’ll telephone them to say you’ll be there this afternoon.’

Daisy went to the cloakroom to fetch her uniform jacket and cap, deep in thought. Although Mrs Green had been dismissive of her concerns, she couldn’t help wondering if she was being sent away for asking too many questions.

Shrugging, she picked up her handbag and went through to the canteen to say goodbye to Lily and June.

‘They’re sending me to Eastchurch,’ she said.

‘Lucky thing – if you see Roland, give him my love and tell him to write,’ Lily said.

‘Don’t be daft, Lily. How can you say she’s lucky? It’s dangerous – all those raids,’ June protested. She turned to Daisy. ‘Why are they sending you?’ she asked.

'They're short-handed.'

'I'll worry about you.'

'So will I,' Lily said. 'I'm sorry for being so thoughtless. It's just – I haven't heard from Roland and I'm worried.'

'I know you are. I'll look out for him.'

'Thanks. Tell him I miss him. I know it's difficult with the raids and all, but I need to know if he's all right.'

'I will. And don't worry about me. My dad thinks they'll leave the airfield alone now - turn their attention to the other bases,' Daisy said.

To her relief there was no one there when she got home. She hadn't looked forward to telling her parents where she was off to. Dad wouldn't be happy about it. She would leave them a note. She went upstairs to pack a spare uniform shirt and clean underwear. A few toiletries and her remaining store of makeup went into the bag and she sighed, looking around the room she had shared with Sylvia for most of their lives.

She grinned, imagining the letter she'd write to her sister. She may not have been able to join the WAAFs, but she would be serving on an RAF station like her. She wasn't worried about further air raids. From what her father said, the last raid had completely wrecked the airfield and the few personnel left were engaged in clearing up and repairs. Surely Dad was right in thinking the Luftwaffe would turn their attention elsewhere now.

She went out of the back door and let herself into the alley that ran along behind the houses. It was a bit of a short cut to the High Street and she would avoid the sight of the bombed houses at the end of the road.

The bus came along just as she got to the stop. It was almost empty, and she was glad no one she knew was on it. She wasn't in thc mood for chatting. She stared out of the window, although she scarcely took in the familiar view of the marshy fields, giving way to the low hills that formed the eastern end of the Island. She was reliving that last conversation with Mrs Green. The supervisor seemed angry with her for mentioning the missing goods and she couldn't help wondering if she was involved. She couldn't really believe it. Mrs Green was so strict and her eagle eyes missed nothing that went on in the canteen. No. It must be the manager. He was the one who ordered the stores and kept an eye on supplies. It would be easy for him to siphon off a few extras for his friends and family. Rationing was getting worse and people might not be too worried about where their 'little extras' came from.

Daisy remembered her mother talking about something a neighbour had said. It was easy to get round the rules if you knew the right person, she'd whispered, tapping her nose. Mum had been indignant. 'As if I'd do such a thing.'

Was Mr Browning a 'right person', she wondered.

The bus started up the hill that led to Minster Hospital and Daisy shivered, thinking of the injured airmen who were taken there after the last raid. A bit later the bus lurched to a halt and she realised they had reached Eastchurch village. She hadn't been to this part of the Island since last summer, just before war was declared. She and Bob had walked along the cliffs all the way to Warden Point and then made their way to a pub in the village for a drink, before going home on the bus.

Sighing nostalgically, she got off the bus and began the half mile walk to the airfield. As she approached her mood changed, and she looked around in dismay. Curls of smoke still rose from the stricken aircraft and men were working frantically to repair and rebuild the surrounding buildings.

She went into the NAAFI building and knocked on the door of the office but no one answered. As she hesitated, not knowing what to do, a girl in NAAFI uniform entered the building.

'You must be the new girl,' she said.

'I'm Daisy. I've been working at Sheerness.'

'Barbara,' the other girl said with a smile. 'I don't know why they sent you. Most of the personnel have gone since that last raid. There's just a few mechanics and communications chaps left. And the maintenance staff, working on the buildings.'

'Who else works here?' Daisy asked.

‘There’s only me and the RAF cook now. Mr Browning, the manager, comes up a couple of times a week to check on me.’ She laughed. ‘You know Mr B I guess.’

‘I do. I don’t think he likes me.’ Daisy thought it best to keep her real feelings to herself.

‘Don’t worry about that. He’s a grouch. Always finding fault. Still, you must know that.’ She sighed. ‘Anyway, I do the best I can.’

‘I’m sure you do.’

‘Well, don’t listen to my grumbles. Come on, I’ll show you to your billet. It’s not far.’

‘Is it all right to leave the canteen unattended?’

‘There won’t be anyone in till later. I need to show you the way.’ She took Daisy’s bag and locked the door.

As they set off down the lane, Daisy said, ‘I’m sure I can find the way. Is it in the village? I know the place quite well.’

‘Are you a local then?’

‘Lived on the Island all my life. I used to walk all over here with my boyfriend.’

‘Lucky you. Where is he now?’

‘Abroad.’ Daisy didn’t want to go into details and changed the subject. ‘Where are you from?’

‘London. My mum was quite pleased I got a posting down here. She thought it would be safer.’ Barbara gave a rueful laugh. ‘Little did she know.’

‘It must have been awful.’

Barbara shuddered. ‘I’d rather not talk about it.’ She pushed open a farm gate and led the way past a barn to a row of cottages. ‘Here it is. Mrs Lucas will make you welcome. I’ll leave you to settle in,’ she said, handing Daisy her bag. ‘Come back when you’re ready and I’ll show you round.’

Daisy knocked on the cottage door and introduced herself.

Mrs Lucas was a thin woman with grey hair in an untidy bun. She welcomed Daisy kindly but bit her lip, her forehead creased in a worried frown. ‘I don’t know what they’re thinking, sending young girls like you and Barbara to work here. I know there's a war on and everything and everyone's got to do their bit but...' She led Daisy up a narrow flight of stairs into a low-ceilinged room with a dormer window.

'Oh, what a pretty room,' Daisy exclaimed, taking in the flowered curtains and matching bed spread.

'Barbara's just across the landing,' Mrs Lucas said. 'I hope you'll be comfortable.'

'Oh, I'm sure I will.' Daisy put her bag on the bed and went across to look out of the window. The room faced south and she could see across the fields to low wooded hills. The sun glinted on the narrow stretch of water that separated the Island from the mainland of Kent. It was hard to believe that only half a mile away was a scene of such devastation.

'I've made some tea,' the landlady said. 'Would you like a cup?'

Daisy was gasping for one, but she thought she ought to get back to the NAAFI and find out what her duties would be. She had a feeling her posting here would be very different from working in the busy, bustling Sheerness canteen.

She soon settled in and began to enjoy the more relaxed atmosphere. As Barbara told her, there were very few customers and there had been some talk of closing down after the last raid. But the powers that be thought it would be good for morale to stay open and give the remaining personnel somewhere to go and relax in their off duty hours.

So far, she hadn't encountered Stefan, the Polish pilot, or Roland. She hadn't really expected to as officers did not use the NAAFI. But, mindful of her promise to Lily, she hoped she would bump into him, so that she could tackle him about his treatment of her friend. Maybe she'd voice her suspicions too. She had been keeping a careful eye on Lily and was almost sure she was right. If so, Roland ought to be made aware of his responsibilities. But what if she was wrong?

***

Very often Daisy was on duty alone and on busy evenings had little time to think about what was going on back home. She knew her mother would let her know if news came of Bob – not that she expected any. She hadn't really given up hope, just resigned herself to waiting till the war was over. She pushed all thoughts of Chris and her growing feelings for him out of her mind. Bob was her sweetheart, always had been, and she would not betray him by thinking of another man.

When she wasn't working, she sat on the wide windowsill in her room, gazing out over the marshes and remembering the walks she and Bob used to take in the long summer evenings. She enjoyed the solitary walks between her billet and the NAAFI but there was now an autumnal feel in the air and the nights were drawing in. She wondered how she would feel stuck out here in the countryside when the dark winter evenings came.

She and Barbara got on well but they were seldom on duty at the same time, and she didn't feel the same sense of camaraderie as she had with Lily and June. She missed their frequent laughter and teasing. One thing she didn't miss was the manager and his grumpy ways and she had managed to dismiss her suspicions of him from her mind. When, if ever, she returned to Sheerness she would ask her dad's advice. He would know the right person to talk to.

I won't wait till I see him, she thought. I'll write to Dad tonight, tell him what I saw. She would walk in to the village and post her letter tomorrow.

The next day she was just handing over her shift to Barbara when she heard a van stop outside. She went to the door, her heart thumping as Mr Browning got out. She knew he came up to Eastchurch occasionally but hadn't been expecting him so soon.

'Good afternoon, Miss Bishop. I've just come to see how you're managing with just the two of you and a cook.'

'Very well, Mr Browning.'

'I've brought some supplies. Perhaps you'll help me unload.'

She didn't like to say that she was just going off duty and she followed him outside. She picked up a carton of cigarettes and carried them into the building. Mr Browning was close behind carrying two more large boxes.

When they had finished unloading, they stacked the boxes in the small storeroom behind the counter. 'There, that should keep you going for a bit,' Mr Browning said, producing a clipboard. 'Here, just check this stuff off and sign for it.' He leaned closer. 'That way we can be sure there's no funny business.' He bared his teeth in a grin, but Daisy knew he wasn't joking.

She managed to sign her name although her hands were shaking. 'All in order, Mr Browning,' she said as she handed the clipboard back to him.

She watched him drive away and realised her hands were still shaking. Did he realise she was suspicious of him? Had his words been a subtle warning?

Barbara finished serving one of mechanics and said, 'Isn't it time you were off?'

Daisy nodded. 'I'm just going in to the village to post a letter. Can I get you anything?'

'No thanks. Enjoy your afternoon off.'

As she started down the lane, Daisy wondered if she was being overly suspicious. After all, she wasn't absolutely sure the manager was really involved in wrong-doing. It was just suspicion based on the way he'd behaved towards her and the missing stores she'd noticed. Perhaps it had just been a mistake – someone had forgotten to sign when taking stuff out. But it happened too often to be carelessness. And she couldn't help recalling his face when he'd mentioned 'funny business.' For a moment there she had been quite frightened. The manager's words were innocuous enough but the menace in his voice was unmistakeable.

Daisy took a deep breath and told herself she would not be intimidated and would definitely keep her eyes open.

It was a lovely afternoon, still warm and sunny but with a touch of autumn in the air. When she reached the village, she stopped outside the church. It was a typical country church with a lych-gate and a paved path leading to the entrance porch. She went in and wandered round, enjoying the sense of peace and calm. A lump came to her throat when she spotted a memorial to the men of the village who had died in the previous war. How many names would be added when this one was over?

She said a silent prayer and left. When she got back to Mrs Lucas's cottage, she realised the letter to her father was still in her bag. Perhaps she wouldn't post it after all, she thought, telling herself it was her dislike of the man that caused her suspicions. It certainly wasn't because she was scared of him. No, she would wait till she had some real evidence and then report him.

Chapter Eighteen

Daisy had been stationed at the Eastchurch airfield for two weeks and was just settling into the work when there was another raid. This time it was far worse than the previous one. She wasn't on duty and she felt guilty as she crouched in the cupboard under the stairs with Mrs Lucas, her arms around the frightened woman. She wished she could get out there and do something – anything. What was happening to Barbara? Daisy had been due to take over from her just when the raid started. Had she managed to get to the shelter in time? And what about Dad? He was sure to be there, trying to help as he had last time. It was so hard to stay here in the semi-darkness, listening to the noise of bombs and anti-aircraft guns, not knowing what was happening outside.

The raid seemed to go on for hours but at last the all clear went and the two women crept out of their hiding place. Mrs Lucas went straight to the sink and filled the kettle but Daisy opened the back door and stepped outside. Across the fields she could see clouds of smoke and flames, smell the acrid odour of burning.

It was hard to tell from here which buildings were hit and how badly the airfield was affected. She must get up there and see if she could help. There was sure to be injured to deal with. She thrust aside the thought that there would also be fatalities.

When she went back inside, Mrs Lucas was making tea – the universal panacea – but Daisy waved her offer aside. 'I must go and see – Barbara, my father...'

'Stay here, dear. You'll just get in the way. Besides there's nothing you can do.'

‘I can’t sit here drinking tea,’ Daisy said with a sob. She rushed out of the house and up the lane towards the airfield.

Shocked, she hesitated at the gate. Despite her father’s description of the devastation caused by the previous big raid, and the damage she’d seen for herself on her arrival, nothing prepared her for this. Debris from burning planes littered the ground and there were huge craters everywhere. On the far side of the airfield several of the buildings had been completely demolished.

Daisy gasped and started forward. ‘The NAAFI,’ she gasped. ‘Barbara...’

Before she took more than few steps, she heard a shout and turned to see an officer running towards her.

Daisy hardly recognised the man with his blackened face and torn uniform.

‘What are you doing here?’ Roland asked, grabbing her arm.

‘I work in the NAAFI,’ she said.

‘I thought you were based in Sheerness. But you must get away. It’s too dangerous. We think there’s an unexploded bomb.’

‘I must see if Barbara’s all right.’

‘Was she on duty?’

Daisy nodded, unable to speak.

He shook his head. ‘The NAAFI got a direct hit.’

Daisy gasped and felt her legs shake. Roland took her arm and spoke gently. ‘Don’t worry, she may have got to the shelter. Look, you can’t hang around here. Go back to your billet and I’ll see what I can find out.’

‘No, I want to stay. Perhaps I can help.’

‘There’s nothing you can do. Besides, it’s too dangerous.’

Reluctantly she gave in and slowly walked away, pausing frequently to look back at the devastation. Back at the cottage she couldn’t relax, pacing up and down the small kitchen and periodically going outside to gaze towards the stricken airfield.

Mrs Lucas tried to distract her. 'Could you help with the vegetables, dear?' she asked.

Daisy picked up the potato peeler but her hands were shaking so much, she dropped it into the sink with a clatter.

'Never mind, go and sit down. I'll do it,' her landlady said.

'Sorry, I just can't...' Daisy sat at the kitchen table, but a few seconds later she was up again, standing by the back door. She gasped as she spotted a figure walking towards the farm. At first she thought it was Roland coming with news but as he got nearer she recognised her father.

She ran towards him and flung herself into his arms. 'Dad, you're safe. Thank goodness,' she cried.

'Now then, lovie. No need to make a fuss,' he said, gently pushing her away.

'Any news, Dad?'

'Come inside and I'll tell you.'

Daisy could hardly contain her impatience, but she sat at the table opposite her father and waited while he took a long swig of the tea Mrs Lucas placed in front of him.

He put the cup down and wiped his hand across his mouth. 'Not good news, love. I'm sorry...'

'Roland told me about the NAAFI,' she interrupted. 'Is it Barbara?'

'Fraid so, Daisy. Thank God you weren't on duty.'

Mrs Lucas started to cry. 'Such a lovely girl. Oh, this damned war...'

Daisy put her arms round the older woman trying to comfort her. She choked back a sob. 'Poor Barbara. I didn't know her all that well. She came from London – her parents thought she'd be safe out of the city.'

Stan took another slurp of his tea and Daisy saw that his hands were shaking. 'It was terrible – four dead, so many injured, not enough beds in Minster hospital. They sent some to Sittingbourne.'

Daisy didn't know what to say. She took a sip of her own tea, but she couldn't sit still. She stood up. 'What do I do now?' she asked.

'You'll have to come home,' Stan said abruptly. 'You can't do any good here. I've spoken to Sid Browning. You can have a few days off and go back to the garrison later.'

'Mr Browning? What's he doing here?'

'He came up in his van as soon as the all clear went. Wanted to see the damage for himself, see if he could salvage anything, he said.'

'Roland said it was a direct hit. There won't be much to salvage.'

'He said there were a few cartons. He'd just finished loading up the van when I spoke to him.' Stan patted her arm. 'Nothing for you to worry about. Anyway, go and pack your things. He'll give you a lift back to town.'

Daisy shuddered at the thought of being in the van with him and was about to protest. But the buses probably weren't running after the raid. Dad came on his bike and said he had to stay for a while helping with the clearing up.

She turned to her landlady. 'I'm sorry Mrs Lucas, looks like you're losing your lodger.'

'I'm sorry too. It's been nice having young faces around.'

'Would you like me to stay and help with Barbara's things?' Anything to avoid being in the van with that horrible man. But Mrs Lucas refused her help. 'I'll do it, dear. And I'll write to her parents too – much better than an official letter.'

'If you're sure?'

Mrs Lucas nodded and Daisy went upstairs to pack her few belongings. She stripped the bed and folded the sheets and blankets. Looking round to make sure she hadn't left anything, she went downstairs and said a tearful goodbye to Mrs Lucas. Her father took her bag and they walked up the lane to the airfield in silence.

The fire engine was still there damping down the smoking ruins of the NAAFI building and the RAF personnel were busy salvaging what they could of the damaged aircraft.

Near the gate Sid Browning leaned against the bonnet of his van smoking a cigarette. He straightened up as Daisy and her father approached but she ignored him. 'I'll just go and say goodbye to Roland,' she said.

She had to find out about Stefan too. Then there was the question of Lily. Should she tackle him about his two-timing, as well as the coming baby? It really wasn't her business though.

Roland was supervising a couple of mechanics, shouting at them to get a move on. She wasn't surprised at his bullying. It just strengthened her dislike of the man.

She called out to him and he looked up, quickly suppressing the frown of annoyance.

'Oh, it's you. I thought you'd gone back to Sheerness.'

'I'm on my way. Sorry to interrupt your work. I just wanted to know if Stefan was all right.'

'Stefan? Oh, that Pole you danced with. Dead, I'm afraid.'

How could he sound so casual? Perhaps it was his way of dealing with things though.

'Oh, I am sorry. He showed me a picture of his fiancée. So sad. I didn't know him very well but...' As he made to turn back to his work, she caught his sleeve. 'There was something else. Lily asked me to give you her love and say she misses you.'

'All right – you've told me.'

'Haven't you any message for her? She's a bit upset she hasn't heard from you.'

'I've been busy, haven't I? As you can see. Now, I must get on. Goodbye.'

Stung by his abruptness, Daisy went back to where her father and Mr Browning were talking.

'Was that Sylvia's young man?' Stan asked.

Daisy nodded.

'Come on then. I haven't got all day,' Sid Browning said, opening the passenger door of the van.

'Goodbye, Dad. I'll tell Mum you're all right.' She kissed his cheek and climbed into the van, glancing into the back. The vehicle was stacked with boxes.

As they pulled away she said, 'I see you managed to salvage some of the stores.'

‘Yes, good job I came. Those Home Guards and firemen would have had the lot away if not.’

Daisy didn’t reply. If that lot were salvaged from the ruined NAAFI store, she’d eat her hat. Everything she’d seen that morning was black with smoke. Those pristine boxes had been nowhere near the building during the raid. He must think I’m stupid, she thought. Well, he’s not going to get away with it. I’ll find out what he’s up to if it’s the last thing I do.

***

They drove the few miles in silence, the manager scowling, crashing the gears and driving erratically. He slowed down as they drove through Minster past the pub at the top of the hill. A man standing outside waved to them, but Mr Browning ignored him and speeded up.

Daisy was pleased when they reached the outskirts of town and the van slowed to go through the checkpoint near the canal. Soldiers manned the gun emplacements along the canal bank – a grim reminder of how vulnerable the Island was. Sid Browning showed his pass and a few yards further on dropped Daisy off at the corner of her street, braking abruptly and throwing her back in the seat. She got out and, without saying goodbye, he drove off down the High Street with another clash of gears.

She walked up the road, averting her eyes as she passed the ruins of the bombed houses. She’d seen enough destruction today to last a lifetime. She hoped her mother wasn’t at home; she couldn’t cope with her fussing right now.

But Dora was there, bent over the range, taking something out of the oven and Daisy realised how good it was to come home to a loving welcome. The tempting aroma of her mother’s cooking made her realise she hadn’t eaten today.

‘Smells good, Mum,’ she said.

‘Oh, goodness, you nearly made me drop it. I didn’t hear you come in.’ Dora put a pie down on the table.

'Rabbit – for a change.' She gave a little laugh. 'Don't know about the pastry though, not enough fat really. Probably be hard as rocks. Still, there's plenty of greens and spuds thanks to Dad's allotment.'

Daisy put her bag down in the corner and sat down abruptly, her legs shaking. Suddenly, the events of the morning hit her and she struggled to hold back the tears.

Her mother looked closely at her. 'What are you doing home? I didn't expect you. Is everything all right? Have you seen your Dad?'

Daisy nodded. 'He's OK.' She choked on the words and started to cry, releasing the emotions she had managed to hold in check so far. 'Oh, Mum, it was awful,' she sobbed. 'My friend got killed – the girl I work with – and Stefan. They sent me home.' Dora pulled her daughter to her in a hug, smoothing her hair and rocking her as she'd done when Daisy was a child. 'There, there, lovie.'

Finally the storm of tears passed and Daisy sniffed, 'Sorry, Mum. You were asking about Dad. He's all right. He said to tell you he might be late. It's chaos up there.'

'I've been so worried about both of you. When do you have to go back?'

'There's nothing to go back to. The NAAFI's gone, direct hit.'

'Oh, my goodness. You weren't hurt at all?'

'I was in my billet – off duty.' At the thought of Barbara she almost started to cry again. It could so easily have been her. She dried her eyes and sniffed. 'Look, Mum. I don't want to talk about it. I'll go up and lie down for a bit.'

She lay on her bed, trying to stifle the memory of the devastation. She could still smell that awful odour of smoke and something else she didn't want to think about. Poor Stefan, who had danced with her and shown her the photo of his sweetheart - and Barbara who was always smiling. Why them? Why not me?

Gradually she drifted off to sleep. When her mother called up that the meal was ready, she sat up, rubbing her eyes which were red and swollen from crying. She couldn't go downstairs like this. Not for the first time, she wished they had a bathroom upstairs. She hated having to walk through the kitchen to the scullery to wash, especially in this state.

She could hear Jimmy chattering excitedly to her mother and hoped he wasn't ghoulishly asking about the air raid. To him, the war was a bit of an adventure. Thankfully, the reality of it had never been brought home to him. She hoped devoutly it never would.

Pasting on a smile, she went downstairs to face the inevitable barrage of questions.

***

After the meal, when Jimmy had gone off to scouts, Daisy made up her mind to speak to her father about her concerns, thankful that, after a day up at the Eastchurch airfield, he was not on duty that night. Perhaps there was a simple explanation for what she'd seen and Dad could set her mind at rest.

After listening to the six o-clock news, Stan picked up his newspaper but before he could become immersed in his reading, Daisy said, 'Dad, I must talk to you.'

He put the paper down with an irritable sigh, but, as she sat down opposite him, he scrutinised her face.

'What's wrong, love? I know it was hard for you today but you must try to put it out of your mind.'

'No, Dad. It's not that. I'm sad about Barbara and Stefan of course but...' she hesitated. 'It's something else. I think Mr Browning is stealing from the stores.'

'Oh, love, I'm sure you've got it wrong. Anyway, we all know it goes on – a bit of pilfering, a packet of fags here, a tin of ham there. Don't worry about it.' He picked up his paper again.

'No, Dad. It's worse than that – whole boxes of stuff. I saw him loading up his van.'

Stan listened more attentively as she told him about the day she'd seen the van being loaded with stuff for the Eastchurch NAAFI. 'But when I got there, I looked in the stores and there was no sign of any of it. And the chef told me they were short of supplies.'

'Hm. That does sound a bit suspicious,' Stan agreed.

'That's not all. A few weeks ago, June and I saw him outside the pub, taking a box of stuff inside. I didn't think much of it at the time but, added to everything else...' She paused.

'Well, go on, what else?' Stan rustled his newspaper impatiently.

'Dad, listen. This is important. You saw him today – that van was full of boxes. All sorts of stuff – not just cigarettes.'

'He told me he'd managed to save some of the stores after the raid.'

'That's what he said. But he knew about the raid before he got there, and that the NAAFI had been hit. Dad, you saw the damage for yourself – there was nothing to save. And what little there was would have been smoke and water damaged. The boxes I saw were clean, still sealed. No sign of any damage.'

'Perhaps he was making a delivery, didn't realise how bad things were.'

'So why lie about trying to salvage stuff? Besides, he must have known we didn't need supplies.'

'I don't know, Daisy. Anyway, he's probably taken everything back to the store here.'

'I suppose so.' Daisy sighed. Dad didn't seem convinced. Well, she would carry on investigating. When she went back to work tomorrow, she would find an excuse to visit the stores. If the boxes she'd seen in the van were there, she would have to concede that her suspicions were groundless.

She got up at the sound of a knock on the front door. Her mother got there before her and called out, 'It's your friend, Daisy. Shall I ask her in?'

'It's all right, Mum. I'll come out.'

She was pleased to see June standing there but her friend was not alone. For a moment she felt a slight jealous pang. Why were they together? Then Chris smiled and said,

'No duty tonight. We heard you were back. We thought you'd like to come out for a drink.'

'I'll come if you promise not to talk about what happened today. I can't go through it all again.'

'Promise,' June said, and Chris nodded.

Daisy called back down the passage, 'Just going out for a while, Mum.'

They headed up the High Street to the Old House at Home, a quaint old pub with a snug, where they could sit and chat, ignoring the noise from the public bar.

Chris ordered their drinks and brought them over to the table. 'So, how was Eastchurch?' he asked.

'Fine, until today.'

'It must have been awful,' June said. 'Mr Browning told us about it. Lucky you weren't on duty.'

Daisy nodded. 'But we agreed not to talk about it.' She took a sip of her shandy. 'Tell me what's been going on here.'

'Same as usual, I suppose. We've missed you. That new girl Mavis isn't very friendly and Lily hasn't been too well – always having time off. I'll be glad to have you back.'

'Well, I'll be in bright and early tomorrow.'

'I thought they'd give you some leave after what you've been through,' Chris said. 'You need time to get over an experience like that.'

'I'm fine. I'll be better working.'

'Well, I'm glad you're OK. I've been worried about you.'

June grinned. 'He came into the canteen asking if we had any news. When I said I was going to call round, he asked if he could join me, didn't you, Lofty?'

Daisy ignored her suggestive smile. 'You said Lily wasn't well. Is she all right?' She was sure she knew what was wrong and wondered if anyone at work had guessed her friend's condition. She didn't think so – June was sure to have said something.

'Not sure. She's very up and down. And she looks unhappy - probably pining for that Roland.' She finished her drink. 'Anyone for another?'

'No thanks.' Daisy wondered whether to say she'd seen Roland that day. He'd been very offhand – probably because he was busy. But he had looked confused for a moment, almost as if he'd forgotten who Lily was. And he hadn't asked after Sylvia either. Might be best to say nothing until she had a chance to talk to Lily.

The rest of the evening passed pleasantly, June keeping them amused with anecdotes of goings on in the NAAFI and accurate imitations of their customers. She did a good take-off of Mrs Green too, which had them in fits of laughter.

Daisy realised she was enjoying herself, their friendly presence serving to take her mind off the horrors of the day. She even managed to put the problem of the NAAFI manager out of her mind – for a while.

Near closing time, Chris offered to see them both home. June was billeted in one of the big houses on Marine Parade and they left her at her front door. It was full dark now and Daisy stumbled as they crossed the road. Chris took her arm and did not let go. Daisy's resolve to keep their relationship on a 'just friends' basis, wavered as she felt the warmth of his hand on her arm. They walked along in silence until they reached the alley leading to her back garden.

She hesitated with her hand on the back gate. Would he try to kiss her goodnight – and would she let him?

He smiled down at her and said, 'Thanks for a pleasant evening. I hope we were able to take your mind off things for a while.'

Daisy nodded.

'I'm glad you're back in town – even if it was for such a horrible reason.' Chris hesitated and Daisy tensed herself for the expected kiss. 'I've missed you,' he said and, without another word he hurried away.

'Goodnight, Chris,' she called. But he did not look back. Disappointed, in spite of her vow, Daisy walked slowly up the garden path and opened the back door. There were no lights on, so she crept upstairs, anxious not to disturb her brother and her parents.

‘That you, Dais?’ a sleepy voice called.

‘Yes, Dad. Night.’ she whispered, a warm feeling engulfing her. How lucky she was to have someone staying awake until she was safely home.

As she got into bed, she said a prayer of thanks for her loving family and friends as well as praying, as she usually did for the safety of Bob and all those fighting in this dreadful war.

***

Chris walked home mentally kicking himself. When Daisy looked up at him to say goodnight, he had been sorely tempted to take her in his arms and tell her how he felt. He longed to kiss those lovely lips, to run his fingers through her silken curls. But he pulled back in time. ‘Just friends,’ he muttered. How could he be just friends when he wanted so much more?

When he met June tonight and agreed to join her for a drink, his heart leapt when she said she was going to call on Daisy first to see how she was. Everyone was talking about the terrible raid on Eastchurch and his stomach knotted with anxiety until he heard that Daisy was safe.

He kicked a stone in the road and walked on, shoulders hunched. She was safe, that was all that mattered. And if Bob came safely home, he would be happy for her. At least, that’s what he told himself.

Chapter Nineteen

Bob sat at the kitchen table in a lonely farmhouse somewhere in France devouring fresh made bread and soup. His two companions - RAF pilots shot down during the air battle last month – said little, concentrating on their food as if they hadn't eaten for weeks. He had no idea where he was and where he would be next day. They never stayed in one place for long, moving steadily south and west as their rescuers dictated. Bob marvelled that they had not been caught and blessed these wonderful people, who had not given in to their invaders but continued to fight covertly against the enemy.

He had lost weight and his face was thin and haggard, partly from lack of food and proper sleep, partly the ever-present fear of discovery. It was hard to stay constantly alert, nerves jumping at the slightest noise, having to be ready at a moment's notice to move on, usually at night.

This evening, however, he was feeling optimistic. The elderly farmer informed them that a boat was waiting to take them downriver towards the open sea. He hadn't dared to ask what would happen then, but hope flared at the thought he could be home in just a few days. Home to his Daisy. A memory of Francoise crept into his mind, hastily thrust away. He managed to convince himself that he would never see her again so what was the point in thinking of her? Their love affair had been a wonderful interlude in the madness of war and the memories would sustain him through whatever was to come. But sweet Daisy was his first love and he had promised to love her forever – made *her* promise too. She was probably sitting at home now, wondering why he hadn't written, maybe thinking he was dead. He must get home so she could see for herself that he was all right.

Taffy, the Welsh pilot, nudged his arm. 'Wake up, Bob. Time we were moving.'

He wiped the last of his bread round the bowl and stood up, cramming the morsel into his mouth.

The three men crowded in the farmhouse doorway waiting until the farmer beckoned them forward. They crept along a path between rows of grape vines until they reached the river. A man stood on the bank holding the painter of a small boat. 'Come.' A hoarse whisper carried on the still night air. 'Quietly now.'

Bob and his companions shook hands with the farmer and climbed into the craft. The boatman cast off and started rowing, taking them out into the centre of the fast-flowing river. 'We reach the sea soon,' he whispered. 'Quicker if we all row.'

The airmen fumbled with the oars, unsure how to handle them, but Bob had often rowed round the Island with his mates, fishing. He took the oars confidently and soon, helped by the ebbing tide, they reached the mouth of the river.

Just beyond, a large fishing boat rode at anchor. The fugitives climbed aboard and the rowing boat turned back. They set sail immediately, the captain hustling them down an open hatchway. Before descending into the hold, which smelt strongly of a combination of engine oil and fish, Bob took a long last look as the coastline of France disappeared behind them. 'Goodbye Francoise,' he whispered.

***

When Daisy came downstairs next morning dressed in her NAAFI uniform, her mother turned from the stove in surprise. 'You're not going into work today surely?' she said.

Daisy nodded. 'I must. June said Lily's not well so they'll be short-handed.'

‘They’ll manage,’ Dora said, plonking a plate of toast on the table. ‘They can’t expect you to work after what you’ve been through.’

‘Mum. I’ll admit I was upset yesterday but I was nowhere near the airfield when the raid started. I’m all right now. Anyway, being busy will take my mind of what happened up there.’

‘Well, make sure you have some breakfast first. I’ll just go and call Jimmy.’

Daisy sat at the table and picked up a slice of toast, just a scraping of butter and no marmalade. She nibbled at it, helping the dry bread down with a swig of tea. No bacon today either. She’d do better to wait till her break at work and have something to eat then. To please her mother, she forced the rest of the toast down, finished her tea and picked up her handbag.

‘I’m off, Mum. See you at tea-time,’ she called up the stairs.

When she got to work, she was surprised to see Lily in the cloakroom. ‘I thought you were off sick,’ she said, looking closely at her friend. Lily’s face was pale and her eyelids pink from crying. ‘Are you sure you’re well enough to be here?’

‘I couldn’t stay home. Mum’s been getting on at me saying I’m not really ill.’ Lily sniffed and rubbed her hand across her face.

‘So what’s the matter then?’

Lily shook her head and started to cry. Daisy had a sinking feeling; she thought she had guessed what was troubling her friend. ‘Come on, Lily. You can tell me.’

‘I’m pregnant,’ she blurted.

‘Oh, Lily. I don’t know what to say.’ Daisy felt no pleasure in knowing she was right.

‘Why don’t you say what everyone else will when they know? I’m a tart, a trollop, no better than I should be...’

‘No, Lily. I don’t think that.’ She hardly dare ask. ‘Who...?’

‘There’s only been one man in my life as you very well know,’ Lily retorted.

Daisy sighed. 'Roland.' She might have known. Hadn't she mistrusted him all along?

'I love him, Daisy - and I haven't heard from him and with all these raids on the airfield I don't even know if he's all right.'

'I'm sure he's fine, Lily.' Daisy wasn't sure if she should confess she'd spoken to him yesterday and he was very much all right. The only problem was, he'd seemed almost indifferent when she mentioned Lily. She hadn't been surprised – hadn't she seen him with two other girls lately? And then there was Sylvia. How many others had he seduced with sweet talk and promises? She patted Lily's shoulder. 'Dry your eyes and wash your face. Time we were at work. Try not to worry. No one need know yet and I promise I won't say anything.'

'But what am I going to do?' Lily burst into fresh sobs.

'I'll think of something. Come on, be brave.'

Lily dried her tears, splashed water on her face and dried it on the roller towel behind the door. She straightened her blouse and put her overall on. 'You're a good friend, Daisy. I missed you while you were away.' She pulled open the door. 'Come on then. Don't want Mrs G breathing down our necks.'

June looked up from serving a customer. 'What kept you?' she snapped, then spotting Daisy behind Lily she squealed, 'You're back. Thank goodness.'

Daisy smiled. 'Glad to be back.' She took her place behind the counter while Lily started clearing and wiping down the tables. With two of them serving the queue quickly tailed off and Daisy had a chance to speak to June. 'Lily's still not feeling too well.'

'What's wrong with her? If she's ill she should get a sick note.'

'She's tired. You know she has to look after her little sisters and brother when she's not at work.'

'We're all tired, with the raids and all. We just have to get on with it, don't we?' June snapped.

Before Daisy could reply, Mrs Green came through from the office holding a list in her hand. 'I need one of you girls to go over to the stores. Lily, you don't look very busy. Come along, don't dawdle.'

Lily put down the tray she was wiping and took the list from her. 'There's a lot of stuff. I'll have to make two trips,' she said.

'I'll come with you,' Daisy offered. 'If that's all right with you, Mrs Green.'

The supervisor's eyes swept the room noting how few customers there were. 'Very well, but don't take too long.'

In the store Lily looked round in amazement at the stacks of boxes and tins. 'I've never been in here before,' she said. 'How do we know where everything is?'

'The shelves are labelled.' Daisy took the list. 'Beans are up that end,' she said, pointing. 'Bring a couple of cartons and stack them near the door. I'll get the tins of jam and marmalade.' She took down the catering size tins which each held five pounds of preserves. As she put them down, she took the opportunity to look at the clipboard hanging on the nail by the door. There it was. 'Five boxes - beans, peas, tinned peaches, pineapple, condensed milk – and two cartons of cigarettes. For Eastchurch.' She let out a breath. 'All signed for by S Browning,' she murmured. 'So where are those cartons now?' She walked up and down the aisles searching, but there was no sign of the boxes she had seen in Sid Browning's van. The beans Lily carried to the door were a different brand.

'What else?' Lily asked, interrupting her thoughts.

'Cigarettes – over there.'

When they found all the items on the list, Lily said, 'Glad you came with me. I couldn't manage those big boxes.'

They carried everything over to the canteen and Daisy signed the inventory before locking the store door.

She returned the key to Mrs Green, sure she should mention her suspicions. She'd brushed her off last time she'd try to tell her. She had no proof after all. But surely if the van load was really destined for the airfield he would have returned everything to the Sheerness store. And then there was the lie he'd told her father about salvaging stock. What should she do?

For the rest of her shift Daisy could hardly concentrate on her work. She could just ignore it of course, but her conscience told her she must do something. Mrs Green's response set her thinking. Was the supervisor involved as well? She didn't want to believe it. One thing she was sure of. Sid Browning was selling the stuff he'd stolen – it wasn't as if it was just a few cigarettes, the odd tin of peaches for his family. The tightening of rationing meant that many were struggling to feed their families and it was understandable if they bought a few things 'under the counter' as the saying went. But people like the manager were making money out of the war. It wasn't right.

When it was time to go home, she summoned up her courage and knocked on the office door. She had to speak up.

She entered at Mrs Green's call and stood in front of the desk, twisting her hands nervously in her overall.

'Well, girl. What is it?'

When Daisy still hesitated, Mrs Green smiled and said. 'I'm pleased you came back to work today. But if you think it was too soon and you need more time off, that's all right.'

'It's not that, Mrs Green. I went over to the stores with Lily earlier, and I'm sure some of the supplies are missing. I've noticed it before but you told me I was mistaken when I mentioned it before.' She stopped speaking and licked her dry lips.

'Well, go on.'

'I hoped it was a mistake – people forgetting to sign for stuff. But it's happened too often lately, and you know how Mr Browning is about signing. I think someone's stealing.' She couldn't accuse the manager directly, but who else could it be?

'My goodness, Daisy, what an imagination you have.' Mrs Green laughed. 'You've been watching too many films.'

When Daisy made to protest, the supervisor flapped her hand. 'No, it's good of you to come to me with your concerns. But I can assure you nothing untoward is going on here. As you say, it's probably people forgetting to sign.' She sighed. 'I don't say there isn't a bit of petty pilfering from time to time and I'll keep more of an eye on things in future. Now, off you go.'

Daisy left quickly and walked up the road, her mind in turmoil. She couldn't help wondering if Mrs Green was involved too, brushing her concerns aside like that. Well, she'd done her duty in reporting it. What more could she do?

As if that wasn't enough to worry about, there was Lily and her problem. She just didn't see how she could help her friend, short of marching up to Eastchurch and confronting Roland. He would laugh in her face. She just knew he was the sort of man who would blame the girl for getting into trouble. If only she could confide in someone.

***

Daisy was on a late shift the next day and, as the weather was still fine, she decided to join her father on the allotment. There had been no rain for days so she would help with the watering and pick the last of the runner beans for their dinner. It would be a good opportunity for a heart to heart with Dad. This time she would make him believe her suspicions were justified and let him decide what she should do.

To her dismay, her brother was there, helping their father to dig over the plot where the early potatoes had been, ready for winter sowing. There goes my chance of confiding in Dad, she thought.

They both looked up as she approached, and Jimmy grinned. 'Glad you've come,' he said. 'You can help Dad now. I've had enough.'

'You're joking, aren't you? It's too hot for digging,' Daisy said.

‘Now lad, enough of that,’ said Stan. ‘Your sister works hard, and she’s got another shift later on. You just finish that row, then you can buzz off with your pals.’

‘OK, Dad.’ Jimmy resumed his digging while Daisy filled the watering can from the standpipe in the corner. She carried on working until Jimmy called out, ‘Bye, Sis. I’m off.’

She put the watering can down and wiped her sweaty brow with a handkerchief. ‘Time for a rest, Dad. You’ve been out here all morning.’

Stan went over to the little shed at the side of the allotment. ‘I’ve got some tea, love. Want some?’ He pulled a flask out of his bag.

Daisy nodded and they sat on boxes outside the shed, drinking their tea and enjoying the peace and quiet. ‘Bliss,’ she murmured, turning her face up to the sun.

‘Make the most of it,’ Stan said, ‘before the next raid.’

‘I’m trying not to think about it,’ she said.

‘Me too.’ Stan finished his tea and shook the dregs out onto the grass, screwing the lid back on the flask.

As Daisy went to stand up and carry on working, he put his hand on her arm. ‘Wait a minute, lass. Something’s on your mind, I can tell. Why don’t you tell your old dad?’ He looked into her troubled face. ‘You’re not in trouble are you, Daisy?’

It took a second before she realised what he meant, and she laughed. ‘Oh, no, Dad. Not that sort of trouble anyway.’

‘Well, what is it then?’

‘I don’t know where to start.’

‘From the beginning, lass. That’s the best place.’

‘It’s about Mr Browning. I’m sure now he’s stealing from the NAAFI stores - dealing on the black market.’ The words camc out in a rush.

‘So you said yesterday, but what’s changed?’ He grabbed her arm. ‘Don’t tell me you’ve been playing detective. You could get into serious trouble, my girl.’

‘I’m not worried about that. Listen, Dad, I was in the stores yesterday and I had a good look round.’

‘Suppose he’d caught you snooping. Keep out of it, Daisy. It could be dangerous.’

‘I’m not scared of him. Anyway, I was with Lily. Mrs Green sent us to fetch cigarettes and other stuff. And some of the shelves were almost empty. Fags, tinned fruit and other stuff.’

‘Did you check if they’d been signed for?’

‘Of course – first thing I thought of. Mr Browning’s very hot on that. He told me off one day for not signing for cigarettes, practically accused me. But I hadn’t taken any. He made a big fuss about remembering to sign. Then, when I went for some tea the other day, the tin was half empty. You know, it comes in big square tins.’

Stan nodded. ‘Go on. Had he signed for it?’

‘Yes, but it’s always me or Mrs Green who fetches our supplies. Sometimes Harold gets sacks of potatoes for the Sergeant but he’s too dim to do anything on a big scale like this. It must be Mr Browning stealing.’

‘Not necessarily. He *is* responsible for Eastchurch as well. Perhaps he was delivering to the airfield.’

‘That’s what he said when I saw him loading his van that time. But when I was working at Eastchurch the cook was complaining they were short of stores. And one time, June and me were on our way home from the pictures and we saw him taking a big box into the pub.’

Stan nodded and lit a cigarette. ‘Still no proof though, love.’

‘I know. So what do I do?’

Stan blew smoke through his nostrils and thought for a minute. ‘Hang on,’ he said. ‘There was a load of boxes in his van the other day. He told me he’d salvaged them from the bombing raid.’

‘But Dad...’

‘Wait. He couldn’t have. The building was total shambles, I’m positive nothing could have been saved. I should have realised.’

‘That’s what I mean. If he’d picked them out of the ruins they would have been damaged with water and smoke. He’d partly covered the boxes with a blanket, but I could see that they were perfectly all right, not damaged at all. He should have taken them back to the Sheerness stores. But they weren't there today.'

'You're right, love. We'll have to report this.'

'But proof, Dad...'

'You've got a witness – me.' Stan laughed. 'Good little detective, you are. Cracked the case.'

'I'm not sure, Dad. Besides, I'm scared now. Suppose he finds out it was me that told.'

'Don't you worry about that.' He stood up and waved his arms at a man working on the next allotment. 'Ted, over here,' he shouted, then turned to Daisy. 'Mate of mine, Constable Ted Rowe. He'll know what to do.'

A tall, well built man with sandy hair and cheerful grin strolled over to them. His shirt sleeves were rolled up to the elbows and his hands were ingrained with dirt where he had been planting.

'What's up, mate?' he asked.

'This is my daughter, Daisy, works in the NAAFI down the garrison. She's got quite a tale to tell.' He elbowed Daisy in the ribs. 'Go on, gel. Tell him what you told me.'

Constable Rowe squatted down beside her and smiled. 'Well, Daisy, what's been going on?'

After a couple of false starts and prompted by encouraging nods, Daisy poured out the whole story.

The policeman thanked her for her bravery in speaking out and assured her he would look into it. 'We've been aware for some time that there's some black market dealing doing on. The problem is, no one wants to admit they've been buying black market stuff. But it can't go on. Now we know where to start.'

Daisy heaved a big sigh of relief. It was a load off her mind. Now she only had Lily to worry about. How was she going to help her friend?

Chapter Twenty

Lily was just finishing her shift when Daisy came on duty that afternoon and there was no opportunity to speak to her. The canteen was frantically busy, and it wasn't until late afternoon that she was allowed a break. June joined her soon afterwards, flopping down in a chair and arching her back.

'We just seem to get busier. I'm dying for a cuppa.'

Daisy fetched tea for both of them and asked how Lily had been that morning.

'She's still not well but she's managing to do her work all right, keeping out of Mrs G's way.'

'I couldn't believe the change in her, since I've been away. She looks awful, so pale and tired-looking,' Daisy said. 'Have you asked her what's wrong?

'I did but she snapped my head off. I don't know - she hardly talks to me lately. I mentioned going dancing at the weekend but she said she was too busy.'

'I think she's finding it hard coping with the little ones when her mum's at work.' Daisy sighed. So, it seemed Lily hadn't confided her problem to anyone else. But, although there was no real sign of her pregnancy yet, they would know soon enough.

She decided to go round after work and see how her friend was. Perhaps she had plucked up enough courage to tell her parents. Daisy didn't know her friend's family and had no idea how they would react.

She avoided June when they left work and walked across the moat and past the railway station, turning into the maze of narrow streets with their wooden cottages. She knocked on Lily's door, hearing a babble of voices and the high-pitched whine of a tired toddler. She was about to turn away when the door opened. A huge woman, hoisting a small child on her hip stood there. Hard to believe this was the waif-like Lily's mother.

'Who are you?' she said, turning back into the room and shouting, 'Shut up you lot. I can't hear myself think.'

'I'm Daisy. Lily's friend. I was wondering how she is.'

'She's giving the little ones their tea. Nothing wrong with her that I can see.' She pulled the door open. 'Might as well come in and see for yourself.'

Daisy squeezed past Mrs Scott and walked into a cluttered room which seemed to be full of children. Three little girls sat up at the table eating jam sandwiches while a man, presumably their father, sat in the only armchair reading a newspaper. Lily, who was pouring water into a teapot, turned and almost dropped it when she saw Daisy.

'What are you doing here?'

'June said you hadn't been well.'

Mrs Scott put the toddler down and, before Lily could reply, said. 'She's all right now. Been to work this morning haven't you, Lil?'

'I've been working away, Mrs Scott, so I didn't know,' Daisy said. 'Sorry to intrude on your meal time.' She turned to leave.

'That's OK. Might as well stay for a cuppa. Katie, get down and give her your seat.'

One of the little girls scrambled down from the table, till holding her jam sandwich.

'Thank you.' Daisy sat down and accepted the cup Lily pushed towards her. She had hoped for a chance to talk to her friend alone, but it would have to wait. She lifted little Katie onto her lap and the child smiled at her through jam-smeared lips.

Mrs Scott sat in the only other vacant chair and proceeded to feed the toddler.

'That's Donny, the only boy,' Lily said.

Daisy took the little boy's hand. 'Pleased to meet you, Donny,' she said. The other children giggled.

'I'm Katie,' the girl on her lap said.

'I know. And what are your sisters' names?'

'That's Rosie and that's Mary.'

'*Rosemary,'* the older child corrected.

Daisy smiled and said hello to each of them, then drank her tea. 'I should go, Lily. I can see you're busy. Will you be at work tomorrow?' She put Katie down and stood up.

'Don't go yet. Help me get the little ones ready for bed. We can talk later.'

She agreed to stay, although with Lily's parents here, she wouldn't be able to broach the subject uppermost in her mind. Still, just being here would show Lily that she had her support.

The man in the corner crumpled his newspaper and said, 'Haven't those kids finished their tea yet? Come on Mabel, time we was off. Leave it to Lily.'

Daisy was horrified. Surely they weren't going out and leaving her friend to cope with the children?

She felt ashamed of her rush to judgement when the couple put on jackets with ARP armbands and picked up tin helmets from the sideboard.

'Don't forget the blackout,' Mr Scott said, grinning. 'Or I'll be after you.'

Mrs Scott laughed. 'No favouritism, mind.' She kissed each of the children and followed her husband out of the door.

When they'd gone, Lily chivvied the children to finish eating and get ready for bed. It took some time to settle them down, two each head to toe in the two single beds in the back bedroom.

Downstairs Daisy asked. 'Where do you sleep, Lily?'

'In the front room. I used to share with the girls until Donny came along. I'm lucky having my own room but when Donny gets older he'll have it and I'll be back with the girls.' She sighed. 'That's if I haven't been chucked out on my ear.'

'They won't do that surely,' Daisy protested.

'I don't know. Dad would expect me to marry the father but that won't happen.'

Daisy knew she was right but she couldn't say so.

'I've got to face it, Daisy. Roland doesn't care for me.' She choked on a sob. 'He hasn't been in touch for ages and he's only up the road in Eastchurch. It's not as if he's away fighting like your Bob.'

'He could have been caught in that raid.' She ought to tell her he was safe, but before she could speak, Lily went on.

'But even before that, he hadn't written or come into town to see me. He could have let me know if he was all right. Oh, Daisy, suppose he's...'

'He's not dead, not even injured. I saw him, Lily.'

'Why didn't you tell me then?' Lily sat up straight, accusation in her eyes. 'You should have told me, not left me wondering.'

How could she explain? Daisy faltered to find the words. 'He said...'

'You actually spoke to him?' Lily was still angry.

'That's why I didn't mention it. He was horrible, Lily. Sounded as if he didn't even remember your name. So offhand. I didn't want to upset you. And then, when you told me about...' She gestured towards Lily's stomach.

Her friend dried her eyes, her voice softened. 'I guess I knew really. I was going to write and tell him, but it wouldn't have done any good.'

'He ought to be told though, accept responsibility.'

'No. I'll manage.'

'Do your parents know?'

'Mum does – she guessed. I think she's going to break it to Dad while they're out tonight. Calm him down before I have to face him.'

'What you said earlier – about getting chucked out?'

'No, I didn't mean it. They'll probably send me to my Gran's so the neighbours don't know. Mum worries about what the neighbours think.' Lily gave a little laugh. 'That's the least of my worries.'

Daisy knew she was thinking about the baby and was about to ask what would happen to it, when the sirens started up.

'No peace for the wicked,' Lily said, jumping up. 'Let's get the kids down the shelter.'

It was a scramble to get the children out of bed and into their clothes. 'Glad you're here. Hard to manage on my own,' Lily panted, hoisting little Donny onto her shoulder and grabbing Katie's hand. Daisy followed, hustling the other two children along to the shelter at the end of the road. Searchlights lit up the sky and she could hear the ack ack guns up on the seafront. She wondered if Chris was on duty tonight.

They stayed in the shelter till the all clear went. Dusk had turned to dark night while they were inside and they looked around, grateful that there were no flames or smoke lighting up the sky. This time the town had been spared.

'You'd better get on home. Your mum will be worried,' Lily said.

'I'll stay and help with the kids if you like,' Daisy offered.

'It's all right. I can manage. I'm used to it.' Lily gathered the children to her and set off down the road, turning to give a little wave.

Daisy walked home quickly, sure footed in spite of the dim light from her torch. She had walked these streets so often she could find her way blindfold.

Her father and Jimmy were in bed when she got home but Dora, still in her WVS uniform, sat at the kitchen table, her hands clasped round a mug of cocoa. She looked up as Daisy entered the room, her eyes red-rimmed with fatigue.

'You all right, Mum? You didn't have to wait up,' she said.

'Just tired, love. But you know I can't settle till you're home safe.'

'Sorry, I should have let you know I'd be late.'

'Working?'

'No. I popped in to see Lily, helped her get the little ones ready for bed.'

'They expect too much of that girl. She's working full time isn't she - and you said she hasn't been well?'

Daisy was almost tempted to confide the reason Lily had been unwell. But she had promised not to tell, although she knew her mother wasn't the sort to gossip. But she would be shocked and, after all, what good would it do?

'Time we were both in bed,' she said, taking her mother's cocoa mug and putting it in the sink.

Tired as she was, Daisy couldn't get to sleep as the events of the past few days went round and round in her head – the dreadful air raid and loss of her new friend, Barbara, the vindication of her suspicions regarding the NAAFI manager's dealings, and most of all Lily's news.

She sighed and turned over. At least Mr Browning would be dealt with now that her father's policeman friend was involved. As for Lily, what could she do but stand by her and be a true friend?

Chapter Twenty One

Despite the nauseating smell which permeated the boat's hold, Bob found himself drifting into a half-sleep. He was aware of the two airmen talking quietly, the gentle motion of the fishing boat, the chug of the engine.

He stirred as he realised the engine had stopped and he held his breath in the sudden silence. Had the boat been intercepted? He heard voices, then the hatch was thrown open.

'Up, come up.' A hand beckoned them, and the three men scrambled up the ladder into the fresh air. 'Safe now,' the fisherman said.

'Where are we?' Bob asked, looking around him for landmarks. It was still dark, but a faint pink tinged the eastern sky and he made out the grey bulk of a low-lying coast.

'We'll put you ashore here, but you'll have to find your own way from there.'

'Never mind, we're home,' Johnny, one of the airmen said.

'Home,' Bob echoed. He should be elated at having escaped from occupied France but the lurking fear at the back of his mind came to the surface. Would he be labelled a deserter? Would his story of escaping be believed? Not everyone had been rescued at Dunkirk. Many were left behind and captured, himself among them. It was a pure fluke that he got away. But that was months ago.

As the rowing boat that deposited them on the sandy shore pulled away, he confided his fears to his companions.

'Just stick with us. We'll speak up for you,' Johnny said.

'Yes. First thing is to find someone to report to,' Mike, the other one said.

They trudged up the beach, their feet sinking into the loose sand, only to be halted by a tangle of barbed wire.

They looked at each other helplessly.

'What now?' Taffy asked.

He was answered by a figure which arose from behind a sand dune. Pointing a rifle at them, a voice called, 'Halt. Who goes there?'

The three immediately stopped dead and raised their hands.

'Pilot officer John Clark, and this is Taffy – er - Michael Gray.' He turned to Bob. 'Identify yourself,' he whispered.

Nervously Bob recited his name and number. Surely they weren't suspected of being enemy spies? They were in uniform, after all, even if his was a bit worse for wear after his adventures.

Two more men in Home Guard uniform rose from behind the dunes and moved towards the three of them, pointing their rifles threateningly.

'We'll have to have proof, better come to headquarters,' the leader, a sergeant in the Home Guard, said.

He gestured them to walk in front and pointed them towards the road. A little further on, they came to a squat round building which Bob recognised it as a Martello Tower. When he was small his parents had brought him on holiday to Dymchurch, in Kent, and his dad had told him the strange building was one of several built along the coast to repel a threatened invasion by Napoleon. Is this where they had landed? He was given no time to wonder or to ask questions, as the Home Guard sergeant hustled them inside.

To Bob's surprise they were treated kindly and offered tea and sandwiches, thick slices filled with corned beef and enamel mugs of strong tea. He hadn't realised how hungry he was, and he wolfed the food down as did his companions. When they finished eating, Bob attempted to ask what would happen to them but the sergeant refused to answer their questions. 'Wait till the officer gets here,' he said.

It was a long wait, followed by an even longer interrogation and at the end of it, Bob still wasn't sure if he was about to be court martialled for desertion, or returned to his regiment. His two air force companions, after a similar interrogation, were collected in an RAF van and cheerfully waved goodbye to him.

He sat on a bench inside the Home Guard post, dolefully contemplating his future. Even the thought of seeing Daisy again could not cheer him, confused as he now was about his feelings for her.

***

Daisy had scarcely put on her overall and cap when Mrs Green waylaid her. 'That Lily's late again. Don't know what's got into her – she used to be such a good little worker.'

'Perhaps she's ill. She's been off colour for ages.'

'Nonsense – she's skiving,' Mrs Green snapped. 'Probably out late drinking and dancing and can't get up in the morning. If she keeps this up, I'll have to dismiss her.'

Daisy was relieved her supervisor hadn't realised what Lily's problem was but she tried to defend her friend. 'I think she's really ill but struggles in to work when she's not really fit, as her family need her wages. Anyway, she hasn't been dancing for ages – she has to look after her little sisters and brother.'

'Maybe so,' Mrs Green softened. 'I must admit she has been looking very pale. If she turns up today, I'll give her another chance. But she'll have to pull her socks up or that will be it.'

Lily didn't appear that day and Daisy was really worried. She resolved to go and see her again after work.

June wasn't due on duty until later so Daisy was kept busy at the counter. The new girl Mavis was confined to the kitchen washing up. The morning passed quickly and Daisy was relieved when June arrived and she was free for the rest of the day, thanking her lucky stars that she hadn't been sent to the stores. She couldn't face Mr Browning now that she knew he was about to be exposed as a criminal. She hoped Dad's friend had set things in motion to apprehend him and her mind would soon at rest.

Lily's mother came to the door when Daisy called in on her way home. Leaning against the door post, her meaty arms folded across her ample bosom, she said, 'You're too late. She's gone to her Gran's down in the New Forest.'

'Already? She told me she might be going away.'

'I'm taking the little ones down at the weekend – they'll be better off away from all these raids.'

'I'm sure that's for the best' Daisy said. She was surprised the whole family were going.

'Yes, it will be.' Mrs Scott glanced behind her and lowered her voice. 'She told you, didn't she – about her trouble.'

Daisy nodded.

'Her dad don't know – he'd half kill her. You won't say anything, will you – to them at work?'

'No. I promised Lily I'd keep it to myself.'

Mrs Scott nodded. 'Good, Lily says we can trust you.'

'Give her my love when you see her.'

'I will – oh, and don't be surprised if when we come back she's got a little brother or sister.'

'You mean...?'

Mrs Scott put her hands on her ample belly and nodded meaningfully. 'Yes, there's another one on the way.'

It took Daisy a moment to grasp what she was saying. So Lily's mother intended to pass the baby off as her own. He or she would be brought up as an addition to that large, untidy family.

'I hope it all goes well,' she said. 'I'll miss Lily at work.'

'She'll be back when she's better,' Mrs Scott said. 'I've written to her supervisor.'

Daisy said goodbye and walked home deep in thought, hoping things would turn out all right for her friend. She supposed it was a solution of sorts and, at least, Lily would not be parted from her child. Better than letting it be adopted and spend the rest of her life wondering what had happened to it.

Once at home, she tried to put Lily out of her mind after telling Dora that her friend had been sent to the country to convalesce. 'She's been ill on and off for weeks, so her mum thought it best to take her away.'

'What's wrong with her?' Stan asked from his corner by the range.

'Nerves, her mum said. It started when she got caught in a raid.'

'Silly girl,' Stan said. 'There's people suffering worse than that in this war. Still, if she's going to go to pieces every time the siren goes, she'll be no use at your work.'

Daisy ignored his comment. No use arguing, especially as she knew the real cause of Lily's 'illness.' Instead, she decided to go and meet her mother from the WVS post in the church hall in Hope Street.

As she hurried down the High Street, she looked up at the sky with its massive barrage balloons hovering over the town. She hoped there wouldn't be a raid tonight, although since that last dreadful assault on the Eastchurch aerodrome, the bombers seemed to have left them alone. The sirens still went off though, as enemy planes approached, making their way up the Thames towards London. Daisy thought of June and Mavis, who had left their families behind in the city, and realised how fortunate she was to have her loved ones nearby, except for Sylvia of course – and Bob.

She tried to put Bob out of her mind, having convinced herself he must have been killed. Surely if he was a prisoner he would have written, if not to her, then to his mother. But Mrs Gardner had only received a telegram saying 'missing'. She couldn't forget him though. He had been part of her life since junior school when he had protected her from bullies and taught her to swim in the murky waters of the North Sea.

Their friendship turned to love – a love made more intense when he joined the Army and they said their passionate farewells. But was it the kind of love that would last forever? Since meeting Chris, she began to wonder.

Still, she had made a promise to Bob and she would keep that promise until she knew for sure what had happened to him. When – if – they met again, she would know in her heart if they were meant to be together.

'Daisy, Daisy love. Where are you off to?' Her mother's voice brought her out of her reverie.

She had been so deep in thought, she almost walked past the WVS centre. Her mother, in her WVS uniform, hurried towards her.

'I was coming to meet you, Mum. Needed to get out of the house.'

Dora linked her arm with Daisy's. 'Nice to see you, love. We don't get enough time these days for a proper chat. Were there any letters at home?'

'I didn't look. Dad would have said if there was one from Sylvia though.' Daisy had long since stopped checking the mantelpiece for a letter from Bob.

'I worry about her,' Dora said. 'Still, she's doing a good job – and she seems to be having a good time. Doesn't mention that Roland though.'

'Perhaps she's found someone else.' Daisy truly hoped so. She couldn't bear her sister's heartbreak if she was still in love with him and found out what a rotter he was.

'I hope so,' Dora said.

'Why?'

'I didn't take to him that time he came to the house.' She paused. 'I don't suppose you saw anything of him while you were up at Eastchurch?'

'Officers don't come in the NAAFI, Mum.' It was true and saved Daisy from having to tell a lie. It wouldn't do for either of her parents to find out how badly he had treated Lily.

***

The next day at work Mrs Green asked them to gather round as she had some news. 'I've received a letter from

Mrs Scott, Lily's mother. As you all know, Lily has been unwell for some time and she has been sent away to convalesce. It doesn't say what she's convalescing from, but I have my own ideas about that.' She paused and looked round at the girls. 'Never mind. We'll cope. We have Mavis now and I'm trying to enlist someone else. Fortunately, since most of the army has left, we are not quite so busy. Meantime we will carry on.' She waved a hand in dismissal and they all went back to their allotted tasks.

Daisy was stacking plates at the end of the counter when June came in with a handful of cutlery. 'What was she talking about?' June whispered. 'About Lily I mean.'

'I don't know, do I?' Daisy did know but she wasn't about to share it with June.

'She never did believe Lily was really ill. Suspicious old cow. I bet it's TB and that's why they're keeping quiet.' She nudged Daisy's elbow. 'Do you know where she's gone?'

'I saw her mother. The whole family's gone to her grandmother in the New Forest.'

'All of them?'

'To get away from air raids, so she said.'

'All right for some,' June said. 'I wouldn't mind a little holiday in the New Forest. We went there once when I was little. Lovely it was. Ponies and deer. Mind you, I don't think it would suit me now.'

'Why not?'

'No dance halls, no soldiers or sailors.'

Daisy couldn't help laughing, relieved that speculation as to Lily's illness had taken a back seat. She was still laughing when she heard the door open and turned to see Chris. As usual he was alone and she felt sorry for him. Just because he wasn't in the same regiment and didn't go out drinking with them, they treated him like an outsider. The only time they spoke to him was to pull his leg.

He came up to the counter. 'What's the joke,' he said.

'Just something June said. What can I get you?' She spoke briskly, determined not to succumb to the fluttery feeling that engulfed her the minute he walked through the door. Just friends, she told herself firmly.

She served him his tea and toast and watched as he carried it over to the table without further conversation. Disappointed, she carried on serving as he sat down and pulled a book from his pocket.

A little later, during the lull of customers, she picked up a tray and started to clear the tables. As she neared Chris's table she saw that the book he was reading was a motorcycle manual.

'Interesting?' she asked, as she picked up his empty plate.

He looked up and smiled. 'Only to a motorbike freak,' he said.

'Oh, yes. A Matchless, isn't it?'

Surprised, he nodded. 'You like bikes?'

'Sort of.' She couldn't tell him she'd made a note of the make of his motorcycle that time he'd given her a ride during the air raid.

'Perhaps you'd like another ride some time.'

'Perhaps.' Before she could say anything else, she became aware of Mrs Green's eyes on her. She hastily wiped the table and picked up the tray. 'Anything else?' she asked.

'No thank you.'

She cleared a few more tables and went through to the kitchen. Her heart thumped wildly and she took a few deep breaths before depositing the dirty dishes on the draining board and going back to the counter.

June grinned when she returned. 'I saw you talking to Lofty. Making a date, were you?'

'Certainly not. I told you, I'm staying true to Bob.'

'But Bob's not here, is he? No harm in having a bit of fun.'

Daisy ignored her and tried to keep busy, avoiding looking at the corner where Chris had been sitting. At the end of her shift she glanced across the room, but he had left.

Summer was truly at an end and there was a distinct nip in the air as she left the garrison and braced herself for the long walk home, wishing she had brought a jacket.

As she crossed the moat, she heard the roar of an engine and glanced round as the motorcycle coasted to a stop beside her. Chris lifted his goggles and grinned at her.

'No dad walking you home this evening?' he asked.

'He only does that on dark nights.'

'Nice that he cares so much. It's a long walk to your house.' He fiddled with the handlebars and cleared his throat. 'Fancy that ride now?' he asked.

She shivered. 'It's a bit chilly.'

'Never mind, you can borrow my jacket.'

She really wanted to accept, remembering how she felt when she wrapped her arms around him and they drove that short distance to the air raid shelter. As she hesitated, he got off the bike and took his leather jacket off, wrapping it around her shoulders. Almost without thinking, she slipped her arms into the sleeves.

'Suits you,' he said with a grin. He swung his leg over the bike and grasped the handlebars. 'Hop on,' he said over his shoulder.

She climbed on and, without being told, put her arms around his waist, clinging on as he kick-started the bike. The journey was over too soon and they stopped in front of her house. She would have liked to linger but she could see her brother peering out of the window. She got off the bike and took the jacket off, handing it to Chris, hoping he would put it on and be away before Jimmy came out. She knew she'd be in for some teasing from him, coming home on a soldier's motor bike.

Too late, the front door opened and her brother ran up to the motorcycle running his hands over the petrol tank. 'Smashing,' he said. 'I thought you'd be riding an Enfield or a BSA. But Matchless is good.' His eyes gleamed with excitement. 'Can I have a ride?'

Chris grinned. 'Sorry, not today. I've got to go – duty calls.'

'I've seen you, up at the gun place,' Jimmy said.

Daisy grabbed his arm. ‘Chris hasn’t got time to talk to you. Buzz off,’ she said.

‘Leave him. He’s just interested in bikes. I was like that at his age,’ Chris said. ‘Sorry, Daisy, I must go. You working tomorrow?’

He leaned towards her but she stepped away and just nodded. She couldn’t speak. Being so close to him on the bike stirred up those feelings she had been trying so hard to ignore. She pushed Jimmy towards their front door and followed him inside.

He rushed ahead, chattering excitedly to his parents about the motorcycle and the soldier who brought Daisy home. ‘He might let me have a ride,’ he said, his eyes lighting up.

‘Oh, no, he won’t.’ Dora looked up from her ironing. ‘Too dangerous, my lad. Tell him, Stan’

‘When you’re a bit older, son,’ Stan said.

Jimmy stuck out his lower lip in a sulk and rushed up the stairs to his room.

‘Ignore him,’ Stan said. ‘He’ll get over it.’ He turned to Daisy. ‘Now then, what’s all this about you and that soldier? I remember him accosting you outside the garrison months ago. And now you’re getting on the back of his bike. What’s going on?’

‘Nothing, Dad. He just gave me a lift home, that’s all.’ Daisy was embarrassed. Why had she let Chris persuade her?

‘Well, don’t make a habit of it.’ Stan picked up his newspaper. ‘There’s too many sailors and soldiers in this town,’ he muttered.

Daisy glanced at her mother who was trying unsuccessfully to hide a smile. ‘Don’t take any notice,’ she whispered, then aloud she said, ‘Leave her alone, Stan. We can trust our girl not to do anything silly.’

She smiled at her mother. ‘He’s just a friend, Mum.’ She glanced at the mantelpiece but there was no letter. It was a relief in a way, given how mixed her feelings were. If there had been news of Bob she wasn’t sure she would be able to answer him.

‘Can I help you with that, Mum?’ she asked to change the subject.

Her mother put the iron down and folded the shirt. ‘Nearly finished. Why don’t you put the kettle on? I could do with a cuppa.’

Daisy made the tea and handed a cup to her father who was still deep in his newspaper. He put the paper down and leaned over to switch the wireless on. ‘Time for the news,’ he said.

More doom and gloom, Daisy thought. She put her cup down and picked up the pile of neatly folded ironing. ‘I’ll take this up, Mum. You drink your tea.’

Upstairs, she took her time putting the clean clothing away. She needed time to think. Useless to try and dismiss what she was beginning to feel for Chris, feelings which seemed to get stronger every time she saw him. She hardly dared to hope that he felt the same way. After all, since that night at the pictures he had maintained a friendly but distant stance as if he was quite content with her wish that they remain just friends – that was, until this evening. She had been quite sure that, if not for Jimmy, he would have kissed her. In a way the interruption was a relief. She would have been terribly embarrassed if Mrs Gardner had been looking out of her window too. If ever Bob managed to get home and heard that she’d been seen with a soldier, she could say it was an innocent ride home. But if they’d been kissing it would be a different story.

Suddenly Daisy felt ashamed. How could dreaming of another man be staying true to her first love – the man who at this very moment might be suffering in a prison camp? Next time he asks me to get on the bike I’ll refuse, she thought.

She put the last of her clean clothes into a drawer and went into Jimmy’s room with his shirt and vests. Her brother was sitting at a table in the window making a model aeroplane. He turned as she came in, holding up the model and making engine noises.

‘Spitfire, see, Sis,’ he said, waving it under her nose.

‘Very nice,’ she said.

‘I wanted to be a pilot when I grow up but now I’m thinking despatch rider - like your new boyfriend.’

‘He’s not my boyfriend,’ she snapped.

He laughed and made a *brm brm* sound, holding his hands out as if gripping handlebars. ‘Better not let Bob find out,’ he said.

Chapter Twenty Two

Daisy was really missing Lily. In the months she'd been working at the NAAFI they had become good friends. June was good company when they went out together after work and little Mavis was coming out of her shell a bit now, joining in with the laughter and banter in the canteen.

But it wasn't the same. She could talk to Lily about more sensitive things such as her conflicting feelings for the two men in her life. Letters just weren't the same.

'I've got a job in the Land Army hostel, a bit like the NAAFI but no men, not that any man would look at me the sight I am now,' Lily wrote. 'They said I can go back after the baby's born and Mum will look after it. Well, you know what we arranged for when we come home but while I'm here we've given out that I have a husband in the forces. I'm even wearing a ring, Mum bought it in a pawn shop, said she'd lost hers.'

Daisy smiled as she read Lily's words. She could almost hear Lily's laugh, but she could read between the lines how hard she was trying to sound cheerful. She decided to write back straight away, saying there was still no word of Bob, but she wouldn't mention Chris or 'Lofty' as Lily still called him.

The next day she was on kitchen duty and she was fed up. Every time the swing door opened, she could hear June and Mavis laughing together and wished she was in there with them. Working alone left her too much time to think. Since the conversation with Dad's policeman friend she had been on tenterhooks, hoping to hear any day that Mr Browning had been arrested.

She splashed more Teepol into the sink and swished it round before plunging another pile of greasy plates into the water. She sighed, her thoughts going round in never-ending circles. Would she ever hear from Bob or had he gone from her life forever? And if he had...? If only she could see him, she felt sure she would know at once if she still truly loved him and that her attraction to Chris was just a flash in the pan.

Sergeant Shiner's rough voice intruded on her thoughts. Poor Private Tompkins was getting another telling off. 'Stop day-dreaming lad. There's dinners to cook and I need those onions chopped.'

Onions! Where did they get onions? For a moment Daisy's reflections were deflected as she recalled her mother saying that onions were unobtainable these days. It was hard to understand why there would be a shortage if everyone was 'digging for victory' as they'd been urged to do. Luckily, her family weren't suffering so much as Dad spent every minute that he wasn't on Home Guard duty working on his allotment.

Daisy glanced over her shoulder to see Sergeant Shiner waving a wooden spoon in Harold's face. 'Keep your mind on your work,' he shouted.

Harold nodded but still kept glancing towards the door which led out to the stores.

He looked nervous, Daisy thought, and couldn't help wondering if Mr Browning had involved him in his criminal dealings. What would happen to him if the manager was arrested?

It had been a quiet morning up to now, but the shouting soon died down. The Cook Sergeant didn't usually stay angry for long. Poor Harold still looked very subdued though and Daisy flashed him a smile. He blushed and ducked his head, then went back to chopping thc vegetables.

June came through the swing doors with a tray of cups and saucers. 'Not too busy today. They're all getting ready for the off.'

'Off - where too?'

'We're not supposed to know but it's only exercises – over on Salisbury Plain. Getting ready for abroad.'

'How do you know?' Daisy asked.

'Careless words,' June said, quoting one of the posters hung around the canteen walls. 'They didn't realise I was listening.'

'Are they all going?'

'How do I know?' June grinned. 'Oh, worried about Lanky Lofty are you?'

Daisy blushed. 'Of course not,' she protested. But her heart sank when June said the regiment was leaving.

When it was time for her break she sat in a corner with her cup of tea and forced herself not to raise her head every time the door opened. Her break was over too soon and he hadn't come in. That was when she finally had to admit that it was Chris, not Bob, who was constantly in her thoughts. She couldn't bear the thought of him going away without saying 'goodbye'.

***

Daisy hated coming home to an empty house. All her life her mother had been there with a welcoming smile, a hot drink and tea on the table, a fire in the range and the smell of cooking wafting through the house. And, since his accident, Dad would be there too, sitting in his favourite chair reading the paper and grumbling. But he'd been much better lately. Joining the Home Guard gave him a purpose in life. He still walked with a limp and was sometimes in pain, but having a job to do helped and he was now more like the Dad Daisy remembered from before the accident.

Something good had come out of the war, Daisy thought as she stoked the range into life and set the kettle on the hob. Soon, there was a cheerful blaze and it didn't take long for the kettle to boil. She made a pot of tea, hoping her parents would be home soon. Even Jimmy, such an annoying pest when they were young, would be welcome company. He had grown up in the past few months, proud of his Scout uniform and the work he was doing to help the war effort.

As if her thoughts conjured him up, the back door was flung open and her brother burst into the kitchen in his usual noisy manner. ‘Hi, Sis. What you been up to? Chatting up your soldier boy, I bet.’

‘I’ve been working, as you very well know. More to the point – what have *you* been up to?’ ‘Working - like you. We’ve been collecting salvage.’

‘Well, it’s keeping you out of mischief, I suppose.’ Daisy tried not to smile. ‘Any idea what time Mum and Dad will be in?’

Jimmy shook his head. ‘Hope they’re not long. I’m starving.’

‘You’re always starving. I’ll make you a sandwich. Pour yourself some tea.’ Daisy looked in the larder but there wasn’t much in there. She hoped Mum had gone shopping on her way home. It was getting harder to manage on the rations and Daisy knew she was lucky to have most of her meals at the NAAFI. ‘You’ll have to settle for bread and jam, no butter,’ she said.

Jimmy screwed his face up. ‘No butter!’

‘Last week’s ration is all gone. You can have dripping if you prefer.’

‘No thanks. I’ll settle for jam.’

‘Lucky to have that,’ Daisy said, slapping a couple of slices onto a plate and pushing it towards him. They *were* lucky. Just before Lily had gone away they had been up to the ‘Bunny Bank’ in Minster, a favourite blackberrying area. Mum saved their sugar ration for weeks to have enough for jam making. Looking at the row of jars in the larder, Daisy thought they wouldn’t last long at the rate Jimmy was devouring it.

Dora looked disapproving whcn shc camc in and saw Jimmy finishing off his sandwich. ‘Couldn’t you wait for a proper meal?’ she said.

‘I was hungry. Anyway, I’m off out again in a minute.’

Before their mother could ask where too, he swallowed the last of his tea, grabbed his jacket and rushed out.

‘Oh, that boy! I can’t keep up with him.’ Dora put the shopping bag on the table and sank into a chair. ‘He’ll be starving again when he gets home.’

Daisy poured the tea and pushed the cup and saucer towards her mother. ‘Have a rest, Mum. I’ll get the tea ready.’

‘No love. You’ve been working too. Just let me drink this and then I’ll get going again. It was murder at the grocers. Of course, people get out early and grab all the good stuff. We’ve been so busy at the depot, I couldn’t get away.’

‘Never mind, Mum. I had a meal at work. Jimmy can have mine.’

‘Good girl. Anyway, I managed to get a tin of corned beef. I’ll make hash. I’ve got onions and plenty of spuds, thanks to your dad.’

Daisy unpacked the shopping but the mention of onions, made her recall the chef shouting at poor Harold. And that brought her back to her concerns about Mr Browning. Why hadn’t he been arrested yet?’

The smell of cooking invaded the kitchen as Daisy helped her mother to prepare the meal. Amazing what an onion and an Oxo cube could do to spice up a meal, she thought.

Stan thought so too as he came in the back door, sniffing appreciatively. ‘Something smells good,’ he said.

Daisy was dying to ask if there was any news from Constable Rowe, but she held her tongue until the meal was over and Dad was settled in his chair. He switched the wireless on and, as he twiddled the knobs to find the right station, she sat next to him and asked. ‘Any news about what we were talking about the other day?’

Stan shook his head. ‘I spoke to Ted Rowe yesterday. He’s passed on the information to the higher ups and they’re dealing with it.’

‘I get nervous every time I see the manager in case he suspects me of telling. I thought he’d have been arrested by now.’

Dora came in from the kitchen. ‘Who’s been arrested?’

'No one – yet,' Stan said. 'Don't you worry about it.'

'So what's it to do with our Daisy?'

Daisy wished she'd waited till they were alone to raise the subject. She hadn't realised Dad had kept his suspicions to himself.

She tried to play down her involvement. 'Dad and I were talking to Constable Rowe about the black market,' she said.

'He was just saying what a problem it is,' Stan said.

'So who's going to be arrested? Anyone we know?'

'Of course not. Now, let's drop it shall we? I want to listen to the news.' He leaned over to the wireless to change stations.

Daisy smiled at her mother, who shrugged and picked up her knitting. She half listened to the wireless and her father's frequent comments, addressed to no one in particular. It was like this most evenings when he was home, having a conversation between himself and the news reader. She caught the words 'Rommel' and 'Tobruk'. Why were they fighting in Africa? It was so hard to keep up with everything that was happening. She supposed that was where the soldiers stationed here would be sent next. And so, as so often lately, her thoughts turned to Chris. Was she soon to be parted from him, just as she'd realised her love for him? And then, guiltily, she thought of Bob and how she would face him – if he ever returned.

Chapter Twenty Three

Bob had been back in England for three weeks and still didn't know what was going to happen to him. After being picked up from the Home Guard post on the coast by a couple of military policemen, he had been driven for miles across country with no idea where he was – no streetlights as they passed through towns, no signposts anywhere.

'Are you taking me back to my unit?' he'd asked more than once, only to be met with stony silence.

'Am I a prisoner? I haven't done anything,' he protested, only to be met with more silence.

In the end he kept quiet, staring out at the passing countryside, hoping for a glimpse of somewhere familiar.

They pulled in through the gates of an army encampment and he was taken to the guard house where he'd been held ever since. He hadn't been allowed to talk to anyone or to write any letters. He asked if his mother had been informed that he was back and was told not to worry.

He sighed when the door was unlocked and the redcaps came in. Here we go again, more questioning. He had told his story so many times. Why didn't they believe him? He couldn't prove any of it; his only witnesses were Tom and Sergeant Williams. It was no good. Tom could vouch for the fact that Bob had left his unit to make sure the sergeant was all right if he had survived.

'I'm not a deserter,' Bob protested for what seemed like the thousandth time as they marched him out of the dingy room he'd been held in.

This time it was a different set of officers seated at a long table. A court martial, he knew it. He straightened his shoulders, stood to attention and saluted. He'd show them he was a real solider, not a cowardly runaway.

'Well Private Gardner, we've checked your story as far as we were able,' the Military Police Major at the head of the table said. 'You will be pleased to hear that Sergeant Williams recovered from his wounds and is a prisoner in Germany. Private Waters...'

'Tom,' Bob interrupted.

The officer ignored him and carried on, 'Private Waters confirms your story of going back to assist the sergeant.'

Bob sagged with relief. Tom had got back all right then. 'Thank you, sir.'

'Don't thank me yet.' The Major smiled tightly and rustled some papers. 'You will appreciate we are not at liberty to go into details. Suffice to say we do have means of receiving news from the occupied countries and we are satisfied with what you have told us. In fact, you have given us some very valuable information.'

Bob couldn't imagine what, but he didn't dare ask. 'What happens now, sir?' he felt bold enough to ask.

'You will be returned to your unit. Training is underway for posting overseas.' He stacked his papers in a neat pile and stood up. 'Your debriefing is over. Dismiss.'

'Thank you, sir.' Bob came to attention again and saluted before being led outside. He paused for a moment to breathe in the fresh autumn air. He was free. He was home. Well, not quite home yet. And then he had to face Daisy. What would he say to her? All these months with no word. She must think he had forgotten her. He tried to stifle the memory of those precious weeks with Francoise, when Daisy had been so far from his mind.

The military policemen, their manner a little thawed by his release, conducted him to the stores where he was issued with a new uniform and equipment. It felt good. He was a real soldier again.

The quartermaster handed him a rail warrant. 'Forty-eight hours leave and then report to 54HAA, Sheerness, in Kent.'

His face lit up. He was going home.

***

Daisy mended her stockings for what seemed like the twentieth time. She was due on duty in an hour's time and this was her last decent pair. She heard the back gate clang open, followed by a knock on the back door. No one else was at home and she got up to answer reluctantly, not in the mood for visitors. Who could it be? No one usually knocked.

Mrs Gardner stood there, waving a telegram, tears streaming down her face. For a minute Daisy couldn't take it in. 'Bob?' she whispered. A telegram usually only meant one thing.

Then she realised that Bob's mother was smiling through her tears.

'He's safe,' Mrs Gardner squealed. 'Not missing any more. I can't believe it.'

Daisy's eyes shone with unshed tears and her legs felt weak but she took her neighbour's arm and drew her inside. 'Sit down, you've had a shock.'

'I wanted you to be the first to know,' her neighbour said.

'Is it really true? What happened to him? Is he a prisoner?' The questions tumbled out, not giving Bob's mother a chance to answer.

'I don't know. It doesn't say. Just said 'confirmed no longer missing.' I can't believe it.' She shoved the telegram towards Daisy, who took it and read the brief message slowly.

Bob was safe, thank God. She thought briefly of Chris, who would soon be going off to fight, but quickly dismissed the thought. Bob was safe. She must honour her promise to him.

She handed the telegram back and put her arm around Mrs Gardner's shoulders. 'I'm so relieved,' she murmured. 'All these months, not knowing, worrying.' And she was relieved, of course she was.

‘Perhaps he’ll be able to write now,’ Mrs Gardner said. ‘Prisoners of war are allowed to write letters, aren’t they?’

Daisy nodded but the telegram hadn’t said he was a POW. If he had been a prisoner all this time, why hadn’t they heard from him before now? Why had it taken so long for his mother to be informed? But what else could it mean?

‘You’re bound to hear from him soon,’ she said, giving Mrs Gardner a comforting hug.

Bob’s mother dried her eyes and smiled up at Daisy. ‘You must be so happy. I know how you two feel about each other. Perhaps there’ll be wedding bells when he comes home.’

Daisy returned her smile but with a sinking heart. She would keep her promise, of course she would, and nothing had happened between her and Chris, so she could do so with a clear conscience.

***

Bob boarded the train at Victoria, a through train to Sheerness. He wouldn’t have to make any more changes now. It had been a long slow journey from Aldershot which is where he had at last learned he’d been held all these weeks. Getting across London had taken hours too, the city bustling with people and traffic, buses weaving their way between the bomb craters. He’d been shocked at the devastation.

The train was late leaving but at last it began to move and his heart beat faster with anticipation - and a little nervousness too. How would he feel when he saw Daisy again? Would the memory of that precious time with Francoise fade in time as he settled down to life with his childhood sweetheart? If she had stayed true to him as she’d promised, he couldn’t – wouldn’t - let her down.

The train was packed and he gave up his seat to a young woman with a toddler, spending the journey sitting on his kitbag in the corridor. It felt good to be back in a clean, smart uniform again with his own kit, not having to rely on strangers for clean clothes and shaving gear. By the end of his trek across France they hadn't seemed like strangers though. He marvelled at their bravery, their refusal to bow down to the invaders. They hadn't all been like that though and he had been shocked to learn that there were informers among them. Quick thinking on the part of his rescuers had saved him more than once.

He looked out of the train window, his heart lifting as he began to recognise the landscape around him. What a story he would have to tell when he got home, although he had been warned not to say too much about the resistance people he encountered. He was pleased that the information he'd given at the de-briefing would help others who found themselves in the same position, like those two RAF fliers who had been with him for part of the journey.

At Swale Halt the train stopped, the only sound the hissing of steam, the cry of gulls swooping over the narrow stretch of water. Bob looked out of the window, suddenly remembering that the Halt was a checkpoint. No one was allowed on to the Island without a pass.

A soldier pushed his way along the corridor, checking tickets and passes. He grinned at Bob. 'Been on leave, mate?'

Bob merely nodded, impatient to get going again.

The train rumbled across the Kingsferry Bridge, then seemed to take forever as it crept across the marshes, pausing for a few moments at Queenborough before the familiar sights of home came into view.

He scarcely waited for the train to stop before flinging open the door and jumping down onto the platform. Swinging his kitbag onto his shoulder, he strode out of the station and up the High Street, praying he wouldn't bump into anyone he knew. He couldn't stop to greet anyone. He must get home.

He turned off into the alley that led behind the houses, pausing briefly at the Bishops' back gate. No, he must see Mum first. He pushed the next door gate open and ran up the path. The door was unlocked as it always was, his mother sitting in her chair with her knitting on her lap.

She started up as he came in, a puzzled frown on her face which quickly turned to an exclamation of joy as she realised who it was.

'Bob, is it really you?' Her knitting fell to the floor unheeded as she wrapped her arms around him. 'Oh, Bobby, Bobby, my son, you're really home. I can't believe it.'

Bob hugged her back, a lump in his throat. He could hardly speak. A fleeting remembrance of the last time he had been called Bobby came and went. 'It's so good to be home, Mum.' He gently pushed her away, took out his handkerchief and wiped the tears from her face. 'No need to cry, Mum.' He gave a shaky laugh.

Mrs Gardner hugged him again. 'I thought you were a POW. How did you get home?'

'It's a long story, Mum.' Bob yawned.

'Sit down, love. Tell me about it later. You must be hungry.' She bustled around getting things out of the larder, laying the table, muttering to herself about the lack of food in the house. 'It's the rationing, love,' she said.

'Don't worry about it, Mum.' Bob sat and watched her, an affectionate smile on his face. Feeding him was Mum's way of showing her love. He'd had a good meal before leaving Aldershot, but he would eat whatever she put in front of him. He was impatient to see Daisy but another few hours wouldn't hurt.

As he ate, he told his mother a little of what had happened to him, why he hadn't been among those who'd been rescued at Dunkirk. He couldn't tell her the whole story, just said he'd been captured and escaped.

'We didn't know. They just said missing,' Mrs Gardner said, pouring him more tea. 'Your friend came here – Tom something. He said you went back to help someone.' She ruffled his hair, what was left of it after the severe army haircut he'd had at Aldershot. 'Just like you, I told him. Always trying to help.'

Bob gave an embarrassed shrug. 'That's what we do in the Army – look out for each other.' He finished eating and pushed his plate away. 'That was good. Missed your cooking, Mum.'

'Now, I suppose you'll be rushing next door. Daisy's looking forward to seeing you.'

'You don't mind me leaving you on your own then?'

'Of course not. There's plenty of time.'

Bob hesitated, not wanting to spoil things by telling her he would soon be going away again.

'Go on. She'll be home from work now.' Mrs Gardner gave him a gentle push in the direction of the back door.

***

Daisy knew Bob was home and had been looking out of the kitchen window, expecting him to come round at any minute. Of course, he had to see his mother first and she'd been glad of the chance to catch her breath, to think what she was going to say. But when she saw him pushing his way through the hedge, just as he always had when they were children, the butterflies started up in her stomach again.

She opened the back door and paused on the step. He rushed towards her but stopped dead in front of her.

'Daisy!'

'Bob!'

Then she was in his arms and they both spoke at once telling how much they'd missed each other, how awful it had been, not knowing what had happened to him, how glad he was to be home.

'Did you really miss me?' Bob asked as they broke apart and went into the house.

'Of course I did – and when you didn't write I worried. I felt sure something awful had happened to you.' How could she tell him how angry she was when she hadn't heard from him, how she had convinced herself he didn't care? That had been easier then fearing him dead or a prisoner.

'I couldn't write – surely you understand,' Bob protested.

'I realise now,' Daisy said, 'but at the time... Oh, Bob it was awful.' Tears welled up and Bob wiped them away with his finger. 'I'm here now, no need to worry any more.'

'Let's go in the other room,' Daisy said. 'Jimmy will be home soon and I don't want him pestering us.'

They went down the passage into the little used front room and sat close to each other on the sofa. Bob put his arm around her and drew her close. 'I've been waiting a long time for this,' he said, kissing her and stroking her hair.

Daisy leaned into him, returning the kiss. Wasn't this what she had been longing for all those months? But it wasn't the same. She pulled away after a few minutes, sighing.

'What's wrong, Daisy? Don't you still love me?'

'It just feels strange, that's all. I've imagined this so often – us together, here on the sofa like we used to be before you went away.'

'I suppose I've changed,' Bob said. 'War does that to you. I'm not that carefree lad you said goodbye to all those months ago.'

'I've changed too. We've both grown up, I suppose,' Daisy said. 'And I've had my fill of war too. I lost a friend in a raid.'

Bob was silent for a moment. Daisy studied him, noticing the shadows under his eyes, the loss of weight. She daren't ask what he had been through. He was home safe, that's all that mattered. She may not love him the way she loved Chris, but he was still her Bob, the one who had tied his hanky round her knee when she fell and grazed it, who taught her to swim, had been her constant companion growing up.

She knew she ought to confess that she loved someone else. But she had promised to stay true to him. He would soon be going away again back to the fighting. She couldn't let him go with a broken heart. She would keep her promise.

Chapter Twenty Four

Daisy was counting cutlery into the trays to go on the counter. She wasn't really concentrating, her mind going over and over her conversation with Bob the previous day. They had been interrupted when her parents returned home and Daisy had been relieved that they were spared more intimate conversation.

Bob had given a brief account of his adventures, much to Jimmy's delight, who kept interrupting. Mum plied him with food and drink, while Stan told him about the raids at Eastchurch. It was a normal family evening, but Daisy had been glad when it was over and she saw Bob out. Their kiss on the back step brought all her confusion to the fore again. Thank goodness she had to work the next day. It would give her a chance to sort out her feelings.

But here she was, still dithering over whether she should be honest and tell Bob how she felt.

'You're quiet this morning,' June said, dumping a pile of plates next to the cutlery tray. 'I thought you'd be dancing for joy with Bob home.'

'I haven't taken it in. All these months, worrying, wondering and then, here he is. In some ways it's as if he's never been away. But, June – he's changed. *I've* changed.'

'Bound to with what he's been through. Give it time.'

Daisy nodded and carried on with her work. If only they *had* time, she mused. But Bob told her he had to report for duty the next day. He would be rejoining the regiment over in Wiltshire where they were still training. Then he'd be shipped out again, who knew where? Should she let him go thinking that all was well between them?

How she missed Lily. June was a good friend but she didn't feel the same closeness, couldn't have a heart to heart as she'd done with Lily.

She worked mechanically, longing for the end of her shift. Bob was coming to meet her from work and she had almost decided to speak out, only to change her mind again when she pictured his disappointment.

Mrs Green had the afternoon off and gave Daisy the responsibility of cashing up the till. 'Mr Browning will lock up,' she'd said. 'I know you're anxious to get away now your young man's home.' She smiled sympathetically and went on, 'But we've all got to pull our weight. I know I can trust you, Daisy.'

Daisy nodded but deep down she wondered why, if Mrs Green was being so nice for a change, she couldn't let her go early.

At the end of the shift, June and Mavis said 'goodbye' and left her. Alone in the canteen, she looked round nervously. She hoped she could get finished and away before the manager realised she was still here. She had managed to avoid him since the talk with Constable Rowe and she didn't relish being alone in the building with him.

After cashing up, she went through to Mrs Green's office to put the money away in the safe. Passing through the kitchen she was relieved to see Harold wiping down the cutting boards. She was pleased that there was someone else here and she said, 'Working late, Harold?'

He smiled and nodded. 'Nearly finished. Off in a minute.'

She wanted to ask him to stay and walk with her but feared he would misinterpret her friendliness, so she said 'goodnight' and went into Mrs Green's office.

It didn't take long to tidy everything away and she hurriedly left the room, pausing to grab her jacket and going outside. She hadn't seen Mr Browning and hoped he was still in his own office. Better get away before he comes out, she thought.

As she turned to close the door, she heard a vehicle and caught a brief glimpse of the manager's van. She crept round the side of the building just as Mr Browning got out and went into the store. What was he up to now?

Hearing footsteps behind her, she forced herself into the gap between the store and the canteen, peering out to see who it was. Harold! So he was in on it as she'd suspected earlier.

She waited till he'd followed Mr Browning into the store and decided to leave before she was caught spying on them. But just as she stepped out from her hiding place, the manager came out carrying boxes, Harold behind him. She froze, watching as they loaded the van. He hadn't seen her. She let out a breath and started to move, just as he turned to go back into the store.

A torch beam flickered over her face and she shrank back into the shadows. 'Hey, what are you doing here?' He rushed towards her and grabbed her arm.

Heart beating rapidly and her breath coming in gasps, she managed to stay calm. 'I could ask you the same question,' she said.

'Harold said you'd gone home. Anyway, as I've said before it's none of your business.'

Daisy glared at him. 'No? Well, you can't pretend you're taking stores to Eastchurch this time, can you? The NAAFI up there is still a heap of rubble.'

His grip on her arm tightened. 'Private Tompkins, get back to your quarters. I'll deal with this.'

With a frightened look at Daisy, the young man started to walk away.

Daisy was really scared now. 'Harold, don't leave me with him,' she pleaded.

He shook his head and started to run, disappearing into the gathering darkness.

'Keep your mouth shut if you know what's good for you,' Browning shouted after him. 'Now then, missy. What shall we do with you? They say curiosity killed the cat, don't they?' He laughed harshly and gave her a shove. 'Get in the van.'

***

Bob waited outside the guard room, glancing at his watch. She should have come off duty by now. Where was she? He was tempted to go into the NAAFI and look for her but didn't want to bump into any of his old mates. They'd be clamouring for the story of where he had been all this time and how he'd managed to get back. He was still on leave and time was precious.

He paced up and down. He had to make the most of this time with Daisy. They needed to have a long talk. He had sensed that something wasn't right last night. Perhaps it was just being apart so long that had changed her – changed both of them.

A motorcycle pulled up alongside him and a lanky despatch rider dismounted, pulling off his helmet. 'Waiting for someone?' he asked.

'My girl friend. She's late,' Bob replied. He glanced towards the NAAFI building behind the guard house. 'She works in the NAAFI.'

'It's closed now. Perhaps she's already gone home.'

'No, Daisy would have waited. I'll hang about a bit longer.'

'Daisy – Daisy Bishop?' The man held out his hand to shake. 'You must be Bob. I heard you'd made it back. She'll be glad you're safe.'

'You know my Daisy then?' Bob returned the handshake tentatively.

'We know all the NAAFI girls. I'm Chris, but most of my mates call me Lofty.'

Bob turned round to stare in the direction of the building where Daisy worked. What had happened to her? 'I'm going to look for her,' he said.

As he walked away a van came round the side of the building and drove out of the gates. 'That's the NAAFI manager,' Chris said. 'We should have stopped him, asked if Daisy had left.'

'She's probably gone already. I'll go to her house, see if she's there.' He was beginning to feel anxious. Surely she would have waited. Hadn't she said they had a lot to talk about before he reported for duty the next day?

'I'll give you a lift. Hop on.' Chris replaced his helmet and kick started the engine.

When they reached the house there was no sign of Daisy.

'Perhaps she's working late,' Dora said.

Bob didn't want to worry Mrs Bishop and said he must have mistaken where they were to meet.

'I'll go and meet her,' he said.

To his surprise Chris was still waiting outside. 'Not there?' he asked.

'Perhaps she's walked home a different way. I'll catch up with her, don't worry.'

'Hope you find her. I'm sorry, I have to report back but I'll look in on the NAAFI in case she's working late. It'll be closed now but she might have stayed behind to clear up or something.'

'It's not your problem,' Bob said. 'But thanks anyway.'

Chris hesitated and then said, 'Daisy's very well-liked. I hope she's all right.' He mounted the motorbike and roared off down the road.

***

As he rode slowly through the dark streets, Chris's stomach churned. He prayed that any moment he would see her walking towards him, her handbag swinging from her shoulder, the glimmer of a torch clasped in her hand. But there was no sign of her and no one else about he could ask. 'Be safe, Daisy, my love,' he murmured. He would rather see her happy with Bob than for something unimaginable to befall her.

There had been no air raid siren this evening so that was one less thing to worry about. He recalled seeing the NAAFI van leaving the garrison and wondered if the manager had given her a lift home. But if so, she would have been there when Bob called. Besides, he remembered her saying how much she detested the man. She would never willingly have got in the vehicle with him.

When he reached the guard house he stopped to show his pass and asked the soldier on duty if anyone else had been in or out since the NAAFI had closed.

'Only Browning's van,' he said.

'What about Miss Bishop? Have you seen her?'

'Daisy? No. I did hear her boyfriend was back.' He grinned. 'Bit of a blow for you, eh mate?'

Chris ignored him and rode away. On impulse he stopped the bike outside the NAAFI and tried the door. It was locked. He walked all around the outside of the building, but it was in complete darkness as it should be with the blackout. He stopped by the kitchen window and pressed his ear up against the glass. If anyone was still there, he'd be able to hear them working. Silence. He went back to his bike and rode off towards his billet.

Worry nagged at him as he got ready for bed and he knew he wouldn't sleep although he had to be up at six for parade. He'd be on duty all day and no chance to find out what had become of the girl he had fallen in love with.

Chapter Twenty Five

Every time the van went over a bump Daisy was thrown against its side. Her stomach churned and her head pounded. Where was he taking her? Her hands were tied and she struggled to free herself, but the knots only tightened around her sore wrists. She screamed for help but her voice was muffled by the dirty rag he had tied round her mouth. She gagged against the musty smell.

'No use screaming, girl. There's no one to hear,' Sid Browning gave a nasty chuckle. 'Told you to mind your own business, didn't I?'

The van stopped and she heard his footsteps coming round to the back. The doors opened and she tensed herself, ready to run if she got the chance. Thank goodness he hadn't tied her feet. She could hear music and laughter and guessed they had stopped at one of the many pubs on the Island. Surely someone would help her.

He leaned into the van and, as if he had guessed her intention, he took off his tie and fastened it around her ankles. 'Just in case,' he said with a leer.

She shrank away from him and he laughed, picking up one of the boxes. 'Just got a little business to see to and then I'll decide what to do with you.'

He disappeared and she heard voices and doors opening and closing. While he was gone she made another attempt to free herself, but it was no good. Before she could make any impression on the knots, he was back. Hefting another box onto his shoulder, he grinned. 'Just you lie quiet there, missy, there's a good girl.'

Anger threatened to choke her and she struck out with her feet against the side of the van. No, I won't lie quiet, she thought. She kicked again, grunting with satisfaction at the metallic clang her shoes made. Surely someone would come. But the noise from the pub drowned out her efforts.

She didn't hear him come back as the van door slammed open. 'Told you to be quiet,' Browning said roughly. He closed the door and she heard the lock click. They drove for a few more miles, stopping again to unload more boxes. Each time he left her alone she tried to make enough noise to attract attention, at the same time twisting her hands in an attempt to loosen the rope.

They stopped several times, offloading boxes of goods at each place. Finally, the van was empty and Daisy wondered where he would go now. And what would he do with her? Did he intend to kill her?

She should have been feeling terrified but her fear had subsided, overwhelmed by fierce anger – not just at the way he was treating her but at what he was doing. She thought of the families struggling to feed their children, the merchant seamen braving the u-boats to bring food to them, the soldiers and sailors who relied on the NAAFI for their little extras. How dare he? She kicked the side of the van again and one of her shoes fell off. The tie he had fastened around her ankles was loose. She pushed with her other foot and her feet were free.

She replaced her shoe and wriggled around until her feet were against the rear door. When they stopped, she would kick out, surprise him and hope she could get away. She hadn't a clue where they were, but she knew the Island so well she was sure she would recognise some landmark.

The van drove over a bumpy track and jerked to a stop. Daisy tensed herself, ready to run. The door opened and she kicked out, aiming for Browning's flabby stomach. He grunted and doubled over and she seized her chance.

She started to run, stumbling in the pitch darkness, hampered by her hands still tied behind her back.

'You won't get far, missy.' His voice sent tremors through her. He was closer than she'd thought.

She stopped and looked around her. Where was she? There was no moon and no lights to guide her. With the blackout there were no streetlights, no friendly lamps gleaming in cottage windows. And out at sea the ships that plied the estuary were under orders to show no lights. She heard Browning's heavy footsteps crunching on gravel. Were they near the beach? But she couldn't smell the sea.

She shuffled her feet – only soft earth under them. If she managed to keep off the gravel path, she could move quietly and hopefully get away. Find somewhere to hide until he gave up or until it got light and she could go for help.

As she hesitated, trying to decide which way to go, straining her ears for Browning's footsteps, a hand touched her shoulder.

***

Dora put down her knitting and looked at the clock on the mantel. 'Daisy's late,' she said.

'Do you blame her? She and Bob have a lot of catching up to do.' Stan stood up and stretched. 'She's probably round next door. Stop fretting.'

'It's not like her though,' Dora said. 'It's usually you who worries when she's late.'

'She'll be all right if she's with Bob. I know he went to meet her from work.'

'He didn't see her though. He called earlier while you were still out, asking if she was home.'

'I'm sure they've met up. Still, I'll just pop next door – see if she's there.' He patted Dora's shoulder. 'You go on up, love.'

'No, I'm staying here till she gets home.'

Stan went out the back door and Dora put the kettle on. 'I'll make some cocoa,' she muttered. 'Keep busy till she gets home.' She didn't usually worry about her daughter; it was young Jimmy who usually caused concern. But the lad seemed to have grown up a bit since joining the Scouts and doing his bit for the war effort.

As she set out mugs and put milk on to heat, she thought about her children. How the time had flown.

Sometimes it was hard to believe she had three grown up children – well, almost grown up. She was so proud of them all. She missed Sylvia, of course, up there in Norfolk but Daisy... She didn't have favourites – no mother should – but she and Daisy had become extra close just lately. Dora choked back a sob. Surely Daisy would know she was worrying, would have popped her head round the door to say she would be late. She could almost hear her daughter's cheerful voice – 'just popping round to Bob's, won't be long.'

The milk boiled over, hissing and spitting on the hob. Dora grabbed the saucepan and dumped it in the sink. She looked at the clock again. Stan had been gone a long time.

Just then the door opened. 'Not back yet?' Stan asked.

Dora shook her head. 'She's not next door then?'

Stan hesitated. 'Bob's just come in. He's been out looking for her. Walked back to the garrison and asked the guard. No one's seen her.'

Dora covered her face with her hands. 'Oh, God. What's happened to her?'

Stan eased her over to the couch and made her sit down. He put his arm around her shoulders. 'Me and Bob are going out to have another look round. Perhaps she's had a fall, hurt herself.' He gave her a hug and stood up.

As he hesitated by the door, Dora looked up at him. 'Find her, please,' she whispered.

***

Daisy tried to scream as the hand tightened on her shoulder and swung her round. Browning thrust his face close to hers. 'Where did you think you were going then?'

He grabbed her arm and started to walk, pulling her behind him. A door opened and he shoved her inside, throwing her down in a corner. 'Right, you can stay there till I've decided what to do with you.'

The door slammed and she heard a key turn, then his footsteps crunching away over gravel. It was pitch dark and she stood up cautiously, feeling her way around, trying to make out where she was. She stumbled over something which fell to the floor with a metallic clanging sound. She knelt on the floor, reaching out until her fingers touched cold iron. A spade? Was he going to kill her and bury her here? Her breathing quickened and her heart raced. No, she told herself. If he was going to kill her, he'd have done it already. Well, she wasn't going to sit here awaiting her fate.

Her hand caressed the spade, feeling the sharp edge. She turned it on its edge, holding it between her knees. She rubbed the rope tying her hands against the spade, back and forth, back and forth. She gasped as it gave a little, and she tried to pull her hands apart. But there was still some way to go. Patiently, she began the sawing motion again until at last the threads broke.

She was free. She pulled the rag from around her mouth and breathed deeply, rubbing her chafed wrists. She smiled grimly. The stupid man had forgotten to re-tie her feet.

She stood up, flexing her cramped limbs, and began to explore her prison more thoroughly. When she came to the door, she pushed against it but there was no movement. Frustrated, she kicked it, kicked and kicked until, exhausted, she fell to the ground.

She must have slept for a while and awoke stiff and cold. It must be morning. Faint light filtered through gaps in the wooden walls and she realised she was in a shed, one very like the shed on her father's allotment. Was that where she was? Not her father's, of course, but there were several areas in the town given over to allotments. Did Browning have one?

As the light strengthened, Daisy grew hopeful. These days everyone was growing food, following the government's injunction to 'dig for victory'. Men often spent an hour or two gardening before going off to their regular work. Someone would come.

Chapter Twenty Six

Chris had scarcely slept and he was first out of his bunk when reveille sounded. He hastily washed and shaved and was out on the parade ground impatiently looking around at his mates. Why didn't they get a move on?

Daisy was never out of his mind. Had she got home safely after all? Was he worrying for nothing? He had no right to feel this way. He had seen Bob's distress and felt for him. But the most important thing was that she was safe.

Instead of going to the mess for breakfast he went straight to the adjutant's office for his orders – delivering some important papers to the RAF station.

'Quick as you can, Corporal.'

'Yes, sir.' Chris saluted and marched smartly away.

Yes, he would be quick – but first he would call in at the NAAFI and see if Daisy had turned up for work. Just to see her bustling around, a smile for everyone would set his mind at rest.

He opened the canteen door and looked around. It was too early for customers. He spotted June and the supervisor through the hatch.

He heard Mrs Green shouting. 'Just because her boyfriend's home on leave doesn't mean she can skive off instead of coming to work.'

'But, Mrs Green. Daisy's not a shirker. Besides, she told me Bob had to report for duty this morning. So she can't be with him. She must have a good reason for not turning up.'

'I don't care. We're already short-staffed now Lily's gone. She'll get a piece of my mind when she does deign to get here.' She turned round and noticed Chris. Pointing through the hatch at him she said, 'Well, girl, better get on. Can't you see you have a customer?'

June came through the swing doors. Her face was red and Chris could see she was fighting back tears. 'Mean old cow,' she muttered.

Chris swallowed and asked, 'She's not here then?'

June shook her head. 'It's not like her. She's always on time.'

'Look, I can't stay. I'm on duty.' He hesitated. 'I don't want to worry you, but Daisy didn't go home last night. Bob was supposed to meet her here, but she didn't turn up.'

'Perhaps they met up later. If she was with Bob perhaps she needed a lie in this morning.' She laughed. 'Good luck to her. She's waited for him long enough.'

'You're probably right.' Much as he hated the idea of Daisy and Bob spending the night together, it was preferable to the other thoughts that tormented him. 'Well, I must go. I'll pop in later,' he said.

As he rode through the town and up towards the east end of the Island, he ground his teeth in frustration. Daisy wasn't the sort of girl to spend the night with a man, even if they were all but engaged to be married. But what other explanation was there? He refused to contemplate the thought of her lying somewhere hurt – or worse.

He delivered the papers to the officer in charge and got back on the bike. He should go straight back to the garrison. Instead he turned off at the bottom of Minster Hill and rode towards the coastal defences and the Home Guard post at the base of the cliffs. If Daisy's father was on duty there, he might have some news.

Stan came out and was getting on his bicycle as Chris pulled up. One look at the older man's face told him that Daisy hadn't come home. 'I'm worried about her, Mr Bishop. I called in at the NAAFI hoping she'd turned up, but no one's heard from her.'

'You're not the only who's one worried, lad,' Stan said, running his hand through his sparse hair. 'I'm just off to the police station to report her missing.'

Chris hesitated. 'I've no right to ask, I know, but could you let me - us – all her friends - know what you find out?'

'Of course, lad.' He mounted his bicycle and rose away.

Chris watched him for a few moments and then started his motorcycle, giving Stan a wave as he passed him pedalling against the wind.

Back at the garrison there were more messages to deliver and he had no chance to make his own enquiries until he went off duty later that day. He made his way to the NAAFI, praying that Daisy would be there.

As he opened the door, Bob barged past him on the way out. 'She's not there,' he said.

'She'll turn up, mate,' Chris said, but there was no real conviction in his voice and Bob rounded on him.

'Keep your daft ideas to yourself,' he said and stumbled away.

Chris agreed that it *was* a daft idea, but he had to keep telling himself that she was all right. In fact, he was increasingly concerned that something bad had happened. He remembered Daisy telling him she was nervous of Mr Browning and tried to avoid him whenever she was sent to the stores. But when he'd asked her about it, she had brushed his concern aside, saying she was just being silly. It occurred to him that the manager might have something to do with her disappearance.

And if he had...! Chris bunched his fists and gritted his teeth. He pushed open the door and
marched up to the counter. 'I want to see the manager,' he demanded.

June looked up from serving a customer and stammered, 'I don't think he's here, you'll have to speak to Mrs Green.'

'Junc, that won't do. I must scc thc managcr.'

'Why? Mrs Green deals with complaints.'

'I haven't got a complaint.' He lowered his voice. 'It's about Daisy.'

'What...?'

'Never mind. If he's not here, I'll come back later.'

He stormed out, wondering what to do next. He was off duty till the evening and he was determined to look for Daisy. But where could she be?

He decided to call at her home, hoping for news.

Dora let him, signs of tears streaking her face. She shook her head, then ushered Chris into the kitchen. Stan was sitting at the table with a policeman.

'Come in, Chris. This is Constable Rowe, an old friend.'

'I thought Bob would be here.'

'He's on duty and being shipped out in a day or two. We must find her before he goes. He's in a right state, I can tell you.'

He knew how Bob felt. He was on standby himself, waiting to hear when and where he would be sent. 'No news then, I take it.'

'Not yet, but Ted here says the police are on the lookout for Browning's van. They've now got enough evidence to charge him.'

'Charge him? What's that got to do with Daisy?'

'She's a witness.'

'Witness to what?' Chris was confused. Daisy hadn't told him about this.

'He's been stealing from the NAAFI and selling on the black market.'

So that's why Daisy had been nervous of him; he'd been imagining something quite different. 'Is there anything I can do?' he asked.

'Leave it to the police, son,' Constable Rowe said. 'We'll find him – and Daisy too.'

'Let's hope so,' said Stan and Dora let out a choked sob.

Chris nodded and turned to go. There wasn't much point in staying and there was precious little time to do what he planned. Dora saw him to the door and he took her hands, saying, 'Try not to worry, Mrs Bishop.'

She managed a tremulous smile. 'She was so happy to see Bob. And now this...'

He mounted his motorbike and rode away. Leave it to the police – not likely. Back to the NAAFI first. If Browning thought the police were on to him, perhaps he'd locked Daisy in the storeroom to give him time to get away. He'd tear the place apart if necessary and he wouldn't let anyone stop him.

***

Daisy strained her ears, but all was quiet. She felt all around the walls of her prison, pushing at the planks in the hope of finding a loose board. She must escape before Browning came back. She was now convinced he was going to kill her and bury her body on his allotment. She knew too much.

At least Dad and his policeman friend knew what he'd been up to. It might be too late for her, but they'd make sure Browning got his just deserts. The thought brought no comfort and she shivered. No one knew where she was. Surely they would be looking for her though.

She sank down onto her haunches and put her head in her hands, giving herself up to despair. No use shouting for help. Besides, her throat was raw already. Her hands felt clammy and her heart pounded. He'd be back soon and then what?

She shook her head and sat up straight. She couldn't just sit here and wait for whatever was in store. She must at least try to escape.

Sun streamed through the narrow gaps in the planks, giving her enough light to see what she was doing. Once more she examined her prison, more carefully this time. She pushed at the door in frustration, hearing the padlock rattle against the wood. There was a bolt too, she realised.

She sat down again, thinking hard. There must be a way. She remembered the adventure stories she'd read as a child. The heroes always managed to escape from locked rooms. She'd already felt around on the dusty floor and found nothing, but in desperation she tried again, going over every inch.

Her fingers closed on a small piece of metal. She held it up to the light – a nail. Fat lot of good that was, she thought. Still, better than nothing. She went over to the door again. The padlock was on the outside – no chance of picking that lock. She wiped her damp hands on her skirt and examined the hinges, feeling around the edges in the meagre light. Was one of them loose? She pushed the nail into the tiny gap and wriggled it around.

Almost weeping with frustration, she continued to pry at the loose hinge for what seemed like hours. It just wouldn't budge.

She paced the floor in despair. Browning would be back and she must get away. Then she remembered the spade which she had thrown down in a corner. She grabbed it and raised it to her shoulder. She'd give him a good whack when he came in, take him by surprise and make a run for it. Gripping the spade, she waited tensely for the sound of the van.

After a few minutes she gave an impatient exclamation. 'Idiot,' she muttered, moving closer to the door.

She pushed the edge of the spade into the small gap by the loose hinge and began to wiggle it to and fro. Panting with the effort at last she felt it starting to give. She dropped the spade and worked at it with her hands. Finally, with broken nails and bleeding fingers the hinge came away and she pushed at the door. The bottom hinge still held but she was able to create a gap large enough to squeeze through.

Freedom, fresh air and sunshine. She paused to get her bearings, alert for the sound of a vehicle and Browning's return. She looked around - she was right about the shed being on an allotment, but it wasn't one of those near the canal where her father's was. These plots were alongside the railway line not far from the station.

Most of them were well tended, with rows of bean poles and the feathery tops of carrots poking through the soil. This one was on the far side, away from the road. It was obvious Browning was no gardener. Weeds grew tall among neglected cabbages and cauliflowers. A swathe of bare ground covered in gravel, formed a path through the middle. She could see tyre marks where the van had parked.

Mindful that Browning could return at any minute, she pushed her way through the tall weeds, away from the path, ears alert for the sound of the van.

When she heard the distinctive growl of its engine, she crouched down among the weeds. Then she heard the van door slam and footsteps on the gravel. Had he seen her?

She crawled away, hoping to reach the shelter of a shed near the railway line. She would hide there till he'd gone.

As a roar of rage filled the air, she stopped crawling, biting her knuckles. She dared to look back over her shoulder. He was pacing up and down, shouting. 'Come out, you little bitch. You can't hide forever.'

She crouched lower, hand over her mouth, as he looked towards her hiding place. He took a step forward and she held her breath, beginning to tremble.

Then she heard it. A motorcycle? Yes - and another vehicle. Her heart raced. It couldn't be Chris, could it? How would he know where to find her? But even if it wasn't him, noises meant people, people who would save her.

She dared to stand up and started to run towards the vehicles parked near the entrance to the allotments. She looked back over her shoulder, expecting pursuit. But Browning was getting into his van, slamming the doors and revving the engine in his haste to get away.

Chris ran towards her, holding out his arms and she went into them, letting herself be held by him and sobbing against his shoulder.

'How did you find me?' she croaked.

'It's a long story. The main thing is, you're safe.' He gently pushed her away as someone else came towards them.

'Dad!' She cried, hugging him tightly. 'Oh, Dad. He locked me in. I was so scared.'

‘Brave too, my girl. You got away, didn’t you? Come on, let’s get you home.’ He led her over to the police van where Constable Rowe stood. Browning had been handcuffed and hustled into it by two police officers.

‘Well done, Daisy.’ He patted her shoulder. ‘I’ll come round later to take your statement.’

Chris, who had been standing by, spoke up. ‘Will you let me take her home, Mr Bishop? I’ll look after her.’

Stan nodded. ‘I’ll follow on.’

***

Daisy was exhausted, wishing they would all leave her alone – except for Chris, of course, who held her hand throughout the questioning. First of all, Dora cried all over her, holding her tightly as if she would never let go. ‘Dad told you to leave it to the police,’ she cried. ‘I dread to think...’ and she started crying again.

‘Now then, Dora, our girl’s come home safe. Let her get her breath,’ Stan said, turning to Chris. ‘Take her into the front room, lad. We’ll bring some tea in, in a minute, give Daisy time to get her breath back.’

They sat on the sofa together, Chris’s arms around her, while she recounted her ordeal, how Browning shoved her into the van and drove all over the Island, or so it seemed, before locking her in the shed.

‘How did you know where to find me?’ she asked.

‘We’d been looking for you all night – Bob too, until he had to report back,’ Chris said.

Daisy gasped. She had completely forgotten about poor Bob. ‘Does he know I’m safe?’ she asked.

Stan nodded. ‘I telephoned the barracks.’

Daisy nodded. ‘Thank you. So what happened then?’

Chris took up the story. ‘I went back to the NAAFI to confront Browning. I knew you were scared of him and then your father told me why.’ He glanced at Stan, who nodded for him to continue. ‘He wasn’t there and no sign of his van either. I had a word with Private Tompkins. He was shaking in his shoes when he realised why I was asking about Daisy. Swore he'd been forced into helping. Anyway, he finally admitted that Browning had an allotment and sometimes stored stuff there. I got on my bike and rode straight there.' He squeezed Daisy's hand. 'You can't imagine how I felt when you suddenly ran towards me.'

She smiled. 'Exactly how I felt when I saw you,' she said, blushing.

Dora and Stan exchanged glances but said nothing.

'So how did Dad know to come there?' Daisy asked.

'The police were on the lookout for Browning's van and Ted told me it was spotted going towards the allotments. We alerted his colleagues and rushed over there.' He grinned. 'Chris beat us to it.'

'What will happen to Harold – I mean Private Tompkins?'

'Court martial, I expect – and a spell in Colchester,' Chris said.

'The army prison,' Stan explained. 'And a long spell in prison for Browning too.'

Dora sighed. 'What makes people do things like that? Here we are, all trying to do our bit for the war effort, all pulling together...'

'There'll always be people like him. They see an opportunity to make money easily and they grab it.' Stan stood up. 'I'm going to see your supervisor – explain why you're not at work. I hear she's been giving you a hard time. I'll make sure she knows what a heroine you are.'

He left the room, Dora following. 'We'll leave you two alone for a bit,' she said with a smile.

When she'd gone, Chris took Daisy in his arms. The kiss that followed was all she'd dreamed of.

He released her and looked into her eyes. 'Daisy, my love, never frighten me like that again. I thought I'd lost you.' He kissed her again and she stroked his hair, kissing him back, passionately. She wanted to stay there forever.

'I was scared,' she admitted, 'but angry too – how dare he do this to me? How did he think he'd get away with it?'

She looked into his eyes. 'I prayed you would find me. When I heard your motorbike...'

'Thank God you're safe.' He ran his hand through her springy curls. 'The thoughts that went through my mind when I heard you were missing...' He hesitated, then burst out, 'I know you're promised to Bob but I have to say it, I love you, Daisy.'

'I love you too, but...'

'Bob! Of course. I understand.' Chris stood up. 'I must go. I have to report back.'

'Is it true you're being posted abroad?' she asked. She didn't want him to go but she must speak to Bob before things went any further.

'Afraid so. Soon – a few days at most. But I'll make sure I see you before I go even if it means going AWOL. We've a lot to talk about.'

'Bob's going too. I need to see him – to explain.'

Chris leaned forward and kissed her again. 'I know,' he said. 'But you need to make up your mind.'

She didn't answer, just walked him to the door and watched as he mounted his motorcycle. She knew now, was absolutely certain – Chris was the one. But how could she let Bob down? A tear rolled down her cheek and she closed the door, went into the front room, wanting to be alone. Despite her promise to him, she knew she had to break it.

Chapter Twenty Seven

Bob was in his billet, checking his equipment waiting for the expected order to embark for overseas. The rest of the unit was still in Wiltshire training, but as soon as they returned, he would join them and then they'd be off. They hadn't been told officially that they were bound for North Africa, but they'd been issued with hot weather uniforms suitable for the desert.

Bob couldn't wait for the order to be off, needed to get away. In a way he was glad that he'd be leaving Daisy again. He'd seen how she was with Chris. It was obvious to anyone that she was in love with him – and he with her.

She'd promised faithfully to stay true to him but he couldn't be angry – after all, he'd fallen in love too. Francoise, sweet, gentle Francoise – but brave too, hiding him and others from the Germans, doing her bit for her occupied country. Would he ever see her again?

He had to face the fact that he might not, but he would hold the memory of those precious few days with her in his heart forever.

He tipped the contents of his kitbag out onto the bed and checked them again. It was something to do but it didn't stop the thoughts from whirling around in his head. What should he do? While he'd been travelling across France, he had tried to forget Francoise, concentrating on his longed-for reunion with his childhood sweetheart. And if things had been different, he would have kept his promise.

He still loved Daisy but now he realised it was a different sort of love. He wanted her to be happy and she wouldn't be happy with him, especially if he was forever harking back to those wonderful few days in France. Even in the midst of danger it had been a magical time. Sadly, he acknowledged the end of his dream of a life with his childhood sweetheart.

When he came off duty this evening, he would go and see Daisy, release her from her promise. He wouldn't mention Chris though. And he wouldn't tell her about Francoise – the end of another dream, he thought bitterly.

***

Despite her parents' entreaties to stay at home and recover from her ordeal, Daisy insisted she would be better off being busy and went in to work the following day.

Halfway through the morning, she began to wish she had stayed home. June and Mavis bombarded her with questions each time there was a lull in serving, eager to hear details of Daisy's kidnapping and the subsequent capture of Sid Browning.

'It's just like a film,' Mavis squealed. 'And you rescued by the handsome hero.'

Daisy laughed it off, but Mavis wasn't deterred.

'I can just picture that Lofty bloke roaring up on his motorbike and rescuing you from the hands of the villain.'

'Don't be silly,' June said. 'It was the police that caught him.' She turned to Daisy. 'That's right, isn't it?'

Daisy nodded and June said, 'Still, it is exciting. Nothing like that has ever happened around here.'

I wish they'd shut up and leave me alone, Daisy thought, catching sight of Mrs Green watching through the hatch. They were supposed to be getting the canteen ready for the lunchtime rush, so she gave Mavis a nudge. 'We'd better get on. I'll talk to you later,' she said.

During their break she had to go through it all again but, despite their pleas, she refused to go into detail about Sid Browning's activities. 'I'm not allowed to say anything until the trial,' she told them.

'Will you have to go to court?' Mavis asked.

'I will if he pleads not guilty,' she said.

They finished their meal and the girls reluctantly returned to work. They were quite busy and every time the door opened Daisy looked up, catching her breath and releasing it when it turned out to be yet another unfamiliar soldier or sailor coming through the door. She longed to see Chris, although she knew it was Bob she should be looking out for. She must speak to him, although what she would say she hadn't a clue. Her head told her she must forget Chris and keep her promise, but her heart was saying no.

At last the long day came to an end and Daisy helped Mrs Green with the cashing up, hoping June and Mavis would have walked on without her. She couldn't face yet another interrogation.

Her heart skipped a beat when she left the building and saw Bob waiting outside. He smiled and came towards her, putting his arm around her shoulders as they began the walk home. After his first 'hello' he was silent and they walked along, each deep in their own thoughts.

Daisy assumed his silence was because he would be leaving. He hated farewells. Did he realise her feelings had changed while he was away? Had his feelings changed? They must sort things out before he went.

'When do you go?' she asked.

'Not sure exactly but we're on standby – tomorrow or the next day.'

Daisy's heart skipped a beat. Chris would be going too. Would she manage to see him before he went?

They reached the broad path leading up to the old fairground and instead of continuing along the High Street, Bob suggested they go up to the seafront.

'We're not allowed,' Daisy said.

'Oh, I forgot. Let's sit on the wall for a bit. I don't feel like going home yet, although I must say goodbye to Mum.'

It was a mild autumn evening, but Bob spread his coat on the wall for Daisy to sit on. She looked across at the boarded-up entrance to the fairground, its twin towers a landmark for miles around. 'We've had some fun in there, haven't we,' she said dreamily. 'The big wheel, the skating rink...'

'And the ghost train.' Bob laughed. 'You were so scared.'

Daisy laughed too, remembering how she had clutched at Bob in mock terror as cobwebs clung to her face. 'Happy memories,' she whispered.

Bob nodded. 'But we were just kids. I've grown up a bit since then.'

It was the opening Daisy had been hoping for. 'We're different people now, aren't we?' She turned to face him. 'Bob, I need to ask you...'

'I know.' He took her hand. 'I saw it when you were missing. That Chris was going spare. Such a state he was in. I saw how he felt about you.'

Daisy nodded. 'But Bob, I promised...'

He squeezed her hand. 'And you will keep your promise, I know. That's the sort of girl you are. That's what I love about you.' He let her hand go and stood up, pacing a few steps away and back again. 'You feel the same way as him, don't you?' he said abruptly.

Before she could reply he sat down again and took both her hands. 'It's all right, Daisy, love. You're right. We *are* different people now. We were childhood sweethearts but we've both grown up. I won't hold you to your promise.'

Daisy should have felt relief. No row, no recriminations. Instead an overwhelming sadness swept over her and tears rolled down her cheeks. Dear Bob, she would always love him in a way, but it was Chris who held her heart.

Bob saw her tears and attempted to wipe them away. 'Don't cry, sweetheart. It's what you want isn't it?'

She nodded and attempted a smile. 'I hope one day you find the same sort of love that I have,' she said.

'Maybe.' He shrugged his shoulders and stood up abruptly. 'Time to go. Gotta say goodbye to Mum. Not looking forward to that. You know what my mum's like.'

He took her hand and they walked in companionable silence the rest of the way home, parting at their respective back gates. Daisy watched him turn and wave as he entered the back door of number 41. She waved back and went indoors with a heavy heart. She might never see him again and she was saddened. He would always be her childhood sweetheart, the boy next door.

***

As usual the wireless was on when Daisy went indoors. After hastily splashing her face with cold water from the tap in the scullery she planted a smile on her face and went into the kitchen. They were listening to a play and Dora motioned her to be quiet, pointing to Stan who was sitting forward in his chair absorbed in the dialogue.

'It's nearly finished. I'll make a cuppa in a minute,' she whispered.

'I'll do it,' Daisy said, returning to the scullery to fill the kettle. By the time she'd filled the teapot and brought the tray through the play had finished.

'Had a good day, love?' Stan asked, taking the cup she handed to him.

'I've just said goodbye to Bob,' she said. 'He's next door breaking the news to Mrs Gardner.'

'Poor woman. All that worry to go through again,' Dora said. 'Will he pop in to see us before he goes?'

'I doubt it. We've broken up,' Daisy said.

'Really? I thought – we all thought...'

'I know Mum, but it hasn't worked out. As we've both agreed, we've grown up, we're different people now – the war, everything...'

'And that Chris bloke,' Stan said. 'I knew it. Poor old Bob.'

'Stan, leave the girl alone,' Dora protested. 'Anyone could see how they feel about each other – and he seems a nice lad.'

‘I don’t want to talk about it. He’s going away too, and God knows if I’ll ever see either of them again so please, just...’ Daisy burst into tears and fled the room.

Upstairs she dried her eyes and got ready for bed. She must be up early tomorrow although she wasn’t on duty till later in the day. She had to be at the garrison early, though, just in case the regiment was moving off. She remembered the day Bob left for France, waving from the back of a lorry. She hoped that wouldn’t be her last glimpse of Chris, too.

Chapter Twenty Eight

Chris should have been feeling on top of the world. Daisy had said the magic words. She loved him. He hadn't really dared to hope. A few trips to the pictures, holding hands, a few kisses – sometimes he had been sure he was just a substitute, someone to dally with until Bob came home. However hard he tried to convince himself she wasn't the sort to toy with him, he couldn't help wondering how she really felt.

When Bob turned up out of the blue after months on the missing list, Chris had been devastated. Daisy was lost to him now. But then she'd gone missing and when she was found, he was the one she'd turned to. He recalled those ecstatic moments on the sofa in her front room. He couldn't stop himself from blurting it out. He loved her and then, incredibly she'd said she loved him in return.

Now, though, as he prepared for service overseas – any day now, they said – he wondered if he had a right to feel happy. Could he ask her to wait for him, put her through months, if not years, of uncertainty and worry?

The thought of leaving her was tearing him apart. More so, the thought of not seeing her before he went. Suppose she had changed her mind? When she saw Bob, would he persuade her that she was still his girl, that she should honour her promise to him?

He decided to go over to the NAAFI and try to speak to her. But as he opened the door to his billet, the sergeant major nabbed him.

'Where you off to, Corporal?' he demanded. 'I've got a job for you. Take this message up to Barton's Point – and no stopping on the way.'

‘Very good, Sergeant Major.’ Chris took the despatch case and went back in for his motorcycle gear. Fetching his bike, he put on his goggles and rode towards the main gate.

As he stopped briefly to acknowledge the guards, he caught a glimpse of one of the NAAFI girls going into the stores. From this distance it could have been any one of them, but he would know Daisy anywhere – her confident walk, undaunted by her experiences yesterday, the way she swung her arms. He was tempted to stop and speak to her but, mindful of his orders, he changed gear and swept out of the garrison onto the main road.

Was this the last time he would see her?

***

On her way to the stores, Daisy heard the motorcycle engine and paused. Was it Chris? When it didn’t stop, she swallowed her disappointment and walked on, telling herself Chris wasn’t the only motor cyclist on the camp. She had arrived at the garrison several hours before her duty time this morning but there had been no exodus of lorries so far. Bob and Chris must still be here – that is, unless they had left during the night.

When she went into the NAAFI, arriving earlier than usual there were several of their regular customers already in, eating the hearty breakfast the cook sergeant was known for. So, they hadn’t left yet.

She didn’t like to ask anyone when they were going, knowing that they shouldn’t really talk about it. June had no such qualms and quizzed everyone who came in as she poured their tea and handed them their cigarettes.

‘No news,’ she whispered to Daisy. ‘But I think it will be soon. They all look a bit on edge, although they’re trying to hide it.’

‘I said goodbye to Bob last night,’ Daisy told her.

‘Goodbye for good?’

Daisy nodded.

‘How did he take it?’

'All right. He wasn't surprised, said we'd both changed since he'd been away.'

'So you're a free woman now.' June nudged her, so that she almost dropped the plate she was holding. 'So, what about Chris then?' she said.

Daisy just shrugged. It was all too new to talk about. Besides, who knew if Chris's declaration had just been relief at finding her safe? Feelings had run high during those few minutes in her front room. And he didn't yet know that she had rejected Bob.

She got on with her work, ears tuned for the sound of the door, forcing herself not to turn round in anticipation every time someone came in. Although she longed to see him, she hoped in a way that their next meeting wouldn't be while she was at work. How could she say what was in her heart, kiss him goodbye in front of her friends and all his pals?

She wanted their last meeting to be somewhere romantic, a memory she could treasure in the uncertain years ahead. She pictured him picking her up from work, climbing on to the pillion and clinging to him as he rode the motorbike into the countryside, up towards the cliffs.

She was startled out of her daydream when, towards the end of her shift, Mrs Green called her into the office. What now? she thought. Was she in for another telling-off for not concentrating?

'Close the door, Daisy, and sit down,' the supervisor said. She paused for a moment, lacing her fingers together as her hands rested on the desk. 'Well, you've certainly made a name for yourself, haven't you?'

Daisy looked up, about to protest, but she saw that Mrs Green was smiling. 'Quite the little detective. I knew you were bright, and I should have taken notice of your concerns. I suppose I didn't want to admit that there were such goings on in my NAAFI.'

'I wasn't sure myself, but things started to add up,' Daisy said.

'Well, thanks to you, most of our missing stores have been recovered. I hear several people have been arrested.'

She tightened her lips. 'Such wickedness when we're all struggling.' She sighed. 'Well, something good has come out of it and I hope you'll agree it is good news for you. I've been promoted to manager.'

Before Daisy could take it in, the supervisor continued. 'Which means, Miss Bishop, that you will now take my place as supervisor.'

Daisy gasped. Promotion. She couldn't believe it. It was good news in a way, but she wondered how it would affect her relationship with her colleagues. She stammered her thanks and rose to leave.

'Congratulations,' Mrs Green said. 'You'd better be off now. We'll talk over the details in the morning.'

'Congratulations to you too,' Daisy said.

She left the office in a daze. June was getting ready to leave and looked at her curiously. 'What did she want?'

'I've been promoted.'

'Really? Well good luck. You deserve it,' June said.

Mavis added her congratulations and said, 'You don't seem very thrilled.'

'It's too much to take in. I've got so much on my mind.'

'Chris.' June said.

'Has he been in?'

'Sorry, no.'

Disappointed, Daisy said goodnight to Mavis who was working late, and walked out with June. They reached the Clock Tower where they usually went their separate ways.

'Coming to the pictures tonight?' June asked. 'It'll take your mind off things.'

'I don't know. I thought I'd stay in.'

'Just in case Chris turns up, I suppose?' June said. 'Come on, it's no use sitting at home moping.'

'All right. I'll meet you outside the Rio. I don't know what's on, but I don't really care.'

Only Jimmy was at home when she got in and she was disappointed not to be able to tell her parents her news. They would be thrilled for her. Jimmy as usual was hungry and she made him cheese on toast, giving him the rest of her cheese ration. She didn't feel like eating anyway.

He was still excited by her kidnap and rescue and kept asking questions. 'You're a hero,' he said through a mouthful of toast. 'You should get a medal. I've told all my pals about it.'

'Oh, Jimmy, you shouldn't have. Anyway, it's heroine, not hero – and I'm not one. It was Dad and Mr Rowe who caught the baddy.' She left him to his supper and went upstairs to get ready for the cinema.

'Where you going?' Jimmy asked when she came down.

'Pictures.'

'With that despatch rider, I bet. I can tell you're all moony over him.'

'Well, you're wrong. I'm meeting June.'

When she reached the end the road, she almost changed her mind and went back. She wasn't in the mood for a film or June's company. She forced down the thought – the hope –that Chris might call while she was out.

A few people were waiting outside the Rio Cinema when she got there, but no June. She'd checked the time as she passed the Clock Tower, so she knew she wasn't late. Should she go in on her own and hope her friend turned up later?

She took a couple of steps into the building and looked around for her friend. Still no sign of her. Oh, well, I'll get my ticket, she thought, going up to box office in the centre of the foyer.

As she reached into her bag for her purse, she felt a hand on her shoulder. 'I've already got our tickets.'

She gasped and looked up into Chris's laughing eyes. 'What are you doing here?'

'A surprise,' he said.

'How did you know I'd be here?'

'I got one of my mates to give a note to your friend asking her to arrange for you to be here.'

'June! The sly little thing. She never said a word.'

Chris laughed and took her arm. 'Shall we go in?'

'Oh, Chris, I was beginning to think I'd never see you again.'

'I couldn't go away without saying goodbye. We're off in the morning. I was lucky to get permission to come out this evening.'

The usherette showed them into the back row and they settled into the plush seats, Daisy looking around before the lights went down. She hoped they wouldn't see anyone she knew.

They sat in silence through the advertisements, the newsreel and a cartoon and at last the main film started. Daisy had no idea what it was or who starred in it for, as soon as credits rolled and the music swelled, Chris pulled her into his arms. She lost herself in his kisses which grew ever more passionate and as his hands caressed her, she completely forgot her surroundings. It wasn't her imagined walk along the cliffs and a lie down in the long grass, but this was better in a way. She had been afraid of getting carried away and later finding herself in the same position as Lily. Much as she would have loved to, she was relieved that here they could indulge their feelings but keep a rein on their passion.

It seemed no time before the film came to an end. They broke apart at the sound of seats tipping up and people standing for 'God Save the King.'

Outside, Chris led her round the side of the building to where he had parked his motor bike. 'Your carriage awaits, Madam,' he said, gesturing to her to climb on.

She clung to him, leaning forward to rest her face against the rough serge of his army battle dress. They reached her house in minutes and she reluctantly got off the bike. Chris followed her into the porch and took her in his arms again.

'Oh, God, Daisy, love, I don't want to go. But I must.'

Her tears brushed his cheek as she kissed him. 'I don't want you to go.'

He gently wiped the tears away with his thumb. 'Don't cry, Daisy, love. I want to remember you smiling, that lovely smile, the first thing I noticed about you.'

Daisy managed to smile through her tears, and he kissed her again.

'God knows how long I'll be gone.' He hesitated 'I want to ask you to wait for me, but I know what you went through when Bob was missing. It wouldn't be fair.'

'Chris, darling, I'll wait forever. I promise.'

'If you're sure.'

'I'm sure.' They kissed again, a long, lingering kiss. 'I'm very sure,' This time, she added silently.

It was time to go and Chris got on his motorcycle, leaning down for one last embrace before riding off into the night.

Daisy stood at the gate, watching until he turned the corner. They had only been at war for just over a year but so much had happened in that short time. Who knew how long it would go on, how long before they'd see each other again?

She sighed and wiped away a tear. She had made another promise, but this was one she knew she would keep.

The End

BWL Author
Roberta Grieve

After 22 years of handling other people's books while working as a library assistant Roberta Grieve decided it was time to fulfil a long-held ambition and start writing her own. Her first novel, 'Abigail's secret' was published in 2008 and since then she has had many more books published.

Roberta lives in a small village near Chichester, Sussex, and when not writing enjoys walking her son's dog.

Website: www.robertagrieve.co.uk

Printed in Poland
by Amazon Fulfillment
Poland Sp. z o.o., Wrocław

54464690R00150